Waiting for a Scot Like You

He brought his attention—his every ounce of focus—to her, and her breath caught. "The choice you made, to explore and discover, that's the harder one to make. Yet that's what you did. You chose the courageous path." His gaze was warm with admiration.

They neared each other, pulled toward one another with irresistible force.

Beatrice took a step closer to him, drawn by that power. "I want to kiss you, Duncan."

His jaw flexed as his eyes darkened, sending a quake of need through her. "We shouldn't."

She swallowed, pushing down disappointment, yet she had to respect his choice. "I understand if you don't want to."

"I said *we shouldn't*. But I want to," he rumbled. "God, how I want to."

Her pulse went mad, thrumming along her body. "I've adopted a motto these past three years. If there's something that I desire, and if it hurts no one, then I do it."

"Not so simple," he said lowly—yet his gaze burned her.

"It can be," she answered, breathless. "If we let it."

By Eva Leigh

The Wicked Quills of London
FOREVER YOUR EARL
SCANDAL TAKES THE STAGE
TEMPTATIONS OF A WALLFLOWER

The London Underground
FROM DUKE TILL DAWN
COUNTING ON A COUNTESS
DARE TO LOVE A DUKE

The Union of the Rakes
MY FAKE RAKE
WOULD I LIE TO THE DUKE
WAITING FOR A SCOT LIKE YOU

EVA LEIGH

Waiting for a Scot Like You

THE UNION OF THE RAKES

AVONBOOKS

An Imprint of HarperCollinsPublishers

WAITING FOR A SCOT LIKE YOU. Copyright © 2021 by Ami Silber. All rights reserved. Printed in the United States of America. No part of this book may be used or reproduced in any manner whatsoever without written permission except in the case of brief quotations embodied in critical articles and reviews. For information, address HarperCollins Publishers, 195 Broadway, New York, NY 10007.

First Avon Books mass market printing: March 2021

Print Edition ISBN: 978-0-06-293244-0
Digital Edition ISBN: 978-0-06-293245-7

Cover design by Amy Halperin
Cover illustrations by Jon Paul Ferrara
Author photo by Christine Rose Elle

Avon, Avon & logo, and Avon Books & logo are registered trademarks of HarperCollins Publishers in the United States of America and other countries.

HarperCollins is a registered trademark of HarperCollins Publishers in the United States of America and other countries.

FIRST EDITION

21 22 23 24 25   QGM   10 9 8 7 6 5 4 3 2 1

To Zack, and our adventure together

Acknowledgments

This journey back to the '80s has been such a complicated pleasure. I first started reading romance in the 1980s, borrowing my friend's mother's books and reading them during Physical Science class, or late into the night until I gave myself eyestrain headaches (totally worth it). When I began reading romance, it wasn't soon after that I wanted to write them, too. My writing was influenced not just by romance authors, but by movies, television shows, and music videos. It's purely intentional that the Union of the Rakes series was named for a song by my favorite band, whose New Wave videos gave me so much inspiration and helped guide me down a long, winding path that ultimately led to this book in your hands, dear reader.

The complication comes from revisiting many of these films, shows, and videos and seeing not just the parts that I loved and inspired me, but their deeply problematic elements. I say this not to tear down the works that are so important to many, but to recognize that we can and should do better. Being inspired by problematic things means that I have a chance to try to change the narrative, even in some small way. We listen, we learn, and hopefully, we move forward.

With that in mind, I would like to thank the people who helped bring this '80s/Regency fantasy to life . . .

First, to Adrienne H., who loaned me her mother's books, and opened the door to the world of romance novels. I fondly remember going to your house on the weekends and lying on your floor as we both devoured romances, then pausing to have lunch of Pillsbury Orange Cinnamon Rolls, and then returning to our books. Thank you for the gift that is romance. You truly changed my life.

As always, I must give thanks to my editor, the incomparable, tremendously patient Nicole Fischer, who heard my pitch of a mashup between the Regency and the 1980s and encouraged me to go for it. And through the many, many revisions, you were there, offering guidance and support and gentle nudges toward making Lady Farris's story a joyful one.

My agent, Kevan Lyon, has been my stalwart champion for many years, and I'm so grateful for your levelheadedness when I would have gone spinning off into the ether.

Thank you to Megan Frampton and Caroline Linden. You guys helped clarify my vision of Lady Ferris Bueller, and were always available to give me many much-needed pep talks.

My thanks also to Jennifer Prokop, Jen DeLuca,

Elissabeth Legendre, Felicia Grossman, Adriana Herrera, Victoria Dahl, Kenya Goree-Bell, Lorelei Brown, Jackie Barbosa, and Evie Dunmore, who contributed in ways both large and small, offering friendship, reassurance, companionship, and knowledge.

Thank you to Duran Duran. I first heard your music over 35 years ago and I literally have not stopped playing it since then. Watching the tiny cinematic masterpieces that were your music videos shaped me as a dreamer, and as a writer.

Finally, thank you, dear reader. None of this would be possible without you, and the fact that you've chosen my books to help provide solace in the midst of so much chaos is both humbling and empowering. Every dream and every happily ever after are acts of resistance. Together, we fight to change the world.

Waiting for a Scot Like You

Prologue

Eton College, 1797

It was impossible to ignore the hissing.

"Psst! Psst!"

Duncan McCameron kept his head down in a valiant effort to focus on the essay he and the other four boys had to write by the end of the day. The composition was part of their punishment, along with spending hours stuck inside the library, and though Duncan preferred being out on the field kicking a football or running races, he had a reasonable amount of brains and could write a relatively convincing paper.

The essay's topic was who they believed themselves to be. What a ridiculous question. Everyone at Eton knew who they were—they wouldn't *be* here if they didn't.

"Psst!" came the irritating, insistent voice behind him. "Oi—McCameron!"

Duncan twisted in his seat. Peering out from between the library stacks was Theodore Curtis, who smirked at him. He and Curtis had very little to do with each other, since hulking brute Curtis was a rule-breaking troublemaker rumored to be a viscount's bastard. Duncan, on the other hand, was the legitimate second son of the Earl of Glenkirk, a venerable and ancient Scottish title that dated back to Robert the Bruce. But Duncan didn't give a rat's arse about lineage—it was a lad's character that mattered, and Curtis was a scofflaw delinquent to his core.

"C'mere," Curtis said, motioning for Duncan to join him.

Duncan glanced at the other three boys who shared in the day's discipline. Scholarly Sebastian Holloway was bent over his desk, his pen flying across a sheet of foolscap as he industriously labored away at his composition. Lord Clair had his feet propped up on his desk as he contemplated Holloway, likely trying to find a way to get the other boy to write his paper for him.

William Rowe, however, stared at Duncan from behind his shaggy hair, wearing his usual strange little smile.

"McCameron . . ." Curtis said in a singsong voice. "McCameronnn . . ."

Ignoring him clearly wasn't possible, so Duncan shot to his feet and stalked into the stacks.

"Quiet," Duncan snapped. "The senior boy might come back at any minute, and if he finds us talking, we'll get flogged."

"You don't know anything about flogging," Curtis sneered. "*You* never had a cane across your backside."

"Unlike you, I don't make a practice of it," Duncan shot back.

But Curtis didn't seem offended by this remark. If anything, he looked pleased at the notion of cultivating a terrible reputation. That was precisely what Duncan did not want for himself.

"Help me get out of here," Curtis said.

Duncan stared at him. "Beg pardon?"

"Eddings locked the door behind him, but there's a window just up there—" Curtis pointed toward a narrow window set high in the wall. "I reckon with some help I can scramble up there and get out—and you're going to help me, Corinthian that you are. Bet you can climb anything, and I'll need someone up there to help pry the window open so I can wriggle out."

"Bloody hell, Curtis." Duncan gaped at the other boy. "That's against the rules."

"Of course it is, you nitwit," Curtis spat.

"That's the point," a crowlike voice said behind Duncan.

Spinning around, Duncan faced Rowe. The boy stood three feet away, and this close, his angular face and pale eyes looked even more uncanny. Rowe had made no noise as he had approached. Even though Duncan knew the fairy stories he'd heard as a lad had been nonsense, if someone told him that Rowe was a changeling, Duncan would have believed them.

"No point in doing something unless it's against the rules," Rowe added. "Ain't that so, Curtis?"

Curtis frowned in puzzlement, as if he couldn't quite believe that the uncanny Rowe had spoken to him, let alone that his words had made a twisted kind of sense.

But for Duncan, who'd grown up in the shadow of his family's motto—*Dignitas, Honestas, Pietas,* Dignity, Honor, Duty—it was the very opposite of everything he knew to be true.

Rules were in place for a reason. He'd been taught since infancy that rules existed to keep everything running smoothly, and without them, the world itself would eventually fall to pieces.

"What are we doing?" Clair drawled from behind Rowe. Naturally, the school's most popular boy had to be in the thick of everything.

"*We* are doing nothing," Duncan bit out. "Curtis wants me to help him bolt, but I won't do it. Bad enough that I'm here. Not going to make it worse by insubordination."

Curtis rolled his eyes. "God. You are such a goody two-shoes." He sang the last words, digging needles of annoyance under Duncan's skin. "Why don't you loosen your laces? We're all going to die someday, so you might have a bit of fun. For once."

Duncan's spine firmed, and his hands balled into fists. He wanted nothing more than to drive his knuckles into Curtis's smug face—but he couldn't. That's what got him here in the first place. A boy had accused Duncan of cheating at a footrace, and in the next moment, the boy lay on the ground, blood streaming from his nose. That same blood had smeared across Duncan's fist, and only then had he realized he'd punched his accuser.

He had to keep himself under control. Hitting one boy was a mistake, but if he hit another, he'd veer dangerously into anarchy.

Dignitas, Honestas, Pietas.

"Stuff it," Duncan growled instead.

When Curtis groaned in disappointment, Duncan shouldered past Rowe and Clair, then threw himself into his seat. He crossed his arms over his chest and fought the impulse to sulk. Sulking was for babbies, and he was no babby. Hell, he was fourteen years old, and in just a few more years, he'd have a commission and would be an officer in His Majesty's Army. That was his plan, and he always adhered to his plans.

Returning to his essay, he'd known from his earliest memories of arranging his lead soldiers into orderly columns on the floor of the nursery. He'd been praised by his parents and tutors for his exceptional ability to follow instructions—never late for tea, always putting his toys away in precisely the right place, completing his schoolwork on time—which meant that he would be an outstanding soldier and an honor to his family's august name.

Yet these boys—Rowe, Curtis, Clair—sneered at such control and discipline. They seemed to think it less a guiding principle and more of an obstacle.

"I-it's all right, McCameron," Holloway stammered from his seat. "No harm in doing the right thing." He smiled shyly.

Duncan said nothing, but—was Curtis right? What if his whole life slipped by and all he could remember was toeing the line? Or, like Holloway said, was it better to follow the rules and cause no harm?

Damn it, he didn't know, and he hated not knowing.

If only this interminable day would be over so he could leave these boys behind and get on with his orderly, regimented existence. Then everything would be fine.

Chapter 1

London, 1817

Summer in London lay heavy on the city streets, the heat stifling and the atmosphere still and thick. As Duncan walked through Mayfair, the urge to remove his hat and loosen the pleats of his neckcloth tugged on him. But nearly two decades as an officer in the Queen's Own Cameron Highlanders had drilled into him the necessity of maintaining a neat, orderly appearance. Even now, in peacetime, he couldn't let go of almost two decades of training and discipline.

As he made his way toward his destination, he noted laborers working on the front of a house. He envied the men their ability to shuck their jackets and roll up their sleeves.

He envied them for more than their sartorial choices, too. They had work to accomplish, a purpose that got them out of bed each day and ensured they slept well every night.

Duncan couldn't say the same about himself. Hopefully, all that would change soon—which was why he now strode toward Rotherby's home. Knowing that his aimlessness would soon come to an end sped his steps.

A man's shout broke the quiet.

"Watch out!"

Something crashed above him. He caught a glimpse of a piece of scaffolding shuddering loose, which made a stack of bricks atop it tumble toward the edge. The mason managed to stop most of them from falling—but one escaped his grasp. It hurtled straight at Duncan's head.

He dove—the movement instinctive and smooth from years of drills—and the brick fell with a bang to the ground.

When he felt reasonably certain that nothing else would tumble down, he eased to his feet to study the now-shattered piece of clay. If he hadn't moved in time, it would have smashed right into his head, likely spattering his brains across the road.

"Here now," a tradesman huffed, running up, "that were a close one. But you moved like that." He snapped his fingers, then looked at Duncan wonderingly. "Not a scratch to be seen."

"Given all the brushes with death I've had over the years," Duncan said, "meeting my end on this quiet and sunlit Mayfair avenue would have been the height of irony."

Ironic deaths were the most senseless, and if he was going to die, by God, it was going to mean something.

Even so, he couldn't find a thread of fear from this close call with mortality. Having encountered death so many times, he could barely be bothered to acknowledge its presence. Like seeing the same face in the taproom again and again. You nod once in its direction before resuming your ale.

The war had been over for two years, and, presumably, he should have developed stronger ties to life in that time. What did it say about him that all he could muster after nearly meeting his end was indifference?

He *truly* needed something to motivate him. God above, he hoped what Rotherby offered was the answer.

"Suppose," the tradesman said, scratching under his cap, "I can buy ye a pint, if you've worked up a thirst."

Pulling out his timepiece, Duncan consulted its face. "My thanks, but I've an appointment in five minutes, and this little dance with the Devil has cost me time."

"Sure whoever you're meeting don't mind if you wet your gullet first, given that you almost met old Mr. Grim."

"Old Mr. Grim and I are good friends." Duncan returned his timepiece to his waistcoat pocket and dusted a streak of grime off the leg of his trousers. "Just as I'm good friends with the man I'm about to meet. And if I'm late, he'll give me a roasting like a joint of beef." He touched his fingers to the brim of his hat. "Good day."

The rest of the journey to Rotherby's colossal mansion was blissfully uneventful, and within minutes,

Duncan stood beneath the columned portico and knocked smartly on the door.

The butler immediately appeared. "Major Mc-Cameron."

"Symes." Duncan stepped into the vaulted entryway and handed a footman his hat. In early September, there was yet no need for a coat, and Duncan eschewed the affectation of a walking stick. He had functioning legs, didn't he?

"His Grace awaits you in his study."

There was no need to show Duncan the way. He'd been to Rotherby's home countless times—as far back as when Noel had merely been Lord Clair—so he made quick work of the acres of corridors between the entryway and the study. He didn't slow his steps or pause to admire the artwork and priceless decor. As usual, though, he lifted two fingers in an affectionately rude salute to the portrait of Rotherby that had been painted soon after he'd inherited the dukedom.

The door to the study stood open, and Duncan walked straight inside the chamber. He found Rotherby seated at his desk, staring balefully at several mounds of documents stacked in front of him. The responsibilities of a duke seemed vast and generated tremendous amounts of paper.

"Do you think anyone will notice if I burn these," Rotherby asked without looking up, "and then the house down around them?"

"Her Grace might object to losing her home," Duncan noted, dropping into one of the two chairs facing the desk.

At the mention of his wife, a smile flashed in Rotherby's appallingly handsome face. They had been wed a month, after an engagement of mere weeks. "I've six country properties, so that should soften the blow. Still, if you think Jess will be upset . . ."

"She's an adaptable woman, but I don't think arson is something to which she'll readily agree." Duncan had been barely affected by his close call with the plummeting brick, but now that he was in Rotherby's study, with its relative quiet that offered little distraction, energy pulsed through him.

He surged to his feet and, walking to the cold fireplace, he shook out his hands as though preparing for a fight. Surely if he concentrated hard enough, he could light a fire with his mind alone. Given how restless and flinty his thoughts had been for the past two years and three months, it wouldn't quite surprise him if he could conjure flames merely by thinking.

"Soon, I'll be entrusted to one of those homes," he said, affecting enthusiasm. "Again, you've my thanks in offering the position of Carriford's estate manager to me."

The unexpected proposition had been made a month prior, at Rotherby's wedding breakfast. At first, Duncan had laughed, thinking it was one of his friend's occasional forays into whimsy. But no, Rotherby had been in earnest, and after realizing this, Duncan had accepted the position. Second sons generally did not find employment as estate managers, yet his family had always emphasized the importance of making oneself useful. Better to work—at a gentlemanly profession, of course—than be idle.

"I'm acting from pure self-interest." Rotherby waved his hand. "Mr. Gregory will be stepping down as estate manager so he might spend more time with his grandchildren, and as Carriford is the favorite of my holdings, it stands to reason I need someone with a nauseating amount of competency to run the place."

"Mr. Gregory will leave big boots to fill—"

"Ah, they say that the size of the boots isn't as important as the size of one's gloves." Rotherby crossed the room to Duncan and glanced at his hands. "Surprised you could load a rifle with those bangers you call fingers."

"They're still good with the delicate work. Never had a lady complain about them."

Well, that wasn't so. Susannah used to sigh with exasperation because he had large, coarse hands that did not belong to an earl's son. She'd kept giving him gloves in the hope that would make them—and him—a little more elegant.

He forcibly shoved thoughts of her away. That was long ago. It didn't matter anymore.

"But they'll do the job at Carriford," he pressed on. "Been thinking you ought to give me a review in six months, make certain I'm exceeding expectations."

"That's not necessary—"

"It *is* necessary." It was a measure of the durability of Duncan and Rotherby's friendship that he could interrupt a duke without a word of rebuke. "I appreciate everything you've done for me, but whatever I receive I *earn*. This position's no different, even if one of my oldest friends is giving it to me."

"Your father *did* buy you a commission," Rotherby pointed out.

"Because he told me I'd be cut off if I enlisted, so I'd no choice. But I didn't get to be a major by merely screaming at my batman to polish my boots." Duncan propped his elbow on the mantel. "Mark me, Rotherby, I mean what I say. I *must* be employed on a conditional basis contingent on my performance."

He'd been wrestling with this ever since Rotherby had offered him the position. A small voice in the back of his mind had been whispering terrible, insidious thoughts. That his friend was only acting out of charity—even as he hoped this work would give him the focus he'd lacked.

Were Duncan to write up an itemized list of all the activities his life in peacetime ought to include, he had followed that list to the letter. And yet for all his adherence to prescribed behavior, restlessness pushed him from one end of London to the other. The fault had to be something within him, surely.

He needed *something*. Something to occupy his body, and even more so his mind. Nothing seemed to hold his attention anymore, and it was nigh impossible to derive pleasure from any of the things that used to satisfy him.

Rotherby had married four weeks ago, and Holloway had done the same a handful of months before that. With two members of the Union of the Rakes spending more time at home than before, the group had met with less frequency. Yet even before this, when his four friends would spend evenings out on the town, traversing from gaming hell to theater boxes to private parties, Duncan's restlessness grew. He'd keep looking toward the door as if something or someone would walk through it, someone who would hold in their hands the missing piece to Duncan's sense of unease.

The past months had seen him rigorously adhering to schedules. Up at six every morning for a solid two hours taking exercise, then a bath and a light breakfast, followed by work wherein he supplemented his income by reviewing friends' and acquaintances' accounting ledgers. At precisely four o'clock, he rode to Hampstead Heath and back—the crowds at Rotten Row were too thick to permit getting a decent gallop—and a subsequent quick wash before heading out for the evening's revels with his friends. Regardless of what time he went to sleep, he always rose at the appointed hour of six.

Day after day after day.

He'd followed the correct path of a gentleman in peacetime—and should have been satisfied.

Instead, he felt his temper always on the verge of fraying, and when he laughed with his friends, the sound was forced out of him as if he hadn't the necessary chemicals to create the alchemy of laughter.

Perhaps the work as Rotherby's estate manager would be the answer. It had to be.

His friend looked like he wanted to argue against a six-month review, but he must have known the futility of arguing with a Scot, because he eventually threw up his hands. "As you wish, you donkey."

Sticking out his hand, Duncan said, "Shake on it."

"Fine, fine," Rotherby muttered, shaking his hand. "A gentleman's agreement."

"Except before your marriage," Duncan said with a smirk, "you were a duke but no gentleman."

"Jess would be highly displeased if I suddenly developed fussy manners. Although, if she was displeased with me, that might require punishment . . ." Rotherby's eyes glazed as he drifted off to somewhere highly enjoyable.

"God! Don't talk to me of that business!" Duncan grimaced. "We're approaching harvest time, so I'll need a full listing of tenant farmers and their projected crop yields."

Rotherby smoothed a hand down his perfect lapel. "I didn't ask you over here today to discuss the position."

Duncan lifted a brow. "Then, what? Plans for a night out?"

Despite his dissatisfaction, the prospect was a pleasant one. On the nights when his friends were unavailable, he would play billiards at Brooks's, which was only mildly diverting. He couldn't be too surly about the fact that his friends assembled less frequently, not when Rotherby and Holloway seemed happier now than they'd ever been.

"More like a week out." Rotherby lifted his chin. "I need a favor from you."

"Of course," Duncan said without hesitation. Even if he didn't feel indebted to Rotherby, twenty years of friendship meant that the five boys from that day in the Eton library would do anything for the others. The rule was so obvious, no one ever mentioned it. As an afterthought, he asked, "What is it?"

Rotherby walked over to a side table, where he poured two glasses of spirits. That should have been an indication that strange things were afoot in Mayfair. Before his marriage, Rotherby indulged in alcohol at nearly any hour of the day. However, Duncan had noticed that since his wedding, his friend only partook once the sun had set.

He brought the glasses over to Duncan, and they both sipped at their drinks. Regardless of the reason Rotherby had decided to break his embargo on strong drink during the day, Duncan could appreciate the excellent whisky that had certainly come from Scotland.

Every good Highlander knew if it wasn't Scottish whisky, it was merely amber-colored swill.

"A minor thing, in truth," Rotherby said after a moment, his words smooth and easy. "More of a holiday than anything. I've a female friend who's journeying to a house party in Nottinghamshire. She'll have her paid companion with her, but as she's very close with Jess, my friend's safety is extremely important to me."

"And I'm to accompany her on this journey to Nottinghamshire," Duncan said.

"I'll feel more comfortable knowing she has you—a decorated soldier—escorting her. Keeping an eye out for unsavory characters. She's a widow and knows the world, but you never know who's out on the road, eager to take advantage of a woman on her own."

"Reasonable." Duncan took a drink, turning the proposition over in his mind. It did sound quite simple, and with London hot and empty in the late summer, it might be agreeable to take to the countryside. Long hours in a carriage weren't ideal—he'd prefer to ride— but if the company was pleasant, he'd do his best to be a decent traveling companion.

"So, you'll do it?" Rotherby sounded almost indifferent.

"As you said, a week in the country is a holiday. When I return, I'll finalize my plans to move to Carriford." After finishing his drink, Duncan set the glass on the mantel. "Tell me about the lady I'm escorting to Nottinghamshire. In my limited experience, widows make for entertaining company. For some strange reason, dowagers and elderly ladies find me delightful and flirt outrageously. I'm always happy to play the gallant with them. They say it makes them feel young again."

"This widow isn't precisely superannuated." Rotherby strolled to the bellpull. "She's actually here right now, taking tea with Jess in her parlor." When a footman appeared, Rotherby said to the servant, "Have Her Grace's guest brought to my study."

The footman bowed and disappeared to carry out his master's wishes.

"How fares McGale & McGale soap?" Duncan asked as they waited.

Rotherby beamed with pride. "Jess is a wonder. Orders have tripled within the span of a month. At this rate of expansion, we'll be employing all of Honiton and half the neighboring villages."

Duncan nodded in appreciation, though a jab of envy skewered him. He was glad to see his friend so smitten with his duchess, but it also highlighted how empty his own life was, and had been, for far longer than he'd like to consider.

The footman appeared at the door. He stepped aside to permit someone entrance, and a moment later, a striking woman walked into the study in a waft of blue silk, a slight smile tilting the corners of her generous mouth.

It was impossible not to throw an exasperated look in Rotherby's direction. The cursed bastard *knew* how Duncan felt about this woman, and it was clear now that his friend hadn't mentioned the name of the lady he'd be escorting on purpose. Had Duncan known, he would have been far more reluctant to agree to this mission.

"Lady Farris," Rotherby said with a voice as smooth as polished stone, "I believe you already know Major Duncan McCameron."

"Major McCameron." Her smile turned faintly sardonic as she held out her hand. "We met in June."

"Lady Farris." Duncan bent over her hand in a bow, catching the first floral arabesques of her perfume. It wasn't a heavy or cloying scent. Far from it. "It was at Carriford, ma'am."

He straightened and took the opportunity to study her. She was an arresting woman with bold features and slashing dark brows. Silver streaked through her chestnut hair, and there were tiny lines at the corners of her sable-brown eyes. Duncan was rubbish at gauging people's ages, but it was clear that she'd left girlhood behind some time ago. A ripe sensuality clung to her, revealing itself in her full mouth and the way she held herself, as if at any moment she might lean forward and whisper an erotic suggestion into a willing ear.

What would it be like to be the owner of that ear?

He dismissed the errant notion at once, recalling instead how the countess had gone and done outlandish things like climbing trees and sitting on the rooftop to watch the moon rise and laughing with effervescent energy, and she'd simply been *too much*. He'd been unable to stop looking at her, incapable of directing his attention toward anyone else.

She hadn't behaved like a respectable dowager. How was one supposed to talk to a genteel woman who didn't seem to care about decorum or do anything remotely expected?

His friends had even remarked on it, that he'd turned into a gruff, surly bear in her presence, which wasn't his proudest moment. But, damn it, he had been graceless and awkward every time he was near her.

"Your bedchamber was next to mine," she said, "and every time I took a step in my room, I heard the floorboards creak in yours, matching me step for step."

"I sleep lightly, ma'am." Which was true, but that night when they'd shared a wall, he had been acutely aware of her presence nearby. Her own restlessness over the course of that night had fired his own.

"Are you to be my minder, Major?" Lady Farris asked, a note of teasing in her voice.

"I'll be accompanying you to Nottinghamshire, ma'am," he replied with severe politeness. "I expect the journey shall take us four to five days, depending on the condition of the roads. Before we leave, I should like a list of every place along the way where we intend to stop, as well as a listing of inns that would be suitable for a gentlewoman to spend the night. We should have no moment unaccounted for."

Lady Farris's lips quirked. "Does that include timing my visits to the necessary?" When he did not answer, she went on. "For mealtimes, perhaps I ought to calculate how long it takes me per bite of food. But does that include only chewing, or chewing *and* swallowing? Oh, and we should take into account wiping my mouth with my napkin, which I'm certain adds up."

Duncan's jaw tensed as he stared at her. "Ma'am, you must take this trip seriously."

"*Must* I? You're so very adept at seriousness, I'm sure you'll do the job amply for the both of us." There went that smile of hers again, halfway between teasing and mocking.

It was impossible to try to talk sense into this woman, so he didn't bother with an attempt.

"That's an exceptional glower, Major. I would wager that you earned a special commendation in glowering. The Golden Scowl."

Rotherby chuckled, though his laugh turned into a cough when Duncan shot him a glare.

At Duncan's silence, Lady Farris lifted her eyebrow. Turning to Rotherby, she said, "Your Grace, much as I appreciate your efforts in finding me an escort to Nottinghamshire, perhaps we might be able to find someone less"—she eyed Duncan, who stood straighter beneath her perusal—"regimented."

"Major McCameron is the superlative candidate for the job," his friend said smoothly. "In these uncertain times, having a former soldier accompanying you on the road is ideal."

"Oh, very well," she said with a dismissive wave of her hand. "He'll do."

"If you don't want me as your escort," Duncan said tightly, "I'll gladly honor your wishes and remain here in London."

"Lady Farris," Rotherby said with a charming smile, "might I have a word in private with the major?" He already had his hand on Duncan's arm.

"By all means." She swayed over to the bookcase and pulled a volume down from the shelf. It was clear from the speed at which she turned the pages that she wasn't reading a bloody word.

Duncan allowed Rotherby to haul him over to the window, hating how in the countess's presence his body moved as clumsily as his tongue.

"The devil is wrong with you?" Once again, Rotherby's light tone belied the meaning of his words. "The dowager countess is perfectly lovely—"

"Perfectly daft," Duncan muttered. "For God's sake, she climbed one of Carriford's trees. What full-grown adult does such a thing?"

Lady Farris snapped her book shut and made a show of returning it to the shelf before selecting another, her expression determinedly airy.

Rotherby leaned forward and spoke in an insistent

whisper. "I might refresh your memory about the night you and Rowe dared each other to break into the Tower of London to steal a peacock. Thank God I'm a duke, else the both of you would have been arrested." He shot a glance at the countess before returning his attention to Duncan. "Spare me your protestations about indecorous behavior. You can be as wild as a creature freed from a zoo."

Duncan's entire body went rigid. "With the rest of the Union, yes. Beyond that . . ." He tried to exhale, but it felt rough and ragged. Everything in his life felt rough and ragged. "Warfare changes people, Rotherby. It changed *me*."

His friend's gaze softened. "I know."

A thread of gratitude unwound from Duncan's chest. For all his high-handedness, Rotherby could be surprisingly attuned to others' emotions. Well— the Union of the Rakes's emotions. When it came to people outside of their circle, Rotherby easily slipped into ducal arrogance.

Yet if there was anyone Duncan could trust with private truths, it was Rotherby.

"I was responsible for my men," he said lowly. "Not just their movements as soldiers, but their welfare as *people*. I was the one watching over them as they slept, I was the one always thinking about how to keep them fed, how to make sure they didn't run riot in a captured town."

He clenched and unclenched his hands as though

pushing back tides of invisible memories. "Every moment was consumed with my responsibility. I didn't have the luxury of being rowdy, being free."

Glancing out the window at the terrace and the garden beyond, he saw not the handsome and well-maintained green space but the battlefields and ruined towns of the Peninsula. "Can't just shut that off like a spigot."

"Understood." Rotherby placed his hand on Duncan's shoulder and gave a gentle squeeze. "My goal was merely to provide you with a small holiday. I doubt the journey will be at all treacherous, thus enabling you to simply enjoy a respite from the heat and tedium of the city in the summer."

"It's appreciated," Duncan said sincerely.

"However, if taking the countess to Nottinghamshire brings difficult emotions to the fore, you needn't. I release you from any agreement."

Here was an opportunity to walk away, his honor intact. And yet . . . "As you said, the countess is a friend of yours."

"Jess is especially fond of her, and whatever and whomever she values, I value, too. She would be extremely grateful to know that, slim as the chance might be, no harm would come to Lady Farris."

"If the countess's well-being is a concern to your wife, I'll see to it that Lady Farris is kept safe." Duncan didn't consider friendship in terms of a balance of favors. He had no expectations of receiving anything in exchange for the help he'd give one of the Union, and he knew the other men felt the same.

Yet Rotherby had given him a chance to begin again, a chance for purpose and meaning as Carriford's estate manager. Surely a week in the company of the exasperating countess was a small price for an incalculable benefit. Duncan owed Rotherby, and he'd never be able to rise from his bed every morning if he didn't give back the generosity he'd received.

His friend exhaled and gave Duncan a small smile. "She'll be in excellent hands." He turned to Lady Farris. "I believe we are in accord, my lady."

She moved toward them—Duncan had a brief impression of her long stride and the skirts of her blue gown streaming behind her—and said, "Thank you, Your Grace, for arranging this. You should know, Major," she added, turning to Duncan, "if you're in search of a concrete itinerary, you'll be profoundly disappointed. My coachman knows the route, but as to when and where we stop, that is dependent on the conditions of the road and the condition of the horses."

"An estimate of mileage is not entirely out of the realm of possibility," he answered.

"I am not looking for a keeper, Major."

"Nor do I intend to be one, ma'am."

She lifted a finger. "I merely need someone to make certain my coach isn't held up by highwaymen and no one bothers my person."

"All of that will be attended to." He'd no intention

of letting her be harmed on this journey. "You'll be safe in my company. When I accept my duty, I carry it out." He gave her a military bow—and she exhaled. He wasn't certain, but the noise she made sounded as though she found him *amusing*.

His spine turned to iron.

She drew herself up and stroked her hand along her neck, the gesture seemingly habitual. His gaze followed the course of her fingers along her skin, lingering at the places where her fingertips rested. She said, "We depart from my town house first thing tomorrow morning."

"McCameron's punctual," Rotherby answered confidently. "Always exactly where he's supposed to be."

Not so certain of that, Duncan thought as he watched the countess turn and glide from the room.

Chapter 2

What did one pack for an orgy?

It was a question Beatrice Sloane, the Dowager Countess of Farris, had never faced before, and the prospect filled her with giddy anticipation. She flitted from her luggage to her writing desk—where she was halfway through penning a letter to her eldest son—and back. Concentration was in short supply, but it couldn't be helped when she was about to embark on the latest step in her journey of personal fulfillment.

Edward had been dead for three years, and she'd come out of mourning ten months ago. In that time, she'd done everything she could to ensure she had the life she'd wanted but had been denied for decades. Now, finally, she was allowing herself something that she had long dreamt of but never had the ability to make into reality.

"Did you want the slightly sheer peignoir, my lady," Jeanie, her paid companion, asked from the doorway to her private parlor, "or the completely transparent night rail?"

Beatrice paused, quill in hand, and giddily pondered this. Orgies likely required flimsy clothing and undergarments, things that could be easily taken off if not ripped outright.

What a delightful prospect.

"Tell Lucy to include both," she said finally. "It can't hurt to be prepared. Oh, and make sure she packs old ones that will tear easily."

"She'll likely guess why," Jeanie replied.

"Let her guess." Beatrice chuckled. "I haven't precisely been a model of decorum these past ten months."

There had been a handful of rascals—men of the *ton*—who had tried their best to drag her down to their level. Soon after she'd emerged from mourning, a wager had been made to see who would be the first to bed her. Fortunately, a friend had stepped in and kept those blackguards at bay.

Beatrice had vowed then that no one besides herself would ever have power over her body. Which was another reason why she couldn't wait to attend Lord Gibb's house party. *She* would be the only one deciding who she'd fuck.

Jeanie nodded before ducking out of the parlor and into the adjoining bedchamber where her maid supervised packing for the journey and the orgiastic house party at the conclusion of that journey.

Beatrice allowed herself a small laugh—a giggle,

really—before attempting to marshal her exhilaration so she could finish writing her letter to Anthony. She had to inform him that she would be on holiday for the next fortnight. Of course, she'd never tell him where, precisely, she was going. Some things a son did not need to know about his mother, especially the fact that she was about to participate in a week of utter, filthy debauchery.

Once the letter was finished, Beatrice sanded it and summoned a footman, who took the folded paper and bore it away.

Jeanie returned to the parlor, smoothing a hand over her wheat-colored hair. "Lucy packed your thinnest shifts. She had a fair idea as to why you requested them. I think she's going to run to her confessor the moment we depart."

"Poor lamb." Chuckling, Beatrice perused her bookshelf. She had a library downstairs, but this bookcase contained several of her more racy volumes, including the latest from the Lady of Dubious Quality. It was always a good idea to keep such reading near to one's bed. "Which book should I take? *The Highwayman's Seduction* or *To Seduce a Rake*?"

Jeanie raised a brow. "Do you think you'll have much time for reading?"

"Doubtful, but just in case I find myself lacking inspiration, I can always consult its pages." Given how many times she'd read *The Highwayman's Seduction*, she was already well familiar with its contents and could reenact scenes from it based purely on memory. *To Seduce a Rake* it was, then.

She set the book into her smaller traveling case, beside the velvet-lined box containing no fewer than a dozen sea sponges and a bottle of vinegar. The proprietress of the Orchid Club had strongly recommended them as relatively effective contraception, and at the age of forty-six, Beatrice had no desire to carry or raise more children. Two adult sons and an adult daughter were more than enough. Even if her body could withstand the ordeal of pregnancy, her mind and emotional fortitude could not.

"My placement agency would die of apoplexy if they knew I was accompanying you to Lord Gibb's week-long bacchanal." Jeanie smiled.

"Join the festivities," Beatrice said brightly. It wasn't common practice to include one's hired companion in a multiday orgy, but then, that was a topic seldom covered in etiquette manuals.

This was truly going to happen, and best of all, she was making it happen for herself. She didn't have to ask for permission or wait for approval or anything other than gratify her *own* desires.

"Appreciated," Jeanie said with a wave of her hand, "but I've never been much inclined to that sort of activity. I'd rather stay in my room with a cup of tea and a book—*not* one by the Lady of Dubious Quality."

"Aren't you shocked by my decision to attend Lord

Gibb's saturnalia? Shouldn't I be tatting lace or doing something else appropriate for a respectable widow?"

"Given what you've said to me about your married life," Jeanie said, her hands on her hips, "I'm cheering you on. You got yourself into the investment Bazaar, and that took backbone, but that was business, and this'll be pleasure."

"Quite a lot of pleasure." Beatrice bounced on her feet. "Oh, Jeanie, I cannot wait. Besides, I haven't the patience for learning how to tat lace."

Chasing cock, on the other hand, was definitely worth the effort. Especially as she hadn't known anyone's cock other than Edward's, and even that had made itself a stranger for the last few years of their marriage.

"And then you get to visit with your sister." Satisfied with its contents, Beatrice closed her traveling case.

"It's been an age," Jeanie said. "And I'm to retrieve you from Lord Gibb's after a week, which is more than enough time for Mary Ann and me to realize why we don't share a roof." She clapped her hands together. "Sisterly annoyance notwithstanding, I do predict that this little excursion will be quite delightful. We'll have fun, you and I."

"Perhaps not as much fun as we were hoping," Beatrice said, recalling the prior day's meeting at the Duke of Rotherby's home. "As of yesterday."

"Why ever not?" Jeanie asked. "What happened?"

"I did," Major McCameron said, appearing in the doorway. He was neatly, if plainly, dressed and had a pack slung over one wide shoulder.

There was nothing wrong with Major McCameron's appearance. He was actually quite, quite arresting. His features were slightly craggy, but that gave him a rugged, masculine air, and his reddish-brown hair was worn in short waves that appeared to have been ruthlessly tamed by a comb. When she'd stood close to him the day before, she noted he wasn't much taller than her. His eyes were a shade of vivid blue she'd seen nowhere on earth, piercing in their intensity.

"How did you get up here?" she asked. She hadn't even heard him in the hallway.

"The staff downstairs seemed preoccupied with making your vehicle and trunks ready. I waited a full five minutes in the entryway without being greeted by a single servant, so I went on reconnaissance."

He glanced around her parlor. She could just imagine how he judged the room. After she had moved out of Farris House and into this relatively snug town house, she'd indulged her own aesthetics, no longer subject to Edward's approval. The private parlor, like the rest of the house, was a kaleidoscope of color, and for this chamber, she'd chosen lemon-yellow walls with accents of vivid cobalt ceramics. The ceiling had been painted coral, which wasn't harmonious with the other hues, but it made her smile every morning to see it.

The major, however, was not smiling. But that hardly mattered. *She* liked it.

"Jeanie," Beatrice said, making certain to put sunshine in her voice, "this is Major McCameron. Major, my companion, Miss Jeanie Bradbury."

"Ma'am," Major McCameron said with a clipped bow in Jeanie's direction. He turned to Beatrice and said brusquely, "We need to leave soon if we're to make good time on the road."

Right. Of course. Despite his attractiveness, he had the personality of an angry, fussy badger.

She laughed at his attempt to force her into obedience. "We leave when I want to leave. No sooner, no later."

"Tell me about this carriage of yours." He folded his arms across his chest, causing the fabric of his coat to mold to the taut lines of his arms. "How old is it? Is it sound? When was the last time it was given a thorough going-over by the coachman?"

She blinked at him. "I have no idea. That's Wiggins's area of expertise, not mine."

"Have you packed the right gear for a journey of this duration?"

"If traveling dresses and a pair of cunning kidskin boots count as gear, then yes." His glowers couldn't touch her, so she shrugged into her pelisse. "It's just a trip to Nottinghamshire, Major. We're not waging war."

"We need to be prepared for every eventuality. Fortunately, I've made certain to bring all the essentials. A flint, my spyglass—"

"None of which will be necessary," she said as she buttoned her coat. "There are excellent coaching inns along the way which will see to our every comfort."

"Unforeseen things happen. Circumstances change."

Frustration welled acidly, but she wouldn't let it win. Tugging on her gloves, she said brightly, "Major, this journey will be a delightful adventure."

"You don't know that, ma'am."

Oh, for the love of—

She turned in a circle as though trying to see something on her back. "Why, look, I'm no longer in leading strings." Facing him, she said, "As I said yesterday in His Grace's study, I'm not in the market for a minder."

His lips firmed into a line, which was a shame because when he wasn't frowning he had an extremely fine mouth. "Apologies, ma'am," he ground out.

"The carriage is ready, and your trunks are aboard, my lady," her footman said, poking his head in. "Shall I tell Wiggins and Green to wait?"

For a moment, she considered asking her coachman and the postillion to conduct a last-minute inspection of the vehicle. At once, she dismissed the idea. She wouldn't let the major into her head. He would *not* have any sway in how she conducted her business. Especially when she saw him looking at her pointedly, as if trying to mentally herd her toward making the choice that *he* wanted.

It had always been a challenge to accompany Edward out of the house. He'd grow sullen with her if she kept him waiting, but then he'd become snappish and demand patience if she was dressed and ready to go before him. Now it was her turn to let her *own* clock determine her pace.

"We're coming down now," she said, tugging on her gloves. Glancing at McCameron, she added in a jaunty tone that she was certain would annoy him, "With or without you, Major."

He grunted in response and hefted his pack higher.

Fine, if that's how he wanted this dance to go, she'd call the steps.

Without another word to him, she walked into the hallway. Jeanie followed at once. A moment later came the major's solid footfalls.

The carriage waited outside, with Wiggins at his place on the driver's seat and Green in position on the front horse. The housekeeper and maids stood on the front step, with the footman standing ready to hand the ladies into the vehicle.

"Enjoy yourselves in my absence," Beatrice said cheerfully to her staff. "I fully anticipate you having some grand parties. Mind, keep the festivities confined to belowstairs."

"Yes, my lady," the staff chorused.

McCameron glowered at her, likely appalled that she would permit her servants such liberties, but she didn't give a fig about what he thought. She sailed past him and toward her carriage.

But before the footman could help her up into the vehicle, McCameron was there, offering his hand to assist her. She looked down at it for a moment—given that he wasn't an especially tall man, he had rather large hands, and he wore no gloves—then lightly rested her fingers in his palm.

Looking up into his face, she could see that his eyes were not just brilliantly blue, but they also contained tiny flecks of gold in a corona around his large, dark pupils.

She tried her best not to lean too much on him as she climbed inside, but it was impossible to miss how effortless it had been for him to bear her weight.

Beatrice settled on the squabs of the carriage, then edged closer to the window to make room when McCameron helped Jeanie into the vehicle. As much as she didn't want to, she couldn't stop herself from watching as the major climbed aboard, catching quick impressions of fabric stretching across taut muscles.

"All secure, Major?" she asked him sunnily once he'd taken his seat opposite her.

His response was again another grunt.

"You're welcome to close your eyes once we're underway," she said with treacly sweetness. "Might as well get some rest, Major McCameron. I hate to disappoint you, but we are going to have a *very* enjoyable journey."

With that, she knocked on the roof of the carriage. A moment later, they were underway.

Jeanie nodded off long before the major so much as blinked. In truth, they had barely reached the northern edge of the city before Beatrice's companion was asleep and very gently snoring.

Without that option, however, Beatrice was left with only Major McCameron for conversation. The landscape itself was not remarkable enough to demand attention, and as she couldn't read in a moving carriage without feeling ill, there was really nothing to do except attempt to speak to the infuriating man.

"Have you done much travel since the war?" she asked.

"No."

She waited a moment, but it gradually became clear he did not intend to elaborate.

Trying again, she asked, "Have you known the duke for long?"

"Yes."

Once more, silence fell.

"Are you now determined to answer me in single syllables, Major?"

To this, he didn't say a word, only tightened his jaw and scowled at her.

"When my children were little," she said brightly, "and we had to amuse them on long carriage rides, we used to sing a song about what we observed out the window. Would you like to sing that song now?"

"I'm four and thirty, ma'am."

She couldn't resist a triumphant smirk at finally provoking him into speech. But she couldn't ignore the fact of what he'd just said. "Gracious. Thirty-four. That makes me old enough to be your . . . aunt."

"Aunt, ma'am?"

"This isn't the Middle Ages, Major McCameron. I did not start having children at the age of twelve." A thought occurred to her. "Are you married, Major?"

"No, ma'am."

"Do you have any children?"

"None, ma'am."

"That you know of," she added.

He shook his head. "I am careful, ma'am."

"I'm certain you are." Unfortunately, this line of inquiry made her consider whether he had lovers, and if so, who they were, and what it was like for them to have him in their beds.

Boring. She was quite certain of that. He'd be mechanical and rote, with nothing resembling actual lovemaking. It would be brief and cursory, and then he'd click his heels together in a military salute before quitting the bedchamber.

"Forgive me, ma'am," he said on a growl, "but other than the fact that I was a major in His Majesty's Army and your awareness of my friendship with the Duke of Rotherby, you know nothing about me."

"That was quite a soliloquy," she said.

"It won't happen again." Seemingly tired of glaring at her, he looked out the window.

"Goodness," she said and sighed. "You *are* grumpy."

His blue gaze swung sharply back to her. "*Excuse me?* You're calling me a . . . a pig?"

She gaped at him. "I did no such thing. I said you were grumpy."

"Precisely," he bit out. "*Grumphie* is a pig's name—in Scotland."

"Ah." She sat back against her seat. "I didn't know that. I only meant that you were quite cantankerous and sullen."

He narrowed his eyes. "That isn't much better, ma'am."

She exhaled. "This has to rank as one of the most frustrating conversations I've ever had, and, given that I did raise three children, that's saying something."

"As I said before, ma'am," he rumbled, "I am not a child. I'm a grown man."

He did not need to remind her of that. Even though it was still morning, and probably not long after his shave, his reddish beard was already starting to appear on the angles of his jaw and cheeks.

"Was your training strictly in field tactics," she asked, tilting her head, "or did it extend to the negotiating table?"

He raised one of his eyebrows. "I arbitrated but never surrendered."

"Did you take prisoners?"

"When necessary."

"And denied them bread and water, I'd wager."

"Oh, no, ma'am." He leaned forward slightly, bracing his forearms on his thighs. "If someone does what I tell them to do, I treat them very well."

She couldn't stop her laugh. "What a positively despotic attitude. What if you're met with resistance?"

"That depends, ma'am."

"On what?" She didn't want to be intrigued, and yet each laconic statement from him pointed to depths she hadn't anticipated.

"On whether or not they can meet me blow for blow on the battlefield. I respect a worthy opponent." A corner of his mouth hitched, which did nothing to soften his features. He looked, in fact, like a man eager for combat.

"Prepare yourself, then, Major," she said, smiling. "Because you have met your match." She steepled her fingers, tapping them against each other as a throb of something moved her. Something that felt suspiciously like anticipation.

Chapter 3

Duncan leapt from the vehicle before it had come to a complete stop at the coaching inn. Though he and the countess had reached a kind of détente, he wasn't used to sitting still for so long, and his body buzzed with the need to move.

Still, he wasn't a churl and waited to help Lady Farris and Miss Bradbury down. When the countess set her hand in his, it was the briefest of touches, but a quick pulse of awareness vibrated through him.

He straightened, the movement sudden and automatic.

She looked at him then, her lips parting, a stain of pink forming on her cheeks. Goddamn it, but she felt it, too. That was bloody inconvenient.

"Stopping for luncheon, sir?" A freckled woman in a tidy cap and apron hurried forward to speak to the major. Behind her, a man and a boy trotted out of the inn itself, which seemed a fine, well-maintained roadside establishment. "We've a lovely private room."

The innkeeper's presence seemed to break the thrall that had fallen between Duncan and Lady Farris. She immediately released her hold on him as she stepped down.

Before Duncan could speak, Lady Farris replied, "The taproom, if you please." She smiled at the proprietress.

The innkeeper raised her brows in astonishment at the countess's request, and Duncan shared her surprise.

After he helped Miss Bradbury down, he turned to the countess. "Don't know how long you've been out of mourning," he said lowly, "but you might not know that ladies don't usually take their meals with the public." He knew this thanks to his mother and his three sisters, who were always decorous about where and when they ate.

Humor flashed in Lady Farris's eyes. "It's been ten months since I left behind my lavender and gray, Major McCameron. I know the customs of mourning. But I've never eaten in a taproom before, and today's the day I do."

He pulled his timepiece from his waistcoat. "I've budgeted half an hour for us to take our luncheon, and we'd have faster service in a private room."

"Oh, Major, you are setting yourself up for a long and frustrating journey if you think I'm to be ruled by your clock." She plucked the watch from his hand and tucked it back into the pocket of his waistcoat, giving his abdomen a pat as she did so.

He stilled beneath her fingers.

Her gaze flew to his, and for the barest moment, they both froze. Her hand lightly pressed against his stomach, yet he sensed her touch everywhere, as if his body had been dozing before but was now fully awake.

A throng of people passed by the coaching yard, laughing and singing patches of song. At the sound, the countess pulled away from him, leaving a palm-shaped imprint of heat on his skin. Still, they stared at each other as though ensnared and unable to break free from the net surrounding them.

Dimly, he heard Miss Bradbury ask, "Where are those folks headed?"

Duncan managed to drag his gaze away from Lady Farris to watch more people walk by the coaching yard. They wore large straw hats, with sheaves of green wheat woven around the crowns, and in their hands they waved streamer-adorned sticks.

"Local custom, madam," the innkeeper answered. "A fortnight before the wheat is harvested we have a procession. We sing songs and the like."

"How enchanting," the countess said and perhaps he imagined it, but she sounded slightly dazed, as if she was still reeling in the aftermath of their brief physical contact.

"If you're in not too much of a hurry to get back on the road," the innkeeper said, "you ought to stay and watch."

"That depends on whether or not the schedule permits it," Lady Farris answered, shooting him a dry look.

And then she sailed toward the inn, with Miss Bradbury, the innkeeper, and her family following. The countess made an impressive figure as she marched away, her shoulders back, her steps confident.

He stood there, watching the space she'd occupied, his mind continuing to remain the consistency of porridge.

Finally, his brain congealed, and he became aware of Wiggins gazing at him. Looking up at the driver, Duncan asked, "Need anything?"

"My thanks, sir. We'll see to ourselves." The coachman touched his fingers to his tricorn before urging the horses in a walk toward the stables.

For several moments, Duncan stood alone in the yard, gathering himself. He stared up at the cloudless sky, brilliant in its late-summer hue. There had been skies overhead like this in Portugal and Spain. Some of the worst things he'd ever seen had been beneath perfect blue skies. Blood looked especially vivid in the sunlight.

He shook his head. He'd survived, hadn't he? He'd even kept a good number of his men alive. There was nothing to complain about. In truth, he should rejoice that he'd made it out the other side to take this journey with Lady Farris. He could bear all of this with calm and patience. She would breeze in and out of his life, and he could go on with the path he'd set for himself—and hope that it settled the restlessness within him.

After taking a deep breath, he headed inside.

Lady Farris and Miss Bradbury sat at a small circular table at one side of the taproom. Within the chamber itself was a collection of groups and individuals, including shopkeepers and plowmen and travelers, all partaking of a midday meal. A trio of tradesmen—their clothing dusted with plaster—were seated near the countess and kept glancing at her with the same kind of prurient interest men had used for millennia when looking at women. For her part, Lady Farris either didn't observe or pretended not to.

But Duncan noticed. He walked up to the tradesmen and said in a mild but firm voice, "Eyes to yourself, gentlemen."

"We can look, can't we?" one of them said over the rim of his tankard.

"You can," Duncan agreed. "But then I'd have to introduce your face to my fist, and the sound of a nose breaking can put delicate constitutions off their luncheon." To make his point, he rested his fist, knuckles down, on the tabletop.

The men all glanced down at his hand. One of them cursed softly, having no doubt seen the scars that marked his knuckles.

"Earned these scars," Duncan said. "Beginning with the Battle of Bussaco. Bit of hand-to-hand combat with a French soldier intent on slitting my throat. Given that I'm alive and having this friendly chat with you now, you can well imagine how things ended for that soldier."

One of the men swallowed audibly. "We'll keep our eyes on our table."

"Good lads." Satisfied that the situation was under control, Duncan walked to Lady Farris's table and seated himself.

"Were you talking to those men, Major McCameron?" the countess asked.

He grunted. If he told her what he'd been doing, she'd no doubt chastise him for looking out for her best interests. She'd likely consider such measures unnecessary. But he'd given Rotherby his word that he'd protect Lady Farris, and even if he hadn't promised his friend, he would have done it just the same.

Glancing at Miss Bradbury, she said brightly, "As usual, his conversational skills are delightful."

To her credit, Miss Bradbury did not voice her agreement. Instead, she adjusted the folds of her fichu.

"Talked just fine with those tradesmen," he noted.

"Speaking in the common tongue of grunts." The countess batted her lashes at him as if in challenge.

"You've never heard a Shakespearean sonnet until you've heard it grunted," he answered. *"Be wise as thou art cruel—"* he grunted *"—do not press my tongue-tied patience with too much disdain—"* he grunted once more.

A smile bloomed slowly across her face, a true smile,

and something hard and insistent throbbed in his chest. He dug his knuckles into it, trying to banish the sensation. It had to be because he was hungry since his breakfast had been long ago and spartan.

"*O! learn to read what silent love hath writ,*" she said, eyes sparkling. "*To hear with eyes belongs to love's fine wit.*"

No denying it: the quick, insistent flare of hunger wasn't for food.

The innkeeper appeared beside their table. "It's our cook's habit to make one dish a day. Today's is Bedfordshire clanger."

The countess's expression brightened. "I've never had a Bedfordshire clanger."

"'Tis very humble fare, madam," the innkeeper said apologetically. "A shortcrust pastry with savory filling at one end, sweet at the other. I can have Cook make you something special."

"No need." Lady Farris smiled warmly. "A Bedfordshire clanger sounds just the thing, and I'm sure your cook makes a delicious one."

The innkeeper beamed. "Oh, it is, my lady. I'll bring them out right away. An ale for you, sir?" she added, looking at Duncan.

"That will suit," he answered.

"For me, as well," the countess said.

"Wouldn't you prefer a lemonade, madam?" the innkeeper offered.

"Ale," came the cheerful but firm reply. Lady Farris's

gaze was on Duncan as if daring him to contradict her request.

"Lemonade for me," Miss Bradbury said.

The innkeeper murmured something indistinct before fading away to fetch their food and drink. After they were left alone, the countess's companion quietly excused herself and headed toward the back of the inn, where presumably the necessary was located.

"You've much familiarity with ale?" Duncan asked once Miss Bradbury had gone.

"Not a bit," she answered and chuckled.

"Possible you'll regret your choice," he felt obliged to point out.

"It *is* possible," she replied, "but the only one who'll suffer for it is me. No one's life or happiness hangs in the balance, so it's a risk worth taking. What about you, Major?" She rested her chin on her fist. "When was the last time you did anything risky? Reversing the order in which you put on your stockings doesn't count."

From her smirk it was clear that she believed she knew him and understood all there was to comprehend about who he was. But she didn't know him truly, and the need to shock her down to the tips of her own stocking-clad toes was sudden and devilish.

"I clambered up a courtesan's balcony to steal a garter and a kiss." Granted, he'd been dared by Rotherby to do so, and that had been last December, which didn't make it particularly recent, but she didn't need to know that.

Her eyes went wide. Perhaps what he'd said was shocking, but damn if it wasn't worth it to see the look of astonishment on her face.

With what sounded like deliberate nonchalance, she said, "Stealing merely a kiss?"

"There was the garter, as well. As for other things . . ." He held her gaze. "I never steal them. They're always given freely, and with great enthusiasm."

A slight flush rose up in her cheeks. "Sound quite certain of that."

"I am, ma'am, and unless you were in the room with us, you've no reason to doubt me."

The bustle of the taproom ebbed as he and the countess stared at each other. What had started as a throb in his chest spread throughout his body.

"So, Major McCameron," Miss Bradbury said as she returned to the table, "you were in the army. The 79th Regiment of Foot, correct? I believe I read that it was also known as the Queen's Own Cameron Highlanders."

Fortunately, the companion's reappearance quieted his body's attempt to mutiny. "Aye, ma'am."

"You fought mainly on the Peninsula?" Miss Bradbury asked.

"Mainly, aye." Though he respected her endeavor to converse, he'd no desire to elaborate on his years of service. Besides, what he'd seen and done in Spain and Portugal were not fit topics for a roadside luncheon with ladies.

"And you were at Waterloo, correct?"

"Aye, ma'am." He'd fought with the ferocity of a man with no hope. His fiancée Susannah's letter had arrived three days before, and with that letter, he'd lost the future he had assiduously planned. In a way, he owed Susannah for freeing him from fear. Had he believed that a wife and the prospect of a family awaited him on the other end of the battle, terror would have shadowed him through every moment, imagining that he had so much more to lose.

Damn—memories of the war were strong today. Some days, he barely thought of it. There were others, however, where he had to spend hour upon hour exhausting himself at the sporting academy just to keep the thoughts at bay.

He had no physical outlet now, trapped as he was for hours in a carriage. That left ample space for images, sounds, even phantom smells to crowd his mind. Miss Bradbury's questions weren't helping, either.

"The longest day of my life. And the end of many others'." He stared down at his hands resting on the table, and though they were clean now, he'd seen them many times caked with dirt or rusty with blood.

"Forgive me, Major," Miss Bradbury said kindly. "My curiosity gets the better of me sometimes, and I forget that there are things people do not wish to discuss—especially men who have gone to war."

"My thanks, ma'am." His gaze flicked toward the countess, who looked at him with a soft sort of curiosity. It wasn't invasive, her interest; more considering, and a thread of gratitude unspooled—both for Miss Bradbury's concern as well as her mistress's gentle assessment.

Fortunately, the talk of war stopped when their food arrived, along with ales for Duncan and the countess and Miss Bradbury's lemonade.

"This side has the mince pork," the innkeeper said, pointing to one end of the pastry. "The other side's the sweet plum." She hovered nervously as Lady Farris took her first bite of Bedfordshire clanger.

Duncan had to admit, he was curious, too, what the countess's reaction might be. She likely wasn't familiar with plain country cooking.

After chewing and swallowing, Lady Farris looked at the innkeeper. "Before we leave," she said gravely, "I ask that your cook writes down the recipe that I may pass it along to *my* cook."

"Of course, my lady. Happy to, my lady!" Excitedly, the innkeeper hurried away.

"Do you truly like it?" Duncan asked after the woman had gone. "Or were you merely being polite?"

She lifted one brow. "Would you ever accuse me of *merely being polite*, Major?"

He raised his hands. "Fair enough."

"But it is delicious," she continued after taking another bite. "Flavorful and rich but not heavy." She cut a piece from the end that contained plum and popped it in her mouth. Clearly, she didn't care about moving back and forth between luncheon and dessert.

Her eyes closed, and she made a small, pleasured hum that shot right to Duncan's cock. "The plums are a marvel. It's as though someone took the essence of late summer and baked it into a shortcrust. What do you think, Major?"

He didn't expect her to ask his opinion. Quickly, economically, he cut himself a piece from the savory part of the clanger. "It's good."

"And?" She propped her chin on her palm.

He chewed. "I like the taste of it."

"Does the flavor bring anything to mind? Any descriptors besides *good*?"

Setting his fork down, he said, "Ma'am, I've spent over a decade bolting down rations as quickly as I could. There wasn't time to learn gastronomic appreciation."

"We have time now." She gestured to his tankard of ale. "Have a drink. And perhaps, whilst you're drinking, take a moment to truly be there with the ale. Pick out its different flavors. Surely many ingredients go into brewing ale."

"Water, barley, hops, yeast." He could not understand where she was going with this, but there was no harm in following along for a moment or two. Bringing his tankard to his lips, he drank. All he could taste was a standard ale, no different from any he'd had over the course of his life. "It's . . ."

She leaned closer, attentive.

"It's fine," he finally said.

With a rueful smile, she shook her head. "I did my best."

"I cannot unlearn more than fifteen years of training in a single luncheon."

"Well, you're trying," she said, "and that's something."

His food was getting cold, so he resumed eating. He did, however, point his fork at Lady Farris's own tankard. "Your turn. Let's hear *you* express the ale's inner beauty."

Her nostrils flared, and he could not quite tell if his challenge irritated or aroused her. God knew, when it came to her, he himself couldn't tell the difference.

With a queenly air, she picked up her tankard and sipped. Difficult not to watch her throat, which he saw now was long and sleek. She swallowed, and he was flooded with wanting to feel the texture of her bare skin. He had a fleeting impression that it would be soft beyond imagining—her life was surely one of limitless privilege and ease—and he craved the feel of it, his hand curving around her throat as he held her still for a kiss . . .

Duncan mentally shook himself. That was a trail down which he would not venture.

Slowly, she said, "It tastes . . ."

Right—they were discussing the taste of ale. He focused his attention on her face and refused to think at all about her silken neck.

"It's slightly bitter," she continued. "Not enough to be unpleasant, but it contrasts well with the subtle fruitiness. There's some sweetness, too . . ."

"Most likely the malt." He peered at her. "You've had ale before, surely."

Her smile turned almost shy. "This is my first." She suddenly laughed, the sound a rough tumble of velvet. "Here I thought I'd left virginity behind long ago."

The heat he'd felt when watching her drink the ale surged higher, and the air went thick.

"My lady," Miss Bradbury said with a shocked laugh. "You're embarrassing Major McCameron."

"I'm made of stern stuff, ma'am," Duncan said. He took a sip from his tankard, though the ale didn't cool him. "It takes far more than that to embarrass me."

"And yet your ears have turned pink," the countess observed, her lips curling.

Damn his fair skin. "The room is warm."

"I find it quite pleasant and cool." She took a bite from the plum side of the clanger. "You must know, Major, that you cannot say such a thing in my presence without me taking it as a personal challenge."

"You must know, ma'am, that I've successfully defended towns and cities across the Peninsula. Fending off your attempts at embarrassing me will be easy."

Her smile widened. "Oh, now, you *are* challenging me."

It was only when he saw how her eyes sparkled that he realized he smiled back at her. Rearranging his features into a neutral expression, he brought his attention to his meal.

The countess seemed to understand that their conversation had come to its conclusion. But rather than tease him over this, she turned to Miss Bradbury and began to chat. He tried not to pay attention to what they discussed—it had nothing to do with him—but it was difficult not to hear how she talked about her children, two of whom, he learned, were married, with the youngest still at Cambridge.

Her voice was full of affection when she spoke of them—Anthony, the eldest and now the earl; Victoria, the middle child and her lone daughter; and John, the boy who seemed to have a predilection for making trouble. Already, she'd had to threaten that his brother would curtail John's allowance if he continued to play pranks on the other students.

"That's several smiles in the span of an hour, Major McCameron," she noted. "I must confess it alarms me—I am so unused to seeing such things on your face."

"Cannot be helped, ma'am." He took a drink of ale. "They have a will of their own and appear when properly provoked."

"And what provoked this last smile?" Her own, he noted, had a charming lopsided quality that was far more genuine than he'd seen in most nobly born people's expressions.

"Your son, ma'am. John. He seems to have inherited his mother's predisposition for disobedience."

She laughed. "The punishment bestowed upon parents is to have children much like themselves."

"Any of your children like their father in temperament?"

Her lips pursed. "Fortunately, no." Before he could gently prod for an elaboration, the countess waved at the passing innkeeper, signaling for her to come to their table. When the innkeeper appeared, Lady Farris said, "Please, might I personally give my thanks to your cook?"

Briefly, the other woman looked surprised but then said, "Of course, madam. I see you're all finished with your meal," she added, glancing at their empty plates, "so if you'd like, please follow me."

Duncan rose as Lady Farris and her companion got to their feet. He stood by the table as the countess and Miss Bradbury began to trail after the innkeeper, but then Lady Farris stopped and faced him.

"Do come with us, Major," she said.

"I don't think that's needed," he answered.

She tilted her head. "How many inn kitchens have you seen?"

"Well . . . none."

She glided toward him and then looped her arm through his. The equanimity he'd managed to achieve shattered at the feel of her, soft and curved, and if the rosy stain in her cheeks was any sign, she wasn't quite calm, either.

It did not console him.

"Look lively, soldier," she said, her voice slightly breathless. "You're coming with me."

Chapter 4

The inn's kitchen bustled with activity as two young women filled plates with Bedfordshire clangers and hurried them out into the taproom. An adolescent boy peeled and chopped onions, occasionally stopping to drag his sleeve across his watering eyes. Overseeing all of this was a man with impressive gray side whiskers, who used a wooden peel to ferry clangers in and out of the oven.

For all the commotion, it didn't match the spinning confusion and sensation careening through Beatrice as she tugged Major McCameron deeper into the kitchen with her. While he did have impeccable posture—clearly a vestige of his military service—he was now so upright he verged on stiff.

Come to think of it, he'd been that way ever since she'd put her arm through his.

Perhaps her touch made him uncomfortable. At once, she released him, and his chest rose and fell in an exhale.

Was he relieved? Yet his comments to her back in the taproom came back, comments that were almost flirtatious. *As for other things . . . I never steal them. They're always given freely, and with great enthusiasm.*

"This is Mr. Baines," the innkeeper said, interrupting Beatrice's thoughts. "Our cook."

Beatrice gave him a wide smile as the man in the apron bowed. "Your food was delicious. It was my first Bedfordshire clanger, and I am both enthralled by the taste of it as well as mystified by how you're able to fashion it."

"If you like, madam," Mr. Baines said heartily, "I can show you. Better yet—would you like to try your hand at making them?"

Excitement bubbled. "May I?"

"We're losing time on the road," the major murmured. "We need to leave now and—"

"The road isn't going anywhere," she replied affably. "I've never had the chance to make a Bedfordshire clanger, but now that it has presented itself, I'm not losing the opportunity."

She went to stand by Mr. Baines, who had taken up a position at a long heavy wooden table. She gestured for Jeanie to stand on the other side of Mr. Baines. Catching a fragment of Major McCameron's irritated muttering, Beatrice ignored it and turned her attention to the cook.

"We start with a shortcrust pastry," Mr. Baines explained. "I've some already made, if you like."

"I confess I've never made shortcrust pastry," Beatrice said with a laugh. "It always seems like magic." She glanced up at the major, who stood with his arms crossed over his chest, looking slightly annoyed. In response, she gave him a cheerful salute.

"No magic in it at all," Mr. Baines answered. "We'll need butter, flour, salt, and cold water." As he spoke, he gathered the needed supplies in bowls and pitchers, placing them in front of her and Jeanie.

He described how the butter was to be incorporated into the flour using one's fingertips, and Beatrice dug her hands into the ingredients. She rubbed the cool butter into the powdery flour, relishing the contrast of textures.

"Slowly drizzle the water into the mixture," Mr. Baines instructed. "Then knead it together."

"Major McCameron," she said, "I'll need your help." With her chin, she gestured for him to stand beside her.

He frowned but marched over to her. "Aye, ma'am?"

Holding up her hands, she said, "I'm covered in butter and flour and will make a horrible mess if I put my hands on that." She glanced at the water pitcher. "If you please, give me a good drizzle."

The pleat remained between his brows, but he did as she asked, adding the water in a slow but steady trickle into the bowl. As he did so, she worked the mixture with her hands.

"Remarkable how everything comes together," she

exclaimed. "Like alchemy. Major, you must experience it for yourself. Get your hands in here."

"I . . ."

"Ever made shortcrust before?" she challenged playfully. At his silence, she continued, "Thought as much. Give it a try—I promise it's an almost entirely painless experience. Unless . . ." she eyed him ". . . you're worried about maintaining your spotless appearance. Don't want a fleck of pastry on your cuffs. It might not pass muster, and that would be a disaster."

His blue gaze flicked toward her, as if he was well aware that she was deliberately teasing him, and she waited for him to again remark that they were wasting time.

Instead, he shucked off his coat—the movement did wonderful things with his clothing pulling across his shoulders and arms—and rolled up his cuffs to reveal veined forearms lightly covered with reddish-gold hair. They were capable looking forearms. Very capable indeed.

"Challenge accepted, ma'am," he growled and plunged his hands into the bowl.

His blunt-tipped, slightly calloused fingers tangled with hers. Heat shot up her hands, along her arms, and rocketed through her body. She'd never believed fingers could be so masculine, yet now she had proof that they were—that *his* were. Yet they were dexterous, too, as he worked the water into the pastry with adept, efficient movement.

How could she *not* imagine what it would feel like to have his hands move with the same capability on her body? How could she not watch the flex and play of his muscled arms as he turned the act of making pastry dough into something unexpectedly sensual?

Her throat went dry, so she licked her lips—and he stilled beside her. His gaze fastened on her mouth.

"How does it feel?" she asked, hearing the huskiness in her words.

His expression sharpened, becoming almost predatory. His voice a deep rumble, he said, "Ma'am?"

"The . . . ah . . . pastry. You've never made it before. I wondered . . . I wondered how it felt." How could she feel so undone? She planned on attending a weeklong orgy, and yet this simple act of having her hands interwoven with his made her at a loss for both breath and words.

"Surprisingly good," he answered in that rough burr.

My goodness, did that sound delicious. Far more delicious than anything she'd eaten today, or any day.

"Ah, you have it perfectly done," Mr. Baines boomed. "We can move on to rolling out the crust and filling it."

As Beatrice blinked back to rationality, Major Mc-Cameron backed away, reaching for a towel. He made quick work of cleaning his hands before rolling down his sleeves to, unfortunately, cover his forearms. "From here out you'll likely have no need of my services."

That word, *services*, brought too many images to her mind, too many thoughts she wasn't supposed to have about him. Yet she made herself nod and smile brightly, pretending that this stop at the inn's taproom hadn't been unexpectedly revelatory. Because when he pulled on his coat and strode from the kitchen, disappointment needled her, and she realized that she actually might enjoy his company.

She might enjoy *him*.

SITTING alone in the taproom, Duncan tucked his watch back into his waistcoat, and the unlikely twin emotions of impatience and sensual awareness stung him.

They ought to have resumed their journey by now, and he couldn't help noting the ticking down of each dawdled minute. At the same time, the mundane gesture of handling his timepiece brought to mind the countess's hand on his stomach, which plunged him deeper into the memory of their fingers entwining as they'd made pastry. The desire to have her hand, her fingers, on his bare skin came on so fiercely it stole his breath.

Another drink of ale ought to steady him. Yet it didn't.

He shoved his tankard away. Drowning these unwanted needs in drink was no solution, and he had a duty to uphold. He couldn't keep Lady Farris safe if he was sottered.

"Ah, Major, thank you for waiting." Miss Bradbury approached, wiping at a spot of flour on the front of her skirts.

"It's my duty to do so," he said, standing. "Is the class in cookery finished?"

"We made our very own Bedfordshire clangers, and Mr. Baines was gracious enough to write down the recipe." She patted her reticule.

Duncan glanced past Miss Bradbury. "Where's your mistress?"

"She said she would meet us in the yard."

He exhaled. At least this would be the end of the distractions, and they could get back on the road. It wasn't as though he disliked learning how to make pastry, but it had nothing to do with reaching their destination, and it made little sense that they'd spend time doing anything other than trying to get to Nottinghamshire.

Sounds of music and singing came faintly from outside, and he recalled that the town's harvest procession would be happening shortly. Hopefully, they could avoid the worst of the traffic and get out of this place quickly.

Gesturing to the door, he said politely, "After you, Miss Bradbury."

They reached the yard, where Wiggins, Green, and the carriage awaited them. There was no sign of Lady Farris, however.

"Have you seen the countess?" Duncan asked the

coachman after peering into the vehicle and finding it unoccupied.

"Thought I caught a glimpse of her, sir," Wiggins answered. "But she hasn't come by."

Duncan paced back to where Miss Bradbury waited. "Where the deuce could she be?"

"I think I know," the companion said with a small smile. She pointed toward the street that ran past the yard.

Noise from the procession grew louder, and he turned to see townsfolk in wheat-covered hats pass by. Some played fiddles and fifes, whilst others sang and twirled streamers in the air.

Duncan's heart pitched. Lady Farris walked with them, her bonnet traded for one of the straw hats, and joining in the song as she, too, waved a stick adorned with ribbons. Her smile was wide, and even from this distance, it was clear to see the joy in her eyes as she took part in the procession.

"What in Hades is she doing?" he muttered.

"Enjoying herself," Miss Bradbury said. Her gaze was fond as she watched her employer march past. Lady Farris smiled and waved at them as she continued on.

He could only watch her go by, mystified, and also . . . quietly . . . envious. She did look as though she was having a wonderful time, fully immersing herself in yet another experience. What would it be like, to simply wish something for himself and then make it happen?

And yet— "It's not *done*," he burst out. "You don't

just decide to join a harvest procession on a whim. She doesn't even live here. This makes no sense."

Miss Bradbury gave him a sympathetic look. "Major McCameron, you must understand that there's a purpose to her actions."

"Not that I can comprehend," he said.

"It's not my tale to tell," the companion said softly. "But believe me when I say that she has earned every moment of frivolity and happiness." She shot him a sideways glance. "Perhaps all of us have."

He continued to watch the procession and the parade of people in their festive hats, brightening the air with their multicolored ribbons. His gaze returned again and again to the countess and the smile she wore, so exuberant, completely lacking in self-consciousness. Something tugged in him, an urge that began in the middle of his chest and surged lower, coursing down his legs.

One of his feet moved in the direction of the stream of townsfolk. He stared down at it, mystified. Was he . . . was he trying to join the countess? It was as if his lower body acted without receiving any command from his head. As though he *needed* to be part of the festivities.

The only parades he'd marched in had been of the military nature. Those had possessed purpose. They were significant and had an objective. No logical reason why he'd want to be a part of this local harvest procession for a place where he didn't reside . . .

Except there was that tug again. Made all the stronger by the expression of pure delight on Lady Farris's face.

Join her.

He glared down at his feet. Instead of heading toward the procession, he turned his back to it.

"I'll wait by the carriage," he said to Miss Bradbury, grinding out his words. Regret at his rudeness jabbed at him as he marched away. Yet watching the countess indulge her own need for happiness, regardless of rules, frayed at his temper. She did whatever she desired—and somehow, the universe continued to function without spinning into chaos.

He couldn't be sure what would happen if he did the same. The prospect unsettled him, just as *she* unsettled him. As he approached the carriage, he vowed that he'd hold even tighter to the rules that gave his world much-needed structure.

Because it was far too troubling to consider the alternative.

SOMETHING had unsettled Major McCameron. Since they'd gotten underway, he'd kept his words to a minimum, his arms crossed, his gaze fixed on the passing landscape.

His humor wasn't her responsibility, and yet it was clear he was troubled.

"Such a forbidding expression, Major," Beatrice said as the carriage swayed down the road. "Are you stewing over the fact that luncheon took far longer than you'd wanted?"

"I'm here to get you safely to your destination, ma'am. That's the only thing that concerns me." His voice was all military precision.

"Your dedication to duty is admirable," she answered, "but I couldn't resist. My first time making shortcrust pastry and Bedfordshire clangers. The first time I'd ever walked in a procession. So many wonderful chances to do things I've never done before."

He made a noncommittal noise, but his brow furrowed.

"Surely there's *something* you haven't experienced but *want* to," she urged with a smile. "Let me guess. You've always wanted to ride in Astley's Amphitheatre. I can just see you standing on the back of a wild stallion as it thundered around the ring, the audience's applause showering down on you."

The crimp between his eyebrows smoothed, and a corner of his mouth twitched, dislodging a fragment of pleasure from her heart so that it bounced around her chest.

"Never been a dream of mine," he said, "but I'll take it into consideration."

"Oh, I know!" She tapped her fingers together. "You fantasize of living in Paris and becoming a painter who keeps tongues wagging with his scandalous behavior— and you walk around wearing grape leaves in your hair."

His lips quirked as if he fought to keep from smiling. "Only thing I know how to draw are battle plans, and those were never praised for their artistic panache. One of my captains said my scrawls looked like they were done by a barely domesticated member of the canine family."

"You could learn," she pointed out. "And you would look quite fetching with a crown of grape leaves." She curled her fingers against her palm to keep from reaching for his hair and running through the reddish waves—both because it would likely annoy him to have his locks mussed as well as her own sudden need to know its texture.

Perhaps he read her need to tousle his hair, because his hand came up to lightly touch one curl that fell across his forehead. "Sounds positively neoclassical, but I'm not suited for the aesthetic life. Give me a fortification to take or a battlement to storm."

She peered out the window. "Alas, we seem woefully short on such martial objectives."

His shrug drew her attention to the width of his shoulders, and she had no doubt that he hadn't been one of those officers who ordered his men into danger whilst remaining safely behind. He would have led the charge and gotten just as dirty, just as bloody as the soldiers he commanded.

When she'd met other officers at sundry balls and dinners, they didn't have haunted eyes and haunted words. They were exactly the sort of commanders who let their men plunge into battle as they kept themselves secure. Not Major McCameron.

His words from their luncheon drifted back—*The longest day of my life. And the end of many others'.*

The things he'd seen . . . the things he'd done . . .

"It must be a challenge," she murmured, "the transition to life in peacetime."

He inhaled, his chest broadening with the movement. At first, she believed he would give her a quick dismissal—men did not like to admit that they struggled. But then he said lowly, "Aye, ma'am. Rotherby—I mean, the duke—thought this trip to Nottinghamshire might serve as something of a holiday for me."

She'd observed His Grace interacting with the major, how comfortable they had seemed with each other, which appeared to be born from years of camaraderie. Major McCameron had been far looser in the duke's presence, less of a soldier and more of a man in the company of a trusted friend.

The contrast in the major's behavior had been startling, fascinating. There were layers to this man she hadn't initially seen.

He likely needed diversion and pleasure just as much as she did. This journey might be a way for her to experience new things, but there was no reason why she couldn't ensure that he enjoyed himself, too. Seeing him lose a little starch might be gratifying.

And alluring.

A bleat of an animal broke into her thoughts, and

she glanced outside to see a field dotted with fleecy sheep. It made for a charming picture, the green meadow adorned with white wooly creatures, although a breeze swept into the carriage, carrying with it rather pungent scents.

Jeanie, who had been reading up to now, set her book aside and frowned as she stared out the window. She pointed and said with concern, "See that ewe? She's big with a baby."

Both Beatrice and the major looked, and sure enough, there was a sheep that looked quite swollen. It paced restlessly, lying down and then standing up, making sounds of distress.

"Something's wrong with it?" Beatrice asked.

"She seems ready to drop," Jeanie said worriedly, "but can't. And I don't see any sign of a farmer. If she doesn't get help soon, the baby will die, and she might, too."

"How do you know this?" Major McCameron wondered.

"Grew up on a sheep farm," Jeanie replied, still frowning anxiously. She gnawed on her bottom lip as they neared the ewe. "Poor creature."

"You can help her?" Beatrice pressed.

Her companion nodded without hesitation. "Been some time since I did any lambing, but I'd know what to do. Wish I could."

Beatrice knocked on the roof of the carriage. "Wiggins, pull over!"

Almost immediately, the vehicle rolled to a stop, and Jeanie shot Beatrice a grateful look. She removed her spencer, bonnet, and gloves and then stepped down. Once outside, Jeanie clambered the timbered fence that bordered the meadow.

The major exited the carriage before turning to help Beatrice out, and they approached the fence. She was grateful that he didn't say anything about adhering to a schedule. Instead, they both watched with mute fascination as Jeanie approached the agitated ewe, murmuring soothingly.

It happened far faster than Beatrice would have expected. Fortunately, the sleeves of Jeanie's dress were quite short, and with incredible calm, she knelt and eased her hand into the ewe's birth canal. Jeanie did some careful manipulations, and then two miniature hooves appeared, followed by a tiny muzzle. Finally, the whole diminutive creature emerged, dark and wet.

"Might want to look away for the next bit," the major said.

Beatrice squeezed her eyes shut but it was too late—she saw the slippery mass of the afterbirth slide out. "Oh, God."

"Thought you were a mother," Major McCameron said with wry humor.

"Haven't spent much time observing that part from this angle." She swallowed, and her head spun.

The major disappeared into the carriage for a moment, then returned with his hat, which he used to fan her face. "Better?"

"Think so." She laughed at herself. "My goodness, that was far more gruesome than I'd anticipated."

"You didn't cast up your accounts, which is fortunate, given how much you enjoyed that Bedfordshire clanger."

"Please, let's not mention food right now." Still she couldn't help but smile as she watched Jeanie carrying the damp, fragile lamb to its mother's head. The ewe nuzzled her baby like the proud parent she was.

A barrel-chested man in a broad straw hat trotted toward them, carrying a pitcher of water. "Don't know who you are, madam," he panted at Jeanie, "but I thank 'ee for coming to our aid."

"Lambing season ends in May," Jeanie noted with a puzzled tilt of her head, "and late season isn't until November." She nodded gratefully as the farmer rinsed off her hands and arms.

"Know your sheep, missus?" the man asked.

"Born and bred on a working farm in Gloucestershire," Jeanie said with a touch of pride. "We kept sheep for wool and meat. I've helped many a ewe ean—that means *give birth*," she added for Beatrice's benefit.

"We don't know what happened, but half our flock is set to ean in the next week. We've over a dozen springers. A mystery, and an unwelcome one."

"Why's that?" Beatrice asked. "More lambs seems a good thing."

"Except my wife went and hurt her arm helping birth a slink last night." The farmer shook his head. "The leech said she couldn't use her arm for a month at least. Can't find no one from the village to help on account of most of 'em gone to the harvest festival. Which leaves just me to try to get two dozen ewes through their eaning." He studied Jeanie. "It's a shame you can't help."

"Oh, I would love that, just like old times," Jeanie said eagerly, then shot an uncertain glance at Beatrice.

At once, Beatrice knew what she wanted to do. She waved her companion over to her. Lowly, she asked, "Do you want to stay to help ean the lambs?"

Delight filled Jeanie's face—making Beatrice's own pleasure flare—followed by uncertainty. "Is that . . . is that all right? I don't want to leave you on your own."

"If it would please you to stay," Beatrice said, "and perhaps bring you back to simpler times, I'd very much like you to remain. Besides, I've been working to give myself all the things I have longed for—I can do the same for you."

Jeanie ducked her head, but her smile spoke directly to Beatrice's heart. Why not ensure that Jeanie experienced happiness, too? After all, there was a noticeable shortage of joy in the world. She didn't fool herself into thinking that she herself was the sole benefactor of pleasure, yet if she could do this one little thing for someone she cared about, she ought to.

"If this makes you happy," Beatrice said to Jeanie firmly, "then it's settled. You can stay here at—I'm sorry, your name, sir?" she added in a louder voice for the farmer's benefit.

"Dixon," he supplied. "Arthur Dixon."

"If it's all right with Mr. Dixon," Beatrice said, "you can help him with the lambing. I'll pay you the same amount as if you were with me, as well as your room and board here with Mr. Dixon. Will that arrangement suit you, sir?" she asked, glancing at the farmer.

"'Twill," he said at once. "We've a spare room, nice and snug, with a good bed. And my wife can't help lamb, but she can cook a fine stew. We'll keep you well fed."

Deciding it was best not to consider the meat of which that stew was made, Beatrice smiled at Jeanie. "This should be a nice bucolic interlude before your visit with your sister. You can leave for her home once the lambing is done. Then we can meet again at the conclusion of Lord Gibb's, er, gathering."

Mr. Dixon stamped a foot in approval. "I'll tell Sue." He tromped off toward a trim little farmhouse.

"I'll help retrieve Miss Bradbury's luggage," the major said and moved toward the carriage.

Jeanie clambered over the fence to put on her spencer, and once she'd donned the garment, Beatrice brought her in for a hug.

"Ah, Jeanie, I'm glad for you."

"Thank you so very much." Jeanie stepped out of her embrace. "Only . . ." She looked around, and then, taking Beatrice's hand, led her a short distance away. "It will be just you and Major McCameron for the duration of the trip."

"I own that relations between us were not quite agreeable when we began this morning, but we seem to be thawing toward one another." She wouldn't mention how she still felt the brush of his fingers against hers, even hours later, or how his understated humor combined with his wry smiles made her belly flutter. "Things should be pleasant enough between us for the duration of the trip."

"Might be wise not to tell him exactly where you are headed," Jeanie whispered.

Beatrice smothered a giggle. "My lord, no. I said the situation was thawing, but somehow I doubt he'd be particularly tolerant if he knew that I'm en route to a gathering where my every erotic need shall be met, and in abundance, by a number of willing partners."

She glanced over her shoulder. The major was reaching up to take Jeanie's valise from Green, his movement smooth and athletic. She hadn't been able to see when he had been folded up in the carriage, but now she noted again that Major McCameron's physique was excellent—muscled and lean and exquisitely masculine. There was a kind of vital energy within that seemed barely contained by his garments and the tame countryside surrounding him. In battle, he must have been a marvel to behold.

She'd felt the hard ridges of his abdomen and the blunt power of his hands. What would it be like to learn more of him, to discover all the parts of him that were taut and strong? He kept himself tightly controlled, but what if he loosened his grip on that control—and focused his singular intensity on a lover?

As the thoughts uncurled in her mind, he turned to face her, and she was caught on the azure blue of his eyes.

Her stomach leapt and awareness danced through her, and it dawned on her then that in her determination to make Jeanie happy, she had just consigned herself to miles and miles alone with the major.

The prospect was both alarming and thrilling.

Chapter 5

The sun dipped below the horizon, with a faint orange glow against deep indigo heralding the end of what had been an extraordinarily strange day.

Duncan silently exhaled as the carriage came to a stop outside an inn.

Without the presence of Lady Farris's companion, the interior of the carriage had grown paradoxically smaller. He'd been aware of the countess's every movement, every quiet exhalation and shift of her limbs. How could he now catch her scent when before it hadn't teased his senses?

She didn't know it, but thanks to his keen hearing, he'd been able to catch every word of her conversation with Miss Bradbury. Including the fact that at the end of this journey, Lady Farris would be attending a sexual bacchanal.

You couldn't be a man in the upper echelons of society without learning about clubs dedicated to sex and wine-soaked orgies held in picturesque ruins. When he and the other members of the Union of the Rakes had been much younger men, Rotherby had thrown a few wild parties. Such riotous behavior was not entirely unknown to him. He wasn't easy to shock.

Yet knowing that Lady Farris, the woman who sat opposite him in the carriage and whose neck and fingers he'd begun obsessing about, was on her way to be a part of an orgy . . .

He'd been half-stunned, half-aroused for the past few hours.

His mind filled with too many images of her in the throes of ecstasy. Worse still, instead of faceless lovers, he pictured *himself* as the one making her gasp and moan.

Thank God they arrived at The Jewel Inn before he drove himself mad trying to understand what any of this meant.

He was out of the carriage almost immediately, but this time he knew better than to offer his hand to help Lady Farris down. Touching her now would only lead to more confusing sensations and thoughts. So he waited as Green leapt down to assist the countess.

A hound of indeterminate lineage came out to sniff at their heels. He patted the dog on its head and chuckled when it gave his hand a lick of greeting. When he looked up, he found Lady Farris regarding him speculatively.

"Ma'am?"

"You don't laugh often," she murmured, "which is a

shame, because it's quite nice. Reminds me of the way whisky tastes. Rather . . . rough . . . but smooth."

It was a good portrayal of whisky, but heat rushed to his face to hear her describe his laugh. As though she'd been listening carefully to it, to him. The notion was excruciatingly, delightfully intimate.

He cleared his throat, then motioned for her to proceed him. "Shall we go inside?"

As they walked, he caught sight of the stables and saw that they were nearly full. A busy night, and the loud chatter from the taproom's open windows proved that the inn was likely almost completely occupied. Still, the countess's air of gentility and wealth would make certain that there would be some room left for her.

The hound accompanied them, but once they'd crossed the threshold, the dog seemed to decide they were no longer interesting and loped into the nearby taproom.

They were met in the entryway by a middle-aged East Indian woman who wore the apron of an innkeeper.

"Welcome to the Jewel." The woman dipped into a curtsy. "I'm Mrs. Banerjee. Are you staying with us tonight?"

"We are," Duncan answered.

"It's fortunate you arrived when you did," Mrs. Banerjee said. "We have but one room left, and it's yours if you and your wife desire it."

Duncan and Lady Farris shared a look. Without much choice, he gave Mrs. Banerjee a nod.

"Excellent," the innkeeper said brightly. "Mr. and Mrs. . . . ?"

"Frye," Lady Farris said quickly. "Mr. and Mrs. Frye. If we can be shown up?"

"Of course, madam. If you'll follow me," the innkeeper said. "Mind, watch your heads as we go up the stairs. 'Tis an old building, and I cannot tell you how many of my guests, and children, have accidentally concussed themselves."

Mrs. Banerjee took a candlestick and guided them up the staircase, pointing at the low-hanging ceiling as they climbed. At the top of the stairs, she turned down a narrow hallway, and then used the keys at her waist to open a door. She stepped back to permit the countess and Duncan entrance.

"A good room?" Mrs. Banerjee said.

There was a washstand and a small clothespress. A rag rug was spread in front of the cold fireplace.

But that's not what seized his attention.

"There's only one bed," Lady Farris murmured, sounding slightly dazed.

"Well . . . yes," the innkeeper said with a puzzled look.

Duncan swallowed hard, though his throat and mouth remained stubbornly dry. "This will suit. Thank you for accommodating us."

"Yes, thank you," Lady Farris echoed, her gaze continuing to linger on the bed. It was, in fact, not a particularly wide bed. Two people would have to lie very close to each other in order to share it.

"Supper is served downstairs?" he asked.

"The cook goes home at nine, but we serve ale until the last patron leaves."

"Thank you." He dropped a coin into the innkeeper's hand. "Please have our servants bring up our belongings. And have a fire made." Though the day had been warm, a chill had settled with the retreat of the sun.

"Yes, sir." After curtsying, the innkeeper set down the candlestick and darted from the room, closing the door behind her.

The sounds from the taproom grew muffled. It was the first time Duncan had been alone with Lady Farris outside of a carriage, and in the silence that followed, the bed itself seemed to swell and fill the room.

"I'll sleep on the floor," he said decisively.

She pulled her gaze to him. "That won't be very comfortable."

"Wouldn't be the first time I've used floorboards as my mattress." At least the inn's floor was clean and free of vermin, which was a hell of a lot more than he could say about the abandoned slaughterhouse near Badajoz he and his men had been forced to use as their temporary barracks.

"But . . ." She wet her lips, and he tried not to follow

the quick stroke of her tongue as it darted out. "You graciously agreed to act as my escort, and to deny you an actual *bed* is the height of rudeness."

"I'll not think less of you," he said, then added, "if you care at all about my opinion."

"Of course I care about your opinion." She shook her head as though appalled he'd even suggest such a thing. "It's your comfort I'm concerned about."

Absurdly, her apprehension touched him. "Appreciated. But I've every expectation of sleeping soundly tonight, and," he added, "there's enough bedding laid out for us that I can make myself a perfectly snug pallet, with blankets to spare for you."

She looked on the verge of arguing further but then said, "You know your own tolerances best, Major."

Silently, he exhaled. Thank God they wouldn't have to share a bed, because the idea of lying beside her all night, her warmth seeping into him, her nocturnal sighs and murmurs drifting over him while she was close enough to touch . . . it would have been exquisite torture.

"I suppose it would be a fool's errand to suggest that you take your supper up here or at least in a private room instead of in the taproom," he said.

A corner of her mouth lifted. "It would be, yes."

He opened the door and gestured for her to lead the way.

She glided past him, and even though it was the end of a long day, he still caught a touch of her fragrance comingled with the faint musk of her skin. Surely it was because he was hungry that his mouth watered.

Despite the age of the building, the steps were surprisingly quiet beneath their feet as they descended to the ground floor.

Once they reached the bottom of the stairs, he held out his arm to her. She stared at it for a moment before setting her hand on it.

The lightest pressure of her fingers on him, even with the fabric of his coat and shirt as barriers, roused his senses. He'd touched her hand already, felt her palm on his stomach, and had spent most of the day within the confines of the carriage, and yet this physical connection with her shot through him. Any fatigue he might have been feeling disappeared immediately. He became aware of everything all at once—the weight of his garments against his body, the hitch in her breathing.

That catch in her inhalation made it difficult for *him* to draw in air. Yet he was trained to be aware of his surroundings, even down to the minutiae of seeing the flutter of her pulse in her neck. That was all it meant— training and long-held vigilance. Nothing beyond that.

"Could eat a boar," he announced and winced at the loudness of his voice.

"Let's hope it's on the bill of fare," she said in a valiant attempt to match his tone.

Together, they walked into the taproom. It was much like the one in which they had taken their luncheon, though somewhat larger and containing more tables and more people. There was a long bar at one end and a fire at the other. Framed pictures of horses hung on the walls, each with a little placard, indicating that they were horses of some renown. The inn clearly had its share of travelers, because no one gave him or Lady Farris more than a glance as they entered the chamber.

He guided her to a table and held out her seat. With a murmur of thanks, she sank down into it. It was such a mundane thing to do—only today, he'd helped seat the countess and Miss Bradbury—but this time they were alone, which gave the task a domestic, intimate feel.

Fortunately, a man with thinning hair and an apron wrapped around his stout middle approached. He bowed. "Evenin', my lord, my lady. Some supper for you fine gentlefolk?"

Lady Farris rubbed her hands together. "Any roasted boar on the menu?"

Duncan laughed—lowly, but she heard him anyway, and it made her smile.

"We've pork pie, mutton stew, an excellent roast with turnips, and cottage pie."

"Yes," the countess said with a nod.

The server blinked at her. "Madam?"

"I'll try one of each—except the mutton stew. Today I had an encounter with some sheep, so I'd feel like I was betraying them if I made one my supper."

"Those are all mighty filling dishes, madam," the

innkeeper said. "Might be a bit too much for one person."

Her smile was wide when she looked at Duncan, making his stomach tighten in a way that had little to do with food. "You'll share them with me, won't you, my dearest darling? That way we can experience every option. Who knows when we'll come through again, so we might as well take advantage of the opportunity."

"I . . ." It was probably more food than they needed, but her enthusiasm—combined with the sparkle in her eyes—was contagious. He heard himself say, "Why not?"

When the hell do I say things like Why not? Only with the Union of the Rakes did he discard caution and act impulsively, and even then that happened rarely. But when it came to spending time with anyone other than his friends, he trod carefully.

Her smile grew, illuminating the darkest corners of the rusted mechanism that was his heart. "Huzzah! We'll feast like Henry the Eighth! Except we'll refrain from executing our wives."

"Very good." The man bowed and retreated, leaving them alone.

After a serving woman brought them their beverages, he and the countess were silent for several moments, so Duncan offered, "If we're supposed to be married, we ought to talk to each other to complete the illusion."

Her laugh was oddly humorless. "My dearest Mr.

Frye, I can assure you that married couples can spend hours if not days and weeks not speaking to each other. Even the ones that started out as love matches eventually become silent as tombs."

He stared at her, appalled at the picture of life that she painted. If she spoke from experience, how bloody awful. It wasn't the first time she indicated that her own marriage had been less than ideal, if not outright terrible.

His own parents' marriage was a companionable if not passionate union. But Rotherby seemed blindingly happy with his duchess, and when Duncan did see Holloway now, every other utterance out of his friend's mouth was *my darling wife*.

"I've no experience myself," he said.

"No, I don't imagine that you do." The melancholy humor sat on her strangely—utterly antithetical to her usual exuberance. She traced the grain of the wooden table with her fingertip. "Some advice, if you'll hear it: if circumstance does not require you to wed, don't."

He frowned. "But your children married."

"As the earl in need of legitimate heirs, Anthony had to. My daughter Victoria could either exist as a dependent spinster or else find a husband. John is too young to take a wife, but he's freed from the necessity, the lucky blighter."

She has earned every moment of frivolity and happiness. Miss Bradbury's words echoed in his mind as he watched the play of emotion across the countess's face.

"Widowhood is by far the preferable state," she continued with a rueful smile. "For women, in any regard. It is the most freedom we are permitted."

"Hadn't thought of it in those terms," he said quietly.

She shrugged. "Why would you? Women are taught from infancy what men expect of them, how to please them, and know all the stages of a man's life, from their birth to after their demise. I doubt that men are given much education in what it means to be a woman."

He opened his mouth to argue the point, but he had no rejoinder. Because what she said was true, and that truth stunned him.

"Seems a deficiency in boys' education," he finally said. "Mayhap they should include a course on women's lives at Eton."

Her eyes flashed. "This isn't a subject to be mocked."

"It isn't, and I'm not."

"Ah." Tension slowly unspooled from her, though the smile she gave him was ironic. "These past three years, I've been slowly coming to learn that not *every* man wishes to dismiss my opinion."

"Never met the late earl," Duncan growled, "but I suspect the bloke had been something of an ass." When she stared at him, he added quickly, "Apologies. I spoke out of turn. God knows I could go on a tirade about my father's inability to grasp change, yet I'd smear the floor with someone if they called my da narrow-minded."

For a long moment, she said nothing, her expression blank. And then the most incredible thing happened. Her eyes filled with gratitude, warm and genuine and directed at *him*.

"He *was* an ass," Lady Farris said. A giggle bubbled up from her, and she pressed her fingertips to her lips. "Never said that out loud before. Oh, I complained to Jeanie about Edward. But I hadn't had the satisfaction of calling him names. Names he very much deserved."

"I could think of other ones, if you like," Duncan offered.

"Please do," she said with an encouraging nod.

"Fool. Jackanapes." He glanced around to make certain that no one nearby could hear him, then whispered, "Bum-licking bastard."

Her laugh was full and throaty. "Those are very good. Keep going. Be as filthy as you like."

One aspect of being in the military was the abundance of foul language, and he was grateful for his comprehensive vulgar vocabulary if only to make her laugh more. "Arse-pimple. Needle-cock."

A shocked cough sounded beside the table, and Duncan and the countess both turned to see that the server had returned, bearing several plates which he set down between them.

The man's face was the color of beets. "Wine?"

"Aye," Duncan said.

"Be back with that in a moment" came the choked reply before the server hurried off.

It was a mistake to glance at the countess, because the look of hilarity on her face was his undoing. A great, booming laugh leapt out of him, and it showed no signs of stopping, even after the server brought them refills on their wine and disappeared once more.

"I was wrong," Lady Farris said once they had both managed to calm down. "Your laugh isn't nice. It's *gorgeous*."

He didn't know what flustered him more—the eyes of the whole taproom on them or her compliment. Disconcerted, he concentrated on his food, taking automatic bites and following them with swallows of wine.

"Mr. Frye."

He'd just used coarse language without regard for anyone's refined sensibilities. And worse, he'd *liked it*.

"Mr. Frye. Anyone? Anyone?"

Hell—who *was* he?

"Major."

He looked up to find Lady Farris watching him, her lips quirked in amusement.

"Ma'am—I mean, yes, Mrs. Frye?"

She took a drink, her eyes dancing with laughter over the rim of her glass. "You're very focused when you eat."

"Habit, ma'am—my dear."

"I imagine there are other tasks that receive the fullness of your attention," she murmured.

"Wouldn't have been made a major if I had been scattershot in my responsibilities," he answered.

"Do you focus on anything else besides your duties?" she asked coyly. "Something you might consider . . . I don't know . . . enjoyable?"

"I'm no automaton," he answered, yet he bristled at the idea that she might consider him to be nothing more than a machine, without feelings, without needs. A devil suddenly took possession of him, and he said, "There's one other task that receives my complete attention." He lifted one brow.

"I . . . oh." Rose pink stained her cheeks, and she pressed a hand to the base of her captivating throat. She looked goddamned edible.

His mouth watered, and he realized something, something that was both thrilling and deeply unsettling.

He *wanted* the countess. Yet he knew in a bone-deep way that she would completely upend his world. She happily disregarded rules, the very things he relied upon to make sense of the universe. He couldn't permit that—not when he'd fought so hard to keep his world in control.

Chapter 6

Part of Duncan wanted to flee into the night as a measure of self-preservation. But he couldn't leave her on her own to navigate the hazardous road. He'd given his word to both Rotherby and the countess to do his duty by her.

And he was tied to her, drawn by the light she radiated, her sheer joy in living. It was fascinating—he'd never truly met anyone so determined to experience everything life had to offer.

He had to look away from her to find a measure of equilibrium.

Glancing toward the entrance to the taproom, he saw two men standing on the threshold. One was tall, his broad shoulders filling out his coat, and possessing a square jaw that looked as though punches would glance off it without leaving the tiniest bruise. The other man was lean, his features sharp like he'd been whittled, and with eyes so pale blue as to be almost colorless.

Duncan blinked and blinked again. He *knew* those men.

"Excuse me," he said to the countess before leaping to his feet and striding toward the newcomers. "Curtis." He held out a hand. "Rowe."

Both of them seemed surprised to see him at a roadside inn miles from London, but they smiled at his approach.

"The hell are you doing here?" Curtis demanded, pumping Duncan's hand with his usual crushing force. One would never know that the man with the build and might of a pugilist was also one of the country's foremost barristers, whose particular area of expertise was defending those that could not afford counsel.

"Could ask you two the same question." Duncan moved toward his table and said to Lady Farris, "My lady, I believe you've met Mr. Rowe and Mr. Curtis before."

"In June, at the duke's country estate." She smiled up at them. "It's remarkable how attractive your friends are, Major. Between the Duke of Rotherby, Mr. Holloway, and now you two gentlemen, I begin to believe that one of your criteria for friendship is handsomeness."

"Too bad he doesn't apply the same standards to himself," Curtis said.

"I recollect now that I like you very much, Mr. Curtis." She held out her hand, and he bent over it. "And Mr. Rowe, what a pleasure to see you again."

"My lady," Rowe said with a bow. "It's far preferable to look upon you than McCameron."

"That's enough from both of you," Duncan grumbled without anger.

"What an uncommon but delightful thing to meet up with you again," she said warmly.

"Likewise, my lady," Mr. Rowe said.

"Do join us, please." She waved to the table, and in short order, Duncan's friends brought over two more chairs and sat with them. "You three talk like the very oldest of friends. The male combination of insult and affection."

Curtis smirked. "God forbid we should actually let the others know how much they mean to us."

"And let you get inflated ideas of your self-worth?" Duncan demanded and snorted.

"We can't have anyone *value* themselves, Major," Lady Farris said, and the playful swat she gave his shoulder sent hot filaments of awareness through his body.

He shifted in his seat and didn't miss how Rowe gazed at him speculatively.

The countess took a sip of wine before asking, "How long have you known each other?"

"Twenty years," Curtis answered.

"Since we were at Eton," Duncan explained. "Met in the library when we were being disciplined."

Her eyes went round with incredulity. "What on earth could have been *your* infraction? Excessive punctuality?"

Before he could refute that, Rowe said with a grin, "Brawling, if you can believe it."

"I absolutely can*not* believe that." Her look was both aghast and delighted. "Major, there are sides to you that I'm unable to fathom."

"A boy accused me of cheating," Duncan muttered. "Couldn't let that stand."

She clapped her hands together. "Of *that* I am certain. It makes a beautiful kind of sense—you get into trouble for following the rules."

Rowe and Curtis hooted, and Duncan kicked each of them in the ankle. For all their teasing, however, the strangest peace settled over him to have the countess and his oldest friends together and getting along. Granted, they were united in pestering him, but it felt oddly right.

Lady Farris stood, and when Duncan and the others moved to rise, she motioned for them to remain seated. "Much as I enjoy tormenting the major with you, the day has been a long one and I'm for bed. I will bid you all a *bonne nuit*. Enjoy the rest of your evening."

"I'll walk you to the room," Duncan said, getting to his feet.

She held up a hand. "Very courteous of you, but not needed. This is a respectable inn, and I'm relatively certain that my journey upstairs will be a peaceful one. Stay and enjoy your friends' company."

"Very well." In a lower voice he added, "Expect I'll be down here some time, catching up with Curtis and

Rowe and such. You'll want to go to sleep before I return."

"I'll be sure to set aside some bedding and a pillow for you." With a smile and a nod, she left the taproom.

Only when Curtis cleared his throat did Duncan realize that he continued to stare after Lady Farris.

Avoiding his friends' curious gazes, he dropped back into his seat. "Tell me what lures you from the city."

"You first," Rowe said affably.

Duncan hesitated, disliking the thought of lying to his friends. He couldn't very well tell them that he was escorting Lady Farris to an orgy. Neither Rowe nor Curtis were cut from the cloth of staid tradition, but that didn't mean they would greet his news with calm nods of acceptance. And surely the countess wasn't inclined to let the world know about her personal activities.

"Rotherby asked me to accompany the countess on her journey to see a friend in Nottinghamshire," he finally said, which was a version of the truth. "Added security."

"No one better for that job than you," Curtis said, then added because clearly he could not let a sincere comment stand, "you prickly bastard."

Thinking of Lady Farris's comment about male friendship, Duncan couldn't help but snort at this. It didn't seem to matter that they were four and thirty rather than fourteen—if there was an insult to be given, it would be. "And what of you? Why stray so far from your usual disreputable haunts?"

"Rowe's giving a paper—" Curtis began.

"At Sandimas University," Rowe added. "It's about the history of political movements in England."

"And you're his bodyguard?" Duncan grinned as he glanced at Curtis.

His friend shifted uneasily, but Rowe explained with a smile, "He thinks I live in my head too much. Might get on the wrong mail coach or fall into a ditch and forget how to call for help."

"Someone's got to look out for Rowe," Curtis muttered. He cracked his knuckles, a surefire signal that he was uneasy. That shouldn't be, though. Since Eton, Curtis and Rowe had been the closest of friends, nigh inseparable. Surely time on the road together would make Curtis happy, if not less uncomfortable.

Duncan looked back and forth between the two men. Tension hovered in the air, something that made it difficult for Curtis to meet Rowe's eye.

"The road's dusty," Curtis went on. "Need something to drink. I'll fetch ales for us."

Before Duncan could say that it wasn't necessary and that the servers would see to it, Curtis had jumped from the table and strode off toward the bar. As Duncan returned his attention to Rowe, he observed his friend watching Curtis with a look that was both wary and . . . hungry?

"You're not imagining it," Rowe said, still looking at Curtis. "He's tetchy."

"But why?"

Rowe turned his ice-blue eyes to Duncan. "That night at Carriford. Two months ago."

The three of them had been traveling together, coming back from a manuscript archive in Leicester, and had stopped in at Rotherby's estate on the off chance that their friend would be in residence. As it had turned out, Rotherby *had* been there, along with several other guests, including the woman who would one day be his duchess. Lady Farris had also been one of the guests, and, well, Duncan and she had not made a good impression on each other.

"What of it?" Duncan asked.

"Recall that there were only two rooms left for us by the time we arrived. You were in one, Curtis and I in the other. We had to share a bed." Rowe gazed at him levelly, inviting Duncan to realize what this meant.

For a moment, Duncan could not grasp words or how to implement them. It took a full minute before he could fathom what Rowe had said.

"You're surprised," his friend said flatly.

"A bit," Duncan said after a moment. "I knew men during the war, men who preferred the company of their sex. And," he cleared his throat, "Curtis never told me, but I'd guessed that he was one of those men. But—I've seen you with women."

Rowe gave him an enigmatic smile. "It's the *person* that attracts me, not their sex."

"And you find Curtis attractive." Duncan knew he sounded like a dolt, but learning that two of his oldest friends had slept together had fogged his brain.

"Oh, yes." Rowe's grin this time was wolfish. "Without going into that night's details, I can assure you that the sentiment is shared. Only . . ." His smile faded and he frowned down at his hands splayed on the table. "Since then, every word out of his mouth is stilted, and the bastard insists on keeping his hands to himself. Hoping this trip to give my paper can at least salvage our friendship, but . . ." He shrugged, his expression bleak, then he schooled it into neutrality when Curtis approached, carrying three tankards.

"Drink slowly, gents," Curtis said, thumping the ale on the table. "I can only afford one round, and this is it."

Rowe held up his tankard. "A toast. To the Union of the Rakes."

"To the Union of the Rakes," Duncan and Curtis echoed. They clattered their mugs together before taking long drinks. It eased the tension, but only a little, because Rowe and Curtis kept stealing glances at each other. Their gazes would meet and then slide away, then meet again, as though they couldn't *not* look at each other.

For so many reasons, it was strange to be an outside observer to their dance. Though they were his dearest friends, Duncan was shut out from this intimate ballet.

Suddenly loneliness crept through him, as though the tether of human companionship that tied him to the earth had loosened, and he would drift away, unnoted, until he disappeared into the ether.

He wanted *someone* to grab hold and anchor him. But there was no one.

Chapter 7

Judging by the way the major, Mr. Rowe, and Mr. Curtis interacted with each other, with the habits and manners that befitted twenty years of friendship, her presence was not only unnecessary, it might prove a hindrance. She'd had to make similar retreats whenever Anthony or John had come home from school with chums in tow. In those cases, she hadn't taken more than a few steps from the chamber before the room had been filled with a variety of taunts and rude noises. And sometimes smells, God help her.

But Major McCameron was far older than her sons. She'd never forget that. All day, her awareness of the major had grown, as had the subtle shifts between them. He was slowly loosening, releasing the hold on himself. The man she'd met this morning would not have called Edward crude names in a public taproom.

He'd even *flirted* with her. She had no doubt that he wasn't the sort of man to play the glib seducer, which made his words all the more affecting. Perhaps he truly meant them. Perhaps that meant . . . he was attracted to her.

As she left the taproom, a thrill shot along her limbs, concentrating in the soft, receptive places in her body. She was drawn to him, and the contrast between his discipline, so tightly controlled, and the sheer physicality of him, primal and male, was enthralling.

She and the major might not fully understand each other, but understanding wasn't necessary for desire.

Yet after their flirtation, he'd withdrawn. The look on his face had been almost panicked. Perhaps it was for the best that Mr. Curtis and Mr. Rowe had arrived when they had. She had the sneaking suspicion he would have fled—all right, maybe he wouldn't have run screaming into the night, but it had looked as though he *wanted* to.

A little space between her and the major seemed like a good idea.

Before heading up the stairs, she stopped the innkeeper. "I'd like a bath sent up to my room." There would be plenty of time for her to bathe and get into bed before the major returned. No chance of him catching her *en déshabillé*.

Although, the idea of him discovering her without clothing did send a shiver through her—and not in an unpleasant way.

"Yes, my lady. It will be there shortly. I must let you know, though, that we won't be able to take the bath away until morning. I can get some girls to fill the tub, but I need my boys to carry it out, and, on account that they need to be up to meet the first mail coach, they've already gone to bed."

"That will be fine."

Beatrice climbed the steps to the first floor and moved down the corridor to her room. As she walked, a carpet muffled her steps—enabling her to hear the rhythmic squeaking of a bed behind one of the doors.

She couldn't stop herself from pausing and listening, her body tightening automatically in response. A woman's breathy moans were punctuated by a man's excited grunts.

But instead of a few fast squeaks of the bed followed by one long groan from the man, the noises went on. And on. The woman's moans grew louder, throatier. God, it sounded as though she was being thoroughly fucked and thoroughly loving it.

There was a pause, the noises of people shifting, and then the moans began *again*. Holy heaven, they'd changed positions and were *still* rogering each other.

Not once in Beatrice's life had she and Edward had sex for more than a few minutes. She'd read, of course, about marathon sessions of intercourse. In the Lady of Dubious Quality's books, whole chapters had been devoted to a single fuck. Beatrice had believed it to be poetic license. How did people *do* that?

But the couple in this room could. And how she envied them. Her body certainly wanted to be where the woman's was at that moment—her nipples suddenly tight, her quim damp.

Beatrice stroked a fingertip across her collarbone and bit back a whimper. It didn't matter that, in a few days, she'd be at Lord Gibb's, with a buffet of sexual partners from which to choose. She needed sex *now*, preferably the kind that lasted for hours, not minutes.

Her feet wanted to carry her downstairs, into the taproom. Her lips wanted to whisper into Major Mc-Cameron's ear that she wanted him to join her in their lone bed. His words from earlier played through her mind. He was a thorough man—would he be as attentive a lover as the man within the room?

If the look of alarm on his face had been any indicator, he wasn't certain what to do about feeling attracted to her. And suggesting that they become lovers—temporarily—but having him rebuff her was an experience she didn't want.

Very well. She could take care of things herself.

First, she had to walk away and give the two lovers their privacy . . . much as she wanted to hear the conclusion.

Arousal made her legs unsteady beneath her as she quickly hurried to her room. She noted that one of her traveling cases had been brought up, the same with the major's pack. As she waited for her bath, she lit the candle and paced, her body full of restless, responsive energy. A smile touched her lips. How long had it been since she'd had to make her self-pleasuring sessions speedy, lest someone come into the room and interrupt her? The fact that she had to hurry only heightened her need for sensation.

Finally, there was a tap at the door. She opened it to reveal the innkeeper, followed by two girls, who brought in a tub and several cannisters of water. They filled the bath, draping a towel at the foot of the bed, and setting a cake of soap beside the tub.

"I can help you out of your things, my lady," a freckle-faced girl offered after the innkeeper left the room.

"That would be lovely." Beatrice assisted where she could, slipping her arms out of her sleeves and holding steady once the girl had reached her stays. At last, Beatrice was down to just her shift. She gave the girl a coin, and when she was finally alone, she peeled off the wisp of linen. After dousing the lone candle, which permitted the room to be illuminated only by the moonlight spilling in through a narrow window, she stepped into the bath.

The water was warm, not hot, but it was enough. It settled around her body, lapping at her skin, and she glanced at the door. She hadn't locked it, but surely she'd hear if someone—specifically Major McCameron—approached, and besides, he was busy downstairs, enjoying his friends' company. He said plainly he wouldn't be up for a long while.

She stroked her hands down her neck and lower, until, with a low moan, she reached the firm tips of her breasts. Circling her fingers around her nipples, sensation gathered, echoing hotly in her quim. She was ready.

What if Major McCameron came into the room right now? What if he saw her in the bath, completely naked, her hands on her breasts, no doubt as to what she was doing? Would he turn and flee? Or what if . . . he closed and locked the door behind him . . . and watched her?

Thinking of this, she pinched her nipples and bit her lip as she fought to keep from crying aloud. She could picture it now, the major's cock hardening in his breeches, pressing against the placket as proof of his desire for her. He'd battle with his arousal—he was a man of restraint—but then he would be unable to fight it. First he'd stroke himself through the fabric, molding to the shape of his cock, but it wouldn't be enough. He'd curse as his hand fumbled for the fastenings of his breeches. He'd stare at her through half-lidded eyes, caressing his cock as her hand dipped between her legs—both in her mind's eye and in real life.

She gasped when she found herself slick and ripe. Her fingers stroked around her opening and then her bud as she pictured Major McCameron's fist going up and down his cock while he watched her pleasure herself. Would he be silent? No, she wanted to hear him, his grunts of ecstasy, low and animal.

Her caresses grew faster, more intense. The beginnings of a climax gathered, bright but still too distant. She squeezed her eyes shut.

What if . . . the major could no longer stand it? He'd stride forward as she sat in the tub, and then cup the back of her head, bringing her forward until . . . she took his cock in her mouth. And then he'd thrust between her lips, and she'd take it, loving his force, his taste, her own hand still working her quim.

A growl shattered her concentration.

She opened her eyes. Major McCameron stood in the room—staring at her. His cock wasn't in his fist, but there was a definite thick, upright shape snug against his breeches.

Her hands froze. This wasn't her imagination. He was *actually here*. Watching her pleasure herself.

"Holy God!" she yelped, sinking lower into the water.

A second later, he spun around, presenting her with his back. "Didn't see anything," he rasped.

It was a lie, and they both knew it. "Towel. At the foot of the bed."

With his back still angled to her, he edged nearer and reached toward where the towel was draped. Unfortunately, because he wasn't looking where he was going, his hand first touched her shoulder. Her naked, wet shoulder.

Beatrice yelped again, and he made a strangled sound.

"Apologies," he muttered. "Trying to get the—"

"Two feet in the other direction," she said through clenched teeth. It was one thing to deliberately attend an orgy. She wouldn't mind people seeing her naked in *that* context. But having the major interrupt her *now*, without her intending it to happen, that was damned different.

Major McCameron shuffled closer to the bed and mercifully was able to grab the towel, which he thrust toward her.

"I'm getting out," she warned grimly. "Don't look."

"Not looking." His gaze was fixed on the door.

Shaking with lingering arousal, she stood and wrapped the towel around herself. She'd been moments away from a climax when he'd appeared—and her body wanted that release.

"What are you doing up so soon? You said you'd be down in the taproom with your friends." She rubbed the towel over her body as quickly as possible, trying to dry herself so that when she put on her nightgown and rail, they didn't stick to her damp skin. Unfortunately, her nipples were still firm, and the towel's abrasion sent little sparks of sensation through her.

Mentally, she willed her body to *calm down*.

"They went to bed early to catch the morning's first mail coach," he growled over his shoulder. "And *you* said you were weary, so I thought you'd gone to sleep already. There was no light under the door, so, no, I didn't expect to find you in the bath and . . . in the bath."

Shuddering with persistent desire, she might have to dunk herself in the tub again.

"There's plenty of moonlight," she fired back before tearing open her traveling case. Too intent on seizing her nightclothes, she barely noticed as books went tumbling across the floor. As she threw the garments on, she added, "I didn't need a candle."

"Of course," he said, his tone patently disbelieving.

She cinched the belt on her robe. "You can turn around now."

He did so, but his gaze touched on her for a moment before fluttering away like a moth. "I'll just . . . I'll light a candle."

"Unnecessary at this point," she said with a shaky laugh. "You've seen all there is to see."

Still, the candle blazed to life, and after the more subtle illumination of the moonlight, the room felt overbright now. Everything stood out in stark relief—including the fact that his erection hadn't fully subsided. Or the fact that her nipples were still hard as gemstones.

The lingering sensation of his hand against her bare skin made her shiver. She'd learned already that he had a rather rough hand, slightly calloused, but now she knew that it easily covered her shoulder.

He had large hands. She now had visual proof that other aspects of his body were proportionate.

He looked at her, then looked away. "Were you—"

"I'm not responding to that."

"Aye," he said again. A long, awkward pause followed. "Got an early start tomorrow." His voice dipped a full octave. "I'll have the bath removed, and then we should go to bed."

Her heart pitched. "Oh, damn. I'd been so eager to have a bath, I hadn't considered the repercussions. Mrs. Banerjee said that it can't be retrieved until the morning."

"But . . ." He cleared his throat. "It's covering the part of the floor where I intend to sleep."

She inhaled, resigning herself to one irrefutable fact. "We're going to have to . . . share the bed." He was silent for a long time, and she said, "I promise I won't overpower and ravish you."

"You can't overpower me." He lifted a brow.

"There are ways beyond mere brute strength." She crossed her arms over her chest.

His gaze shot immediately downward, and she realized belatedly that her arms pushed her breasts up and against the thin fabric of her nightclothes. It hadn't been deliberate, but it did prove her point because he seemed fascinated by the sight. She had rather dark nipples, and the cotton nightgown barely veiled them.

The sound he made was deep and uncivilized and wildly thrilling.

She *did* affect him.

He ripped his gaze from her breasts, now staring at the bed as if it was a mythical beast capable of devouring men whole. Or perhaps he felt that way about *her*.

She exhaled. "I'm sorry that we cannot remove the bath. There's nothing to be done about it. I don't want to make you uncomfortable, so do as you see best. But I can assure you, despite the spectacle you witnessed moments ago, I am not some libidinous virago incapable of controlling her baser impulses."

A minute passed, and then another.

"As you like." He gave a clipped nod. With economical movement, he pulled off his jacket, then removed his boots before setting them side by side at the foot of the bed. His fingers made short work of the buttons of his waistcoat, which he hung on a peg by the door. He hesitated, then removed his shirt, which he also hung on the peg, before turning back to face her.

Beatrice sucked in a breath. God above, but he was gorgeously fashioned. Whatever he did to keep himself in such excellent physical condition was marvelously effective. Wide shoulders, generously muscled arms, and a sculpted chest adorned with reddish-gold hair. There was no spare flesh on him anywhere— she'd never before seen anyone with such a taut, ridged abdomen, nor had she seen on a living man the defined lines that angled along past his waist and vanished beneath the waistband of his trousers, which hung low on his hips.

One long line, the thickness of a finger, bisected his chest, and a round, raised spot marked the top of his left shoulder. Scars. Evidence that he had been to war and had survived.

"Ma'am."

She blinked, realizing that she stared at him just like the libidinous virago she'd claimed not to be.

"I'll just . . ." She clambered into bed, scooting over as far as she could. After pulling the covers up to her collarbone, she removed her night rail and hung it from the bed post. She turned over onto her side so that she faced the wall, a deliberate movement so that the major could finish undressing without her gaping at him.

The trouble with not watching him remove the remainder of his clothing was that she relied on her imagination to picture him unbuttoning his breeches and stepping out of them so that he wore nothing but his smallclothes.

It was terribly easy to picture him in thin drawers—what his thighs looked like beneath the linen, and his arse, and his cock.

"Are you well, ma'am?"

"Pardon?"

"You groaned."

Had she made that noise aloud? "Merely tired. Please put out the candle before you get into bed." The bed they would share in a moment. Her in a wispy nightgown, and him only in drawers, with hardly any fabric separating their bare skin. Perhaps this hadn't been such a grand idea, after all.

"Aye," he said gruffly, before adding, "ma'am."

It was a calculated use of the term, she understood

that much. Because it created necessary distance and formality, which was badly needed after he'd walked in on her pleasuring herself, and they'd also gawked at each other's partially dressed bodies.

He *did* have a luscious body, and she could easily picture herself running her tongue down his flat stomach and going lower and lower and . . .

She jammed her eyes shut, trying to call to mind soggy stockings, and cold mashed potatoes, and any number of other unpleasant things.

He blew out a breath, and the room was suddenly dark. Perhaps she was safe now that she didn't have to look at him any longer. When she opened her eyes, however, she saw it was not *entirely* dark, with the moon shining through the window. It was bright enough for her to see that indeed, his drawers barely offered concealment—and revealed that, as he noiselessly crossed the room toward the bed, his cock was half-hard, as if he was equally affected by her presence as she was by his.

Pretend like there's a drop of water that snuck underneath your sleeve cuff and it's running down your wrist to your elbow.

That was better. Nothing was more irritating and less arousing than that lone bead of water.

The bed shifted, squeaking slightly, as he lowered himself down onto the mattress. She held herself still as he moved into a sleeping position. Though he was a lean man, he was surprisingly heavy, and she fought to keep from rolling toward him.

His calf brushed hers. It was lightly dusted with hair, and each of those hairs shot lightning through her.

"Sorry," he muttered.

"Oh, I barely felt anything," she said breezily. She feigned a yawn. "What an enervating day. I can barely stay awake."

He grunted in response. That was fine. All of this was fine.

"Good night, Major McCameron," she said, attempting to make her voice sound sleepy. Either she tried to convince him or herself—both were equally probable.

"'Night," he rumbled.

She plumped her pillow, then laid her head down on it. The pillow in and of itself was decent enough, but she couldn't seem to get comfortable on it. For that matter, the strip of mattress she had at her disposal felt rather stiff and unyielding. Or perhaps that was her own body, which she held in rigid, unfamiliar positions to keep from touching the major. And she *would not* allow herself to come into contact with any part of him. Much as she fought against the desire to plaster herself to his broad back, and wrap her arms and legs around him, and rub against his hot skin.

He *was* very warm, his flesh radiating heat that seeped into her own. In a way, it was much more pleasant to share a bed with someone rather than rely on using a bed warmer to chase the chill from the sheets.

His heat offered comfort. For the first time ever, she wasn't truly alone in bed. Granted, she and Major McCameron were the furthest thing from lovers—and yet he was here now. All of his warmth soaked into her limbs, settling her, anchoring her, and she sank down into it.

SHE came awake gradually, settling into peaceful awareness. Sunlight teased under her closed eyes. Had she truly slept the night away? She supposed she ought to get up and get dressed, since they had a distance to cross today, and Major McCameron would likely be irritated with her if she caused any delays. But this was *her* trip to enjoy, and besides, the bed was so warm, and the man who held her was so delightfully solid, so beautifully muscled, his arms wrapped securely around her as though she was precious and he couldn't get enough of her.

Her eyes flew open.

The major embraced her, his chest pressed to her back. Oh, God, was that his cock pressed into her arse? His very erect, very hard cock?

She made the mistake of glancing back at him, and he looked exquisitely rumpled as he slept, his hair mussed and his chin stubbled. There was a small crease between his brows, as if even as he slumbered, he never fully divested himself of his sense of responsibility.

His cock, however, seemed ready for pleasure.

Perhaps this was a sign. A wonderful, wonderful sign that she and the major ought to act on their mutual attraction.

No sooner had the thought entered her mind, the major's body went taut. He sucked in a breath and quickly released his hold of her as though she had been on fire.

"It's just biology," he said tightly, edging away from her.

So, he was awake.

She rolled onto her side to face him and found his expression to be mortifyingly appalled.

"Doesn't signify anything," he clipped.

"What do you mean?"

"You saw your husband when he woke up," he explained. "What happened to his . . . his body."

"Edward and I . . ." She cleared her throat, and busied herself with picking at a frayed thread on the counterpane. Words flew from her mouth, and she hadn't the presence of mind to stop their flow, still too addled from sleep and the feel of his body against hers. "We didn't sleep in the same bed. He'd come to my room on the nights he wanted . . . and afterward, he'd leave. And then, even that stopped soon after the children were born."

Why had she confessed that to him? There was no

possible reason to give him concrete evidence that Edward had never truly been attracted to her. Edward had seen her as many things—muse, mother of his children—but not lover. Not someone to be desired.

"If it's merely biology," she said, attempting an offhand tone, "that must mean you don't find me arousing."

"Not what I said." He raised himself up on an elbow, careful to keep his other hand on his crotch. "I do. Find you arousing."

Her heart pounded with exultation—she hadn't been mistaken last night. "I feel the same way."

He sucked in a breath, and his nostrils flared.

"But it isn't a good idea," he continued, and it sounded as though he strained for a sensible, reasonable tone whilst also shielding her gaze from his hard cock, "to do anything about this attraction we share."

Difficult to hold on to her pleasure in the face of his prevarication. "Why not?"

Major McCameron flexed his free hand, as if trying to keep himself from wrapping it around something. From wrapping it around *her*.

He sat upright and swung his legs around so that he perched on the edge of the bed, his back to her. In the morning light, she could see much more of him, all the shapes of his muscles, and that there were more scars than she'd originally realized. A few came from knives, but there were puckered circles, too, which had to have come from bullets.

She'd heard that the greatest threat to a soldier wasn't the initial wounding, but the fever that often followed. Somehow, he'd lived through all of them, many times. What a will he had to survive again and again.

There was much more to him than she knew, and suddenly she craved all of that, as well. Not merely the use and pleasure of his body but to learn of the man that inhabited that body. The things he'd seen, the experiences he'd endured and emerged from stronger than before. What gave him joy and what brought him sorrow—because certainly he'd known sorrow.

"I didn't plan on this," he said.

"So many unplanned things that can be wonderful. Since we're attracted to each other, we could enjoy the company in bed, and it need not be anything more than that." She reached out to touch his back—his skin was very fair, and there were freckles on his shoulders—but the moment her fingers met his flesh, he flinched.

A combat veteran flinched from her touch.

She'd vowed to make no apologies for herself or her desires, so she refused to let his rejection touch her. But the last sparks of her excitement died.

"You don't want to be attracted to me." She climbed out of the bed and wrapped herself in her night rail.

The major stood and faced her, with the bed between them.

"I *do* desire you," he said roughly. "Yet there's a way I need to live my life. I've spent decades adhering to the rules, being a good officer. The path you're traveling now, doing what you please—it's not my path. I can't . . ." He dragged his hands through his hair. "I can't *function* in that fashion. It unsettles me. It's like the whole world is the edge of a blade, and I'm a moment away from cutting myself into ribbons."

"You can balance on that blade," she said softly.

He shook his head, his expression tormented. "There are *rules*. There's a method in the way things are done. And I need it that way. It gives me . . . purpose. Order."

She drew in a long breath, her heart aching for him. Because this warrior was profoundly shaken. "I understand. Yet, Major, I waited a long time to be able to live *my* life the way I wanted it, free of the rules that are so essential to you. And while I respect your need for order and methodology, that isn't who I am."

"Don't want to make you into someone you aren't," he said gruffly. "No one should."

Be less, Bea, Edward used to say to her. He'd resented her attempts to be anything other than a prop for his self-worth. In the years before she was a married woman, she had been a girl full of excitement about the world, eager to have new experiences and fill her mind with knowledge.

She'd spent the past three years finally being the person she'd wanted to be. The major seemed to recognize this, and though she didn't fit into the neat, contained box of his world, he didn't try to jam her into it. But they were clearly too different, too discordant.

Pulling her night rail snug to her body, she said softly, "Perhaps it's best if we simply continue on as we were. Two people traveling together for a brief time, who will part ways when they reach their destination."

He looked as if he wanted to say more—offer an apology, an explanation—but he stopped himself and then nodded. "That's the wisest choice."

"Go ahead and dress," she said. "I will meet you downstairs."

For a moment, he didn't move, but then he began to put on his clothing. It seemed as though his military habits were deeply ingrained because he was garbed and out of the room within two minutes.

She walked to the window and looked out at a stripe of garden. Unlike the severely trimmed hedges and trees that comprised city gardens, this one was a little chaotic, a little messy, abundant with late-blooming flowers that grew in exuberant profusion.

Much as she felt disappointment that the attraction between her and Major McCameron would go no further, gazing at the garden made her smile.

We're two wild things, she thought. *And all the more beautiful for it.*

Chapter 8

Duncan carried a hamper, following the countess as she selected the best spot in which to eat their midday meal. His gaze kept returning to her, the breeze molding her skirts to her legs, her hips moving with an enticing sway. She inhabited her body comfortably, and now that he'd seen that body not only nude but *aroused*, he cursed himself.

He could have known her feel, her taste. Yet here he was, tight with thwarted wanting, watching her take long strides across the meadow.

Lady Farris was a force unlike any he'd ever known, and she would turn his strictly regulated world on its head. At this tumultuous stage in his life, he needed certainties, order. She offered none of that. It was smarter to limit their involvement—but damn it if the decision didn't twist in his gut.

Because he hadn't been completely honest with her at the inn this morning. There was another reason why he could not become her lover, one that struck at the heart of him.

Though he spent the night with women, he wasn't engineered the way many other men were. Sex meant something to him. He developed yearnings, feelings—which were mostly inconvenient for his lovers, who wanted only a night's pleasure before moving on.

Perhaps, once he had returned to England, he ought to have searched in earnest for a bride. Yet Susannah's rejection had wounded him too deeply to enter into the marriage market, so he'd remained a bachelor who occasionally fucked but hurried on before he started to care.

He wasn't sure why he was protective of that fact. Yet he was. Maybe Rotherby and the others suspected as such—but they didn't talk about it.

He didn't talk about it with anyone.

"Here!" Lady Farris cried up ahead. "The perfect spot." She pointed to a gentle, grassy slope that led to a shining pond.

Beneath his arm, he also carried a blanket, and after setting down the hamper, he spread the cloth out on the ground to keep her clothing from getting stained or damp. Wiggins and Green had remained behind with the carriage, so he and the countess were alone, save for the droning bees and brightly hued butterflies skipping through the air.

Lady Farris bent and untied her boots. She set them aside before reaching farther up her skirts.

"What are you doing?" He winced at his priggish tone.

She said nothing, but then a moment later sighed. It was a sound not unlike what she'd made last night as she'd pleasured herself in the bath, and it stroked across his belly. Then she held up the filmy shape of her stocking, still holding the curves of her leg. She performed the same action with her other stocking, laying them beside her boots and straightening with a triumphant smile.

"Is there anything better than the feel of grass between your toes?"

Having seen her naked, he didn't think that looking at her bare feet could be at all erotic. He was wrong. The throaty noises she continued to make did not help matters, either.

Heat pooled in his groin as she wiggled and curled her toes.

"A bug could bite you," he said inanely.

"Or there could be a venomous adder hiding," she added in a matter of fact tone. "But I can't remember the last time I walked barefoot in grass. Must have been at least thirty years ago. How could I resist the opportunity to do it again?"

A number of dangerous scenarios played out in his brain. Roving bandits might show up and chase them. There could be a freak snowstorm.

"It's not going to happen," she said.

"What isn't?"

"Any of the terrible scenes going on inside your head. They *might*, but then again, they might not."

He frowned at how easily she'd read his thoughts. "We should eat and get back on the road."

She ignored his comment and flicked her fingers at his boots. "Take those off. Sense the grass between your toes. It feels so delicious. Unless," she said with a speculative tilt of her head, "you don't actually like things that feel good?"

"Never said anything like that." Affronted, he straightened. "I like them well enough."

She held up her hands. "It's all right if you don't. You haven't particularly enjoyed the food we've eaten, and you were quite willing to sleep on the hard, uncomfortable floor, so . . ." She shrugged.

Before he knew what he was doing, he'd tugged off his boots and stockings.

"Fine," he said defiantly. "They're off."

A smile curved her lips. "And yet you've arranged your boots very neatly, side by side, and you tucked your discarded stockings into them. All very orderly."

"I was trying to keep everything clean," he muttered.

"Move your toes a bit," she urged, wiggling her own. "Like this."

He had the perverse urge to do no such thing, but he wasn't a stubborn child being forced to finish his oatmeal, so he did as she suggested, giving his toes an experimental wriggle. The grass was cool against the soles of his feet and gave off a verdant aroma.

"What do you think?" she asked, genuine curiosity in her voice.

"It's not quite as soft as I'd have expected it to be, but," he continued when she seemed disappointed by his answer, "the sensation isn't entirely unpleasant."

Her smile widened. "It isn't fulsome praise, but I'll take it."

He took a few experimental steps, finding the grass springy. Its texture tickled a little, making him bite the inside of his cheek to keep from chuckling.

"No hiding it, Major," Lady Farris said. "I can see you fighting a laugh."

"Wonder what my men would've thought of their commanding officer being tickled?" He snorted. "They probably thought I had iron feet."

Though he'd fought alongside his men, he'd been careful that they didn't see him as excessively vulnerable. They'd needed him to be a strong, steady leader, and so only in the privacy of his tent had he ever permitted the doctor to treat his wounds.

She eyed his feet as if she found them attractive, which was bizarre. Men's feet weren't attractive. They were big and a bit hairy and tended to smell if not cleaned regularly.

"Well, you don't have iron feet," the countess said with an approving nod.

"Aye. I'm flesh, like any man."

Her gaze met his. The intimate word *flesh* seemed to still the breeze and turn the meadow into a much smaller, more enclosed space. Last night rushed into his mind and body, remembering her hand between her legs, the other on her breast.

He quickly shook out the blanket. Hopefully the activity covered his half-hard cock, but in case it didn't, he kept his back to her as he rummaged through the hamper.

A few long breaths helped him regain control over his body, and when he turned around, she had seated herself on the blanket.

She patted the fabric. "Sit. I'm famished, and while I still wasn't able to secure us some boar to eat, I think there are some pork pies that will suffice."

He laid out the aforementioned pies, wrapped in paper, as well as some pears, a packet of almonds, a jug of what smelled like cider, and two dented pewter mugs. They quickly began to eat, and he had almost—but not quite—congratulated himself for being unaffected by her, when she made another of her pleasured groans.

"Everything on the road tastes so good," she murmured before taking another bite of pie.

It seemed impossible to contain the joy she felt in living. He admired it—envied it. What must it be like to find the world a place of exciting, limitless possibility?

"I warrant getting free of London's smoke can whet the appetite," he said.

"A prosaic answer, but a credible one." She chewed an almond.

"Aye, that's me," he muttered. "Prosaic and credible." They weren't precisely the most thrilling descriptors, but then, he was a former major in His Majesty's Army, not a retired pirate.

"There are worse things to be than plausible," she said. "For example, if no one ever believed you. Or if your opinions were summarily dismissed on the basis of your gender."

"Fair point."

"Besides," she went on, "I imagine an influential and popular man such as the Duke of Rotherby appreciates having a trusted friend. They're in short supply."

"He has enough arse-lickers—I mean, boot-lickers." Even though he'd used coarse language in front of her last night, he still wasn't used to speaking so crudely in front of a woman.

She laughed. "I preferred the first descriptor. More piquant. And I saw those arse-lickers in action at the business Bazaar. Thank goodness Miss McGale—I mean, the duchess—was there to provide some much-needed authenticity. Well, authenticity of mind and heart, if not identity. It didn't hurt that he fell madly in love with her. Must have been strange, to see your friend—who was no stranger to rakishness—so besotted."

Duncan snorted at the understatement, yet he mulled over what she said. "Strange, aye. Like seeing a tiger suddenly begin to eat exclusively carrots."

"I can't decide if comparing the duchess to a carrot is a compliment or an insult." Her lips pursed into a smile.

"No insult meant," he said at once. "The duchess is a fine woman, sharp as a saber."

"And she loves the duke," Beatrice added pointedly. "Surely a point in her favor."

"Many points in her favor." Duncan ran his hand back and forth over the grass, comparing the feel of it against his palm versus his feet. Contemplatively, he said, "Rotherby's a rogue and a libertine, but there'd always been a part of himself that he kept closed off— even from me and the others. But when the duchess burst into his life . . . it's like he could fully be himself."

He shook his head, irritated with himself. "Don't think that makes any sense."

"It makes perfect sense," she said, quiet. "It's a rare thing, for anyone to find that."

They both fell silent. His own dashed matrimonial hopes were acrid in his throat, and he struggled to swallow them back down where he could taste them no longer. As for the countess, he had no idea what she was thinking—though, given what she'd said about life married to the late earl, he could hazard a guess.

Time to steer the conversation to something more readily navigable. He took a drink of ale and said, "We've more than Rotherby in common. There's Sebastian Holloway, too."

She smiled, spreading warmth through him. "Mr.

Holloway and Lady Grace are what my younger son would call *good people*. I was more than happy to have the opportunity to serve as their patron. They're still in the planning stages of their expedition, but I'm eager to learn about their findings."

"You're interested in the sciences," he noted.

"Not as one with any ability in them. But I appreciate others' work. We're on the cusp of tremendous change, but there's danger in it. I wanted to ensure that there were *some* people who understood its danger and acted responsibly."

He felt his brows climb. "And that falls on you?"

Her smile was self-deprecating. "I'd never believe that I was responsible for protecting the world. What temerity. But I did learn something after my husband passed. My eldest, Anthony, and I went through all of the earldom's holdings and investments." She shuddered. "God. The things we learned. Cotton and sugar plantations, and more. Paying for my gowns, our food, our servants."

She looked ill but continued grimly, "He and I agreed to divest as soon as possible. Yet that didn't seem like enough. So I've set aside part of my widow's portion on repairing some of the damage I'd unwittingly caused and the harm I'd perpetuated. There will always be more and more to do."

He nodded, absorbing what she'd said. "Your presence at the business Bazaar—where you met Rotherby—that wasn't happenstance."

"If there's money to be made," she said firmly, "I can't do it with a blind eye to its origin. And that is where I met the duke and the duchess. She wasn't a duchess then, of course."

"Now you can count them both as your friends," he pointed out.

"Though you might not consider him *your* friend after saddling you with me," she said.

"Two points." He held up one finger. "First, I did consider undertaking this journey as a favor to Rotherby, but I was not *saddled* with you. You're my responsibility, yes, but I'm a grown man and can make my own decisions as to what I do and how I do it."

"As you like," she said evenly, though she seemed pleased by his answer. "But I'm not sharing my pork pie."

"Ma'am," he said gravely, "I vow I will not touch anyone's pie without their express permission."

They shared a laugh, and, with a start, he realized he liked it. He liked pleasing her and watching her smile. He liked hearing her thoughts and being in her company.

Damn good thing they weren't acting on their attraction—he could have been in danger of developing feelings. Given that she was en route to an orgy, it was a fair assumption to believe she was not seeking any kind of lasting connection with her lovers.

"The second point?" she pressed.

Easier to discuss the Union than to think about what

it meant to genuinely enjoy the countess's presence. "Rotherby has been my friend for twenty years, the pompous ass."

"I've never heard anyone say *pompous ass* with so much affection," she teased.

"He'd call me worse if given the opportunity. And I love him like a brother—better than a brother because I chose him and he chose me." Through all the years of Duncan's deployment, he could rely on letters from Rotherby and the other members of the Union, full of good humor and amusing anecdotes that took his mind off the realities of life during wartime.

Whereas his actual brother, Ian, had barely written to Duncan and had never once in all this time acknowledged the fact that Susannah had jilted him.

He could imagine the countess's letters. Witty and lighthearted and containing unexpected insight, just as the woman herself was all of those things.

She was also sensuous as hell. Watching her enjoy her food with unbridled delight, he couldn't stop thinking about her hands on her ripe body, or the sounds she made as she pleasured herself or, God help him, the look on her face as she did so. She gave herself thoroughly to sensation. It was too easy to imagine what it would be like to join her in bed—beyond the awkward sharing of a mattress they'd had last night.

Not rolling her onto her back and tupping her senseless had been, perhaps, the greatest test of his physical ability and restraint that he'd ever known. When he'd awakened with her warm and soft in his arms, his body had responded at once.

Worse, his heart—the stupid fool—had responded, as well, throbbing in his chest with demands of *more*.

He never woke with a woman, knowing deep down that if he did, he'd want more from them besides mere sex. And sex had been all his lovers had been willing to give.

To wake with someone, to greet the day with them and murmur drowsily about dreams and plans, and then, perhaps, share a sweet and tender fuck . . . it was the sort of thing he'd wanted desperately before he and Susannah had married. He'd hoped to share that with her. But he never had, not with anyone. Until this morning.

Eyes twinkling, she said, "It's rare, a friendship like the one you have with the duke, and with the others. And that continued on at university?"

"After Eton, a commission was purchased for me. You know the way of things for second sons."

"John will go into the law. Or he'll run away and join a troupe of strolling players. I'm not certain one is more respectable than the other." She added in a whisper, "I secretly hope that he'll become an actor and scandalize all of London."

He chuckled. "Duty, responsibility. These are important concepts in my family. I always knew I was going to have to make my own way in the world—I've an allowance, but it's deliberately modest. My parents didn't want me growing soft."

"You are assuredly *not* soft," Lady Farris said, looking at his shoulders.

His face heated with embarrassment. His body was merely something he used to accomplish tasks—granted, he'd taken pains to ensure that it accomplished those tasks with the maximum amount of ability and efficiency—but for some reason, all the women he'd ever taken to bed were excessively pleased by his form.

Pressing on, he said, "I didn't want to be one of those officers who just told his men what to do and sat back to collect the glory. Learned about incendiary devices and explosives from one of my men. I thought about how to parlay that knowledge into something I could do now that the war's over but . . ." He shook his head. "I've been adrift since returning to England."

There was no earthly reason why he ought to tell her that, when he himself was only now coming to terms with his restlessness and lack of purpose. Hell, only Rotherby had ever directly addressed those unwonted and unwanted feelings.

And yet here he was, telling her parts of himself he did not quite understand.

"It's been two years," she pointed out gently.

He fought to keep from growling, frustrated with himself. "I know. I'm following all the rules, and yet

I cannot seem to shake this sense of aimlessness . . . I hate it. I hate everything about it."

She slid her hand across the blanket, but then stopped short before she could clasp his. "There's something for you, surely."

"There is." He forced himself to exhale and to not want to feel her touch. "Rotherby offered me a position as the estate manager of Carriford. I'm certain it's the answer."

"*The* answer?" She regarded him, and the skepticism in her expression made his spine tighten. "Is there such a thing?"

"Aye, there is," he said firmly. "And for me, Carriford is it."

The estate *had* to be the solution to his purposelessness, because nothing else seemed right. The possibility that it might not be sent little filaments of panic through him, but he ignored them because finding meaningful employment was precisely what he should do. Surely when he was ensconced at Carriford with an abundance of responsibilities, he would no longer feel as though he was floating through life, grounding himself in order and obligation.

THEY hadn't traveled more than five miles from where they had stopped for luncheon before Lady Farris sat up straighter and knocked her hand against the vehicle's roof.

"Wiggins! Stop the carriage!"

Duncan came to full alert while the coach slowed. "What is it?"

Her face full of excitement, she pointed out the window. "There. I think it's a Roman ruin."

He peered out to see a steep, rocky hill with what appeared to be the remains of stone structures atop it. The hill itself was dotted with scrub and silver birch, but for the most part it was abundant with stones and earth. From the road, it was just possible to see a few ancient walls and the remainder of a column.

He exhaled, tension seeping from him. Merely an old building, and nothing threatening.

"Wiggins, take us to the base of the hill." The smile that wreathed Lady Farris's face would illuminate the darkest corner of any shadowed day. To Duncan, she said brightly, "It looks marvelous. I have to see it."

"This is your journey, ma'am. I'm merely here to make certain it's a peaceful one. Though, I'm slightly disappointed that I haven't been able to prove my manly vigor by fending off a pack of ravenous wolves."

She laughed, and he could fall endlessly into that rich, throaty sound. It was the sort of tone he could hear again and again and never tire of. Unlike some of the people he'd met in society, her laughter was genuine, containing within it true pleasure, as though her surroundings continued to surprise and delight her.

"We shall see what we can do about encountering some vicious animals," she said, "though we *have* met your friends, and perhaps the three of you qualify as some kind of pack of beasts."

"Would you believe that we're far better behaved now than we used to be? The stories I could tell you."

She pressed her hands together. "I will do literally anything to hear about your wilder days."

"A tempting offer. Quite tempting."

The atmosphere in the carriage grew suddenly taut and warm. A picture formed in his mind of her head tipped back as she moaned her pleasure. And he was the one to make her moan.

God help me.

The vehicle slowed and then stopped. "This is as close as we can get, my lady," Wiggins announced.

Duncan opened the door before Green could dismount and provide the same service. He stepped down and offered his hand. "Ma'am."

The moment before her hand slid into his seemed to stretch on and on as he held himself in eager anticipation of her touch. When her fingers did slide against his palm, his entire body roused.

She gave a small shiver, and he knew she felt it, too.

He could not forget last night or banish the image of her pleasuring herself—using the selfsame hand that now rested in his palm. Breathing suddenly became difficult as he fought to rein in his arousal.

Focus on the task at hand, soldier. Right now, it was getting her safely up the hill. "We'll take the eastern slope. It's got the gentlest grade and the fewest rocky patches."

"No need to accompany me if you are less enthusiastic about Roman ruins than I am." She shielded her eyes as she scanned the rise. "I can manage on my own."

"From this vantage," he said, "I count no fewer than four spots where you might turn an ankle."

"If I get into trouble," she answered cheerfully, "I'll call for help, and Green can be up there in a trice. Isn't that so, Green?"

"Yes, my lady." Despite his words, the postillion looked slightly more dubious about the prospect of scrambling up a hill to retrieve his injured mistress. There seemed every chance that a city dweller like Green might hurt himself on unfamiliar terrain.

"No need to involve him," Duncan said firmly. "I'll go with you and can guide you up so that no one gets hurt. Besides," he added when it looked as though she'd object, "the last Roman ruin I saw was Miróbriga, and it's time I saw one under better circumstances."

She was quiet for a moment, then asked softly, "That's on the Peninsula?"

"Near Santiago do Casém. Spent years fighting across Portugal and Spain—I'd heard it said they were beautiful places, but I couldn't tell you if they were. What I saw was not beautiful, and what I did was less so."

The words had come to him before he could think

to hold them back. He glanced at her warily, unsure what she'd do with the information.

Her gaze was soft and full of gentleness, and there was gratitude, too, as if she appreciated what it meant for him to reveal part of himself to her.

His throat tightened—but he didn't look away, letting her glimpse this part of who he was. She didn't turn from him in disgust, and she didn't make a jest in an attempt to skirt away from uncomfortable things because she couldn't bear to dwell in unpleasantness.

After a moment, she waved him forward. "Lead on, Major McCameron."

He released a breath, glad she didn't demand an explanation, appreciative of her acceptance. "Don't suppose you have stouter boots, ma'am."

"These *are* my stouter boots." She held out her foot to examine her footwear. They were cunning little things made of pale blue leather, and he tried very hard not to continue his perusal up past them, higher to her ankle and calf, but he had eyes, didn't he? The temptation to follow the curves of her stocking-clad leg was high—too high for him to ignore. Even the glimpse he'd had back at their picnic hadn't been enough.

Duncan needed to stroke his hand up that leg, up to her thigh, and untie her garter, just as she'd done back at the meadow. Last night, he'd caught glimpses of her leg as she'd lain in the bath, luscious and slick with water. Much as he'd tried to avoid it, he'd come into brief contact with the softness of her flesh. No doubt she was soft all over.

Enough. The mission, McCameron.

As he'd explained, he took them to the eastern slope of the hill, where there was minimal scree and a lady might find easy purchase in flimsy shoes. The day had grown blustery, and winds buffeted them as he led them upward. He kept his pace relatively easy to ensure she stayed close. No sense providing an escort if he bounded up the slope like a mountain goat and left her behind.

Not looking at her, with her skirts blowing against the curves of her body, became even more challenging as she moved beside him. He grew fascinated by the movement of her hips and, yes, even the lush form of her arse and knew with certainty that she would fill his hands abundantly.

"Take that switchback," he said, pointing toward what appeared to be a game trail. "I'll follow."

She saluted—he rolled his eyes at that—and scrambled along the worn patch of earth. And then the stones tumbled beneath her feet, and she stumbled backward.

He moved without thought, darting forward.

She spun and landed in his arms, all of her softness against him, her arms flung around his neck, her breasts snug to his chest.

Her face was inches from his. She had the most incredible mouth, as lush and edible as a basket of summer berries. Nothing could make him look away from her lips, which were parted as she drew in quick inhalations—she panted slightly, either from her exertions, or surprise at her stumble, or his nearness.

He smelled a hint of perspiration comingled with ripe flowers, a scent of pure sexuality.

The desire he'd felt for her last night and this morning had not dulled with time. If anything, it had intensified. He was primed as a rifle, and all it would take was a single touch of her finger to create the spark that ignited the powder.

Hauling his attention up to her eyes, he saw her pupils were wide, and she looked at him as if he was a sweet she'd been denied and now no longer knew why she couldn't eat him.

"Are you hurt, ma'am?"

"Not a scratch," she said breathlessly. The tip of her finger hovered above his jaw, and he burned to turn his face to feel her caress him. Yet she checked herself and lowered her hand. "Given that you've seen me at my most, ahem, *private* moment, and that you prevented me from tumbling down this hill like a wheel of cheese, you need not call me ma'am. I'm Beatrice."

"Beatrice." He liked the feel of her name on his lips and in his mouth. "Duncan."

"Duncan."

It was delicious to hear her speak it. And terrifying that he craved the sound of it so much.

"What a bonnie, braw name," she said with a smile.

"Ach, aye, lassie."

His exaggerated burr had the intended effect of making her laugh, breaking the cocoon of intimacy that had enveloped them. Its absence was a relief and also a loss, and he wasn't certain which was the better result.

Reluctantly, his whole body protesting, he released her so she stood on her own.

"So you aren't hurt at all from that tumble?" he asked.

She bounced slightly on her feet, testing them. "Not a bit. Hale as ever. Shall we continue our climb?"

What he had to do to get her safely up, and despite it being dangerous for him, made him crave her touch even more. Wordlessly, he held out his hand to her.

She did not hesitate and clasped it with her own. His heart thudded and his body grew hot, but he threaded their fingers together before resuming their ascent.

It was surprisingly easy to take the rest of the hill. She relied on him to guide her to the most secure footholds, but he didn't have to pull her behind him. Beatrice moved with energy and purpose, though she breathed heavily from exertion.

His own breath came quickly, and his heart pounded. It wasn't from the climb, but *her*. She was far more thrilling than anything he'd ever experienced.

Chapter 9

A moment . . . if you please," Beatrice gasped. "Haven't much . . . experience climbing . . . rocky hills . . . over the past twenty years." She leaned against a low stone wall to catch her breath, while Duncan watched her, poised and ready to come to her aid if she required it.

She tried to rationalize that her breathlessness had nothing to do with the man who'd helped her up this rise. It didn't come from his care for her safety. It wasn't from the wounded self beneath his warrior's thick armor nor the sheer pleasure of watching a vigorously healthy man use his body to conquer obstacles.

Keep telling yourself that, she thought.

It made a woman wonder what else his body could accomplish.

Her own gown was stuck to her sweat-slicked back, whilst he seemed as calm and composed as if he'd risen from perusing the newspaper in his favorite chair.

"I'll be . . . perfectly fine in . . . just a moment," she assured him, though she panted her words. "Only need to . . . walk." She tried to push off the wall, but her limbs were a touch gelatinous, and he was at her side in a moment, offering his arm for support.

She didn't want to lean on him. There was too much temptation there. She'd already been in his arms earlier, and the experience had been torturously pleasurable. Never before had anyone held her with such perfect expertise, as if he could do so forever without tiring. All his focus had been on her and the moment between them.

Whenever Edward had touched her, he'd done so either being completely attentive to only his own needs or else he'd been distracted, ready to move on to another point of interest. A point of interest that wasn't her.

The hell with Edward. After his passing, she'd created a life for herself that she loved, and she refused to dwell in his shadow.

It felt good to be close to Duncan, even if it led nowhere, so she let him guide her around the site.

"It's in marvelous condition," she said, pleased that she didn't wheeze her words as she looked around.

"Aye, from here I can see there's more than one column, and they're almost complete." He nodded toward them standing in a row in the middle of the hilltop. "This might have been the entrance to a temple."

More remains of walls formed lines in the earth, and

while there were no half-buried statues of gods nor sherds of pottery or bits of bronze, she was transported.

"This place brings to mind images of robed priest-esses performing rites as the pious come to honor their deities," she murmured. A cloud-studded sky spread overhead, creating more mystical atmosphere. "I can almost catch the aroma of incense or perhaps the sharp scent from a blood sacrifice."

She stepped carefully across bricks that were over a millennium old. "The world had to have been a very different place back then, and yet people themselves hunger for the same things: food, shelter, community. Love."

"Aye," he said lowly. "Love."

That word from his lips seemed weighted, a whole history contained within it. But he seemed disinclined to elaborate, and she would not press him to talk about something that might make him uncomfortable.

She slipped from his hold, and she moved toward what looked like the remains of a mosaic floor. The image was of an oak tree—the symbol of Jupiter, ruler of the gods, and a perpetual philanderer—with tiny tiles coming together to form something greater than themselves.

"I'm so glad we saw this," she said as she looked down at the mosaic. She resisted the impulse to dig the toe of her boot into Jove's tiles because she would not destroy them, much as she sided with Juno. "I've learned that you cannot hope happiness finds you.

If you did, you'd wait forever. Opportunities present themselves—to find joy, to help someone—and we have to take them. We have to take them, or we lose those chances to truly live."

She'd almost forgotten that she wasn't alone until she heard Duncan say, "That makes sense, then."

Beatrice looked up at him. "What does?"

"Trying all the food at the inn. Stopping to help at the sheep farm." He made a sweeping gesture with his hand. "Seeing this ruin. All these decisions and impulses. It's a way to create happiness."

Something leapt within her at his understanding. "The only guarantee I have is my own will."

"It's why you're going to Nottinghamshire and that . . ." He cleared his throat, his cheeks reddening, but he continued. "That party."

She pressed her fingers to her lips. Unable to keep the surprise from her voice, she said, "You know about it."

"Overheard you talking with Miss Bradbury. It sounds very . . . energetic."

"That is my wish." She lifted her eyebrow as she waited for his censure. Not that his approval did or did not matter—she was long past seeking validation from anyone—but it wasn't every day that an extremely disciplined soldier learned that an aristocratic widow planned on a week of almost continuous sexual activity.

"I hope . . ." His voice was low and gravelly, but courteous. "I hope it meets your expectations."

Of all the people to appreciate why she did what she did, she had not anticipated it would be this man, here on this hilltop, amidst the crumbling remains of an ancient belief.

"As do I," she answered. "And if it doesn't, I'll find something that does."

"I'm certain you will." He spoke with conviction, as though his belief in her was resolute, and that pleased her.

She walked to the edge of the rise. From here, the view was indeed a marvel. The rolling hills were painted in shades of green, dotted with purple shadows from the massing clouds, and stone walls outlined fields like panes of stained glass. Rooftops were scattered across the landscape, and they could see the very top of a church spire.

"Strange to look at a view like this and not calculate troop positions," Duncan said beside her. It was incredible how noiselessly he could move, another of his many skills acquired through the most hostile situations imaginable.

"I cannot imagine what it must be like to have seen battle," she murmured, "and then come back to this."

"*Disconcerting* is too mild a word for it," he said. "They're both real, that world and this one, but when I was fighting, I could scarce believe in ballrooms and bucolic farms. Now that I'm here . . . I thought I'd find it to be peaceful."

"But you don't." She trod cautiously. The truths he

gave her could not be easily offered, and she had to treat them with care.

"I keep thinking that if I do *this* and then *this*, if I follow a regular pattern and stick to known quantities, then I'll feel . . . aligned." He made a noise of frustration. "I'm furious with myself because for all that I do, all the ways I hold tightly to how things are supposed to be done, I'm still adrift."

Owning this about himself could not be easy, and her heart swelled with the knowledge that he'd given her this trust.

"Extending grace to ourselves is one of the hardest things to do." Her eldest son held himself to such exacting standards, and she'd often comforted him when she would find him in frustrated tears. He'd been an independent child, insisting he could button his own breeches with his chubby little fingers when he'd moved into boys' clothes from a baby's skirts.

"And yet," Duncan said, looking toward the horizon, "you made a choice after the earl's death. It would have been easy to retreat into someplace comfortable, someplace stagnant. You didn't."

He brought his attention—his every ounce of focus—to her, and her breath caught. "The choice you made, to explore and discover, that's the harder one to make. Yet that's what you did. You chose the courageous path." His gaze was warm with admiration.

They neared each other, pulled toward one another with irresistible force.

She took a step closer to him, drawn by that power. "I want to kiss you, Duncan."

His jaw flexed as his eyes darkened, sending a quake of need through her. "We shouldn't."

She swallowed, pushing down disappointment, yet she had to respect his choice. "I understand if you don't want to."

"I said *we shouldn't*. But I want to," he rumbled. "God, how I want to."

Her pulse went mad, thrumming along her body. "I've adopted a motto these past three years. If there's something that I desire, and if it hurts no one, then I do it."

"Not so simple," he said lowly—yet his gaze burned her.

"It can be," she answered, breathless. "If we let it."

He said nothing, holding himself still, like a man preparing to leap into an unknown sea. And then he closed the distance between them in one purposeful stride. At the same moment, his hand cupped the back of her neck, placing her head in precisely the right position to take his kiss.

His lips were firm and direct. There was only a slight hesitation, a silent question if he could lead them to where he wanted to go. In response, she opened to him. His growl resonated through her body, all the way along her limbs, centering in her breasts and between her legs.

She'd had her share of tentative kisses, and indifferent ones. But now that she was an adult woman left to pursue her own desires, she would not hesitate to take her pleasure. When she touched her tongue to his, he met her with equal hunger, thrilling her to the deepest part of herself. There was nothing apathetic or distracted in his kiss. He told her with each savoring stroke that she was all that mattered.

He slid his hand from the back of her neck to encircle her throat, directing her to exactly where he wanted her, angling her head for an even better approach. Yet his grip was careful. Respectful—and commanding. As if the warrior he had been was eager to take up control once more.

She sank into his authority, savoring it. She slid her hands up his chest so that she gripped the unyielding mass of his shoulders, and the feel of his taut, strong body made her liquefy into a pool of need. All she could do was pull him closer to meet his command with her own.

God, yes. This and more of this.

Her moan rose up, the sound of her unbridled desire.

Abruptly, he ripped his mouth from hers and released his hold on her throat. He panted as he stared at her, looking torn between ravishing her on the spot and running like hell.

He did neither, but she could see the struggle in his face and read it in the tension in his limbs.

She certainly didn't want him to be *conflicted* about kissing her.

"Regrets?" she breathed.

"None," he rasped.

She could hear the words he didn't speak: *And yet . . .*

"No denying I want you." His voice was as rough and deep as she'd ever heard it. "But, hell, my mind's a fucking mess, and I don't know what to do with myself."

"I've some suggestions," she said, her gaze raking him. The sky had grown fully overcast, and there was something about the clouds and him mixed that made her hunger blaze. "We desire each other. There's no reason not to yield to that desire."

"I can't just *act*," he snarled, his anger seemingly self-directed. "Not without thinking of the consequences."

She offered him a comforting smile. "I brought some implements with me that can ensure I don't get pregnant."

"Other kinds of consequences." He raked his hand through his hair. "The kind that involves our minds and our hearts. Emotions become involved, and desires for more than a moment's intimacy."

Ah—he worried that she would want more from him than physical pleasure. She knew other widows who had taken lovers, and they'd relayed to her that one thing above all else those men feared was a clinging woman demanding promises of tomorrow.

"Let me set your mind at ease," she said. "Everything between us is temporary. It's only sex. I don't want to *marry* you."

He sucked in a breath, as if she'd rammed a fist into his chest.

Quietly he said, "No one does."

What did that mean?

"Duncan . . ." She'd tried to make him feel more comfortable, but instead she had wounded him. If there was something she could say, some retraction or way to undo the damage she'd caused, she would do it. She didn't want to hurt him, to have his brilliant blue eyes turn to ice and his jaw to go taut.

"We ought to get back to the carriage." He squinted up at the sky. "Weather's coming, and we're going to get caught in it."

"I'm sorry." With a few words, she'd lashed out at him with devastating force.

He gave a brief nod. "I know. But we do need to get off this hill. Now."

At a loss, she turned to make her way down. He was, as usual, almost completely silent behind her, saying nothing, his feet barely making a sound as they descended. It was like being followed by the ghost of a person she had slain through her own carelessness.

By the time she and Duncan reached the carriage, the weather matched the dark, unsettled mood between them. Wind buffeted the trees and blew against the side of the vehicle, and the overhead clouds were heavy with imminent rain. Fortunately, Wiggins and Green had put on greatcoats, and they had their tricorns, but those items wouldn't offer much protection from the elements.

Before Duncan helped her into the carriage, she glanced worriedly skyward. "I fear seeing the ruin has put us in the center of the storm."

"It was going to hit sooner rather than later," he said gruffly. "We were going to get stuck in it, anyway. Nothing to be done but move forward."

She wanted to say more, to express her regret over hurting him with a few words—words that had been intended to offer him comfort but seemed to have had the opposite effect. His stony expression precluded any possibility of attempting to make the situation better. So she climbed into the vehicle, and when he got in after her, she rapped her knuckles against the roof to signal that they should be off at once.

Though it was only midafternoon, thick clouds obscured the sun. The interior of the carriage was shrouded in darkness.

It was a difficult thing to know that you'd wronged someone and there was nothing to be done but wait for them to either forgive you or walk away. In the case of her and Duncan, he could only leave metaphorically, trapped together as they were in this carriage.

The storm hit less than thirty minutes after leaving the ruin. Rain drummed against the carriage, and the vehicle's usual sway turned to a rough rocking from the wind and the now-muddy, rutted road. Peering out the window, she watched trees shudder in the gale, their limbs shaking like frenzied dancers.

She could also just make out the fact that they drove along the edge of a ravine, the ground just beside the road sloping downward into darkness. Thank God Wiggins was an excellent driver—he'd see them through safely, and she would be certain to handsomely compensate him and Green for enduring this weather.

Suddenly, the carriage gave a violent jolt. It came to a grinding halt, and Beatrice was flung forward, sprawling across Duncan's lap. He caught her and braced his feet against the floor to keep them level as the vehicle tilted sharply downward.

"Whoa! Easy!" Wiggins yelled to the horses.

"You all right?" Duncan asked her.

"Only a bump on my shin," she answered, trying to right herself. Her heart thudded in the aftermath of the jolt. "What happened?"

"My guess is a broken axle. Wait here." He set her back on her seat before hauling himself out of the listing carriage, shutting the door behind him to keep out the rain. Then she was alone.

In melodramatic novels, these scenes were thrilling, but she wasn't thrilled at all—this was terrifying. Though things could have been worse, she didn't want to consider those possible scenarios.

She absolutely did *not* want to be by herself in a

carriage that reeled like a drunkard. After nervously tugging her pelisse securely around her body, she pushed open the door and pulled herself from the vehicle.

Almost instantly, the rain soaked through her clothing. Her bonnet did little, and she brushed droplets out of her eyes only to have more and more water run down her face. She shivered from a combination of cold and lingering fear.

Duncan and Wiggins stood next to the front left wheel and, judging by their grim expressions, the situation was dire.

"Is it the axle?" she said above the wind.

Duncan scowled. "It is. And you should be in the carriage."

Suddenly there was a loud cracking sound as a thick branch from a nearby tree snapped off and crashed into the roof of the vehicle. The luggage took some of the force, but a large chunk of the top caved in like a rotten pumpkin.

"Oh my God," she cried. That had been so close, and she'd almost been inside the carriage, almost been . . . She shuddered.

At once, Duncan's arm wrapped around her shoulder. "It's all right. You're safe."

"I nearly wasn't." She took the comfort he offered, leaning into his strength. His hand rubbed up and down her arm, steadying her.

"Unhitch the horses," Wiggins shouted to Green.

She felt Duncan start to move toward Green, but then he stayed where he was, continuing to comfort her.

"You want to help," she said through chattering teeth.

He shot her a look, as though he felt guilty about the impulse to come to the aid of the postillion. "Go and assist him. I'll be fine." To prove her point, she edged away from his hold.

She nodded at him when he gave her another glance, and then he strode toward where Green worked with the animals. In the midst of this freezing chaos, his concern for both her and the others warmed her.

As Wiggins and Beatrice waited, the coachman said to her, "Awful sorry, my lady."

"Nothing to be sorry about." She spread her hands. "This is in the hands of a greater power, and I doubt She even gave us a moment's consideration."

"*She*, my lady?"

"I amend that. When things go well, it's a *She*. When life bedevils us, it's assuredly a *He*." Humor helped to keep her steady.

Wiggins snorted. "My ma would agree with you on that."

A moment later, Duncan jogged up. "Got the horses unhitched, so we ought to—"

Another sharp crack sounded overhead, and an instant later, something warm slammed into Beatrice. She went sprawling in the mud just as an even thicker, heavier branch collided with the carriage. From her position on the ground, beneath Duncan's sheltering body, she watched, aghast, as the entire vehicle toppled over the edge of the ravine. It made a terrible, splintering sound as it slid downward.

She saw this all with horror, yet she was deeply grateful to have Duncan sheltering her. He'd acted immediately to get her out of harm's way and now lay atop her, protecting her from danger. He was heavy and solid, and she made herself concentrate on these details rather than think about their narrow brush with death.

Darkly, she thought that today, the Heavenly Architect was certainly a *He*.

She shuddered, but gave thanks that they had unhitched the horses before disaster struck. Sadly, however, her carriage now lay at the bottom of a ravine—along with the luggage.

Everyone was safe, but still, they had lost everything. She groaned.

Immediately, his hands came up to gently touch her face and stroke along her limbs. "You're hurt?"

"Not a bit, thanks to your quick thinking." She lifted up on her elbows, which was no small feat, given his weight atop her. "You? Are you injured?"

"Wet as a Sunday morning, but otherwise fine." He shifted and rolled to his feet before helping her up.

Mud squished through her boots, yet she was unharmed, as was Duncan, and both Green and Wiggins appeared to be sound, as were the rather frightened horses.

As Green held the animals, she, Duncan, and Wiggins stood at the top of the ravine. It was so dark and rainy, it was almost impossible to see the carriage on its side, some thirty feet below. The cold that congealed in her had nothing to do with the rain and everything to do with the fact that she could have been in the carriage, lying broken at the bottom of a steep gorge.

"Afraid that's a wash, my lady," the coachman said glumly. "Want me and Green to climb down and get your luggage?"

"Risk your necks for a few gowns? Absolutely not." The thought was appalling. "What do we do now?"

"Too far to press forward," Duncan said, his voice firm with authority. "Think we passed an inn a few miles back. Hopefully, they'll have a room for us tonight."

His command immediately calmed her. Yet she had to ask, "And then?"

"And then we'll assess the situation in the morning and determine how best to proceed." He motioned for Green to bring the horses back. "Her ladyship will ride."

She glanced at the animals who, mercifully, seemed calmer thanks to Green's careful attention. "There's only one other horse. But there's three of you."

Duncan, Wiggins, and Green exchanged a look. She read their intent immediately and didn't like it at all.

"I can't ride if you're all on foot," she said, trying to keep her voice level. They'd certainly try to override her if she showed any hint of agitation.

"You're the woman in our party," Duncan said just as evenly.

"Aware of that," she replied.

"And you outrank all of us by leagues," he continued. "We'd feel like regular bastards if you walked with us and," he added as she started to argue, "your shoes are the least suited for miles on foot."

She glanced down at her feet. Her little blue boots, that had looked so charming in the shop window, were utter rubbish at withstanding the elements. They were sodden messes, and she was fairly certain that the decorative heel on her right shoe was on the verge of complete destruction. Walking all the way to an inn whilst wearing soggy leather disasters did not, in fact, hold any appeal.

"I'll ride, but I do so under protest."

"Noted." Duncan said.

Before she knew what was happening, he had his hands on her waist and was lifting her up onto one of the horses' backs. She wrapped a section of mane around her hand, then nodded when Duncan grabbed hold of the animal's bridle. They took one last look at the trench the carriage had dug on its way down the ravine and started back.

The rain pelted them, the wind gusted, and she was horribly cold in her damp clothing. Time stretched on, and she had no idea where they were. They passed what looked like the lane that led to the ruin, but she could not be certain.

Something twinkled off to the right, and hope surged when she was able to make out that it appeared to be a farmhouse.

"Duncan!" she yelled above the storm. He was at her side immediately, and she pointed toward the lights. "We can get dry there."

"Good spotting," he said.

She tried not to preen. "And it's closer than any inn."

They found the track off the main road that led to the farmhouse, and she nearly wept with gratitude once they reached it, its cheerful interior spilling illumination into a muddy yard.

Duncan appeared beside the horse to help her dismount. Her legs were stiff, and her whole body ached, but at last her feet touched the ground. She held onto his shoulder to keep upright. Hard to believe that only hours earlier, she'd gripped those same shoulders during their fiery kiss. At that moment, nothing could be further from her mind and body. All she wanted was a place beside the fire and a mug of tea in her hands.

Together, they strode up to the door, which swung open to reveal a middle-aged man, holding a lantern, and a matronly woman beside him.

"Sir, madam," the man exclaimed, "what happened?"

Beatrice's teeth chattered, preventing her from answering.

"I'm Duncan Frye, and this is my wife," Duncan said. "Our carriage met with an accident. Fortunately, no one was hurt, but the vehicle's a loss, and we're in need of someplace to dry off. And a roof for our horses, if you have it." He glanced back to where Green and Wiggins stood with the animals.

"Can do better than that," the man said vehemently. "You'll all stay the night."

"We'll get you dry clothes," his wife added. "In the meantime, get you in front of the fire. Bill, show their men to the stables."

"Aye, Nell."

When Bill hurried outside, his wife stepped back. "Come in, come in. Straight to the hearth."

Beatrice was too weary to rush toward the fire, but when Duncan deposited her on a bench before the cheerful blaze, she could have wept with appreciation. Nell fussed in the kitchen, clattering pots and pans. Two cats, an orange tabby and a gray one, had been sleeping in front of the fire, but they ambled off in search of solitude when the newcomers took their seats.

Duncan sat beside Beatrice, his legs stretched out as steam rose up from his waterlogged boots. She rubbed her hands together, trying to bring sensation back to them.

"Careful," he said gently. "You could damage them if you rub too hard. Just let them warm gradually."

No doubt he spoke from experience, so she did as he instructed, holding her hands up and letting the heat from the fire penetrate her numbed fingers. They stung as sensation returned.

In the meantime, Duncan knelt in front of her and unlaced her boots. She was far too tired and still too cold to feel anything that resembled arousal as he touched her with impersonal efficiency. He pulled a small knife from an inside coat pocket and used it to cut the swollen ties of her boots before tugging them off. He peeled off her stockings and set them on the flagstones to dry.

He dragged a low stool over, placing it under her feet so that they were closer to the fire.

She couldn't stop herself from hissing in pain as sensation returned to her toes in stinging jabs.

"Aye, it'll hurt." Shrugging out of his drenched coat, which he set beside her stockings, he returned to his seat beside her. "Not for too long."

In response, she mutely nodded but sent him a look of gratitude for all his ministrations.

They were quiet together for several minutes before he spoke. "You were a fine soldier out there. Resilient as hell."

That didn't concern her. What she *did* care about she couldn't keep silent about. "You saved my life. When the second branch came down."

Avoiding her gaze, he muttered and mumbled, grumbling something that sounded like, ". . . nothing . . . duty . . ."

"Let me compliment you." She touched her fingers

to his chin and gently turned him to look at her. In the firelight, his eyes were richly blue, and she found herself riveted by the depths within them.

His gaze held hers for a breath, and then another breath, until she and the major seemed to breathe together, sharing air, sharing time.

Then he lowered his lashes, breaking the connection between them. Ruefully, he said, "I accept punches to the face more easily than compliments."

"I'm too tired to hit you, so just imagine that I've planted my fist in your nose." She took her hand away from his face but couldn't keep from rubbing her fingers together, as if holding in the sensation of his skin against hers.

They gave each other small smiles, which warmed her far more than the fire.

Bill clomped into the room. "Got your men out of the wet, and the horses are stabled. Nell, have you fetched—"

His wife appeared with an armful of garments. "Already seen to, my love. Sir, madam, I'll take you upstairs to change, and then we'll clean your clothes. Hopefully, they'll be dry in the morning."

"We cannot thank you enough," Beatrice said earnestly.

Nell's face turned even more pink. "'Tweren't nothing, my lady. After you change, we'll feed you and your servants, and then we have a nice snug room for you whenever you're ready for bed."

A quarter of an hour later, she and Duncan sat at a table in the kitchen. Her borrowed clothes were a touch snug across the bosom, and the loaned slippers were tight on her feet, but they were warm and dry. Nell provided bowls of stew, fresh bread, and mugs of steaming tea—as well as two tankards of home-brewed ale.

Once Beatrice had shored herself up with her drink, she said, "With the loss of the carriage, I think our circumstances have changed. I've decided to press on to Nottinghamshire. There's a village about a mile from here, and Nell said that the mail coach stops there late in the morning. There's enough money left for me to secure a seat on it."

"Just one seat?" He lifted a brow.

"Two, if necessary, but since I'll be on a public coach, an escort won't be required. Many unaccompanied women travel that way. I assumed you'd want to go back to London."

He shook his head. "I'm sticking with you."

She didn't want to be pleased by hearing him say this, and it was easy to believe that the only thing that motivated him to stay with her on this now rather mad journey was his sense of duty. But after the scene at the ruin, she hoped that it was more than mere obligation that kept him by her side.

"Why are you so determined to reach Nottinghamshire?" he asked softly.

She turned the notion over and over in her mind.

"I've had the goal of attending Lord Gibb's bacchanal for many years," she said pensively. "There's the physical pleasure but . . . it was more than that. It seemed like a place of limitless freedom, the kind of freedom I never had. I've reached a point where I *like* who I am."

"Your own woman," he murmured.

She felt her lips curve, and though he did not smile back at her, his eyes were warm. "I promised myself that, if I ever had the opportunity to go to Lord Gibb's, I would do so and overcome any obstacle that once stood between me and that freedom. It's . . . *thrilling* to know I can do this."

For a moment, he was mute, but when he spoke, his quiet voice held the strength of a vow. "I'll get you there."

"I'm grateful," she said sincerely.

"What of Wiggins and Green?"

"We'll all go to the village, and they'll remain behind. I shall give them funds to engage some local men so they might retrieve my belongings. Hold— what happened to your pack?"

"It was inside the carriage. There wasn't time to retrieve it."

She winced. "Did you have many valuables in it?"

"Some fresh linen, a book, other bits and bobs. And my pistol."

"Once our luggage is retrieved, I'll have Wiggins and Green bring everything to Lord Gibb's, and it will all eventually make the return journey with me to London. My coachman and postillion will be amply compensated for all their labors. You'll be reunited with your weapon, and everything will turn out wonderfully."

One of his brows climbed. He clearly did not possess the same faith she did that things would fall into place and that they would suffer no additional setbacks.

Yet he kept his opinions to himself, and they were able to finish their meal peacefully. With a full belly and her body now finally thawed, weariness dragged at her limbs. She could barely keep her eyes open.

"Mr. Frye, Mrs. Frye," Bill said, approaching the table. "When you're disposed, we've a room ready for you."

Duncan clearly saw how her head kept drooping forward and then snapping up. "Excellent. We'll go up now."

Bill showed them to a room equipped with plain but sturdy furniture, including a spacious bed. Wearily, she shuffled to it and slumped down, sitting like a marionette with its strings cut.

Duncan and Bill spoke in low voices, though she couldn't make out the words. Then the farmer left, and Duncan shut the door.

"Bill rises at dawn," he said, "so I requested that he wake us so we can be sure to catch the mail coach. Didn't ask about a room with another bed, since they're already being so generous."

"'S fine," she slurred. She kicked off her slippers and tugged at her clothing. Duncan turned, presumably to give her privacy, but she didn't give a damn about modesty when she was so bloody tired.

A nightgown had been thoughtfully draped at the foot of the bed, so she reached for it. He shifted from foot to foot as she removed the last of her borrowed clothing and pulled the fabric over her head. Then she dragged herself under the covers.

"Go 'head. I stripped for you, now you strip for me." When he hesitated, she made a show of clapping her hand across her eyes. "Can't see anything."

"You'll peek," he said without much accusation.

"I will," she agreed amenably. With a more level tone, she said, "Unless you truly don't want me to."

There was a pause—a weighted pause that held immeasurable possibility. And, oh, how she loved possibility.

At last, he rumbled thrillingly, "Go ahead."

He began removing his own loaned garments—and suddenly, she wasn't quite so tired anymore.

Chapter 10

Arousal drummed beneath Duncan's skin as he removed his clothing. He kept his back to her. Better to let her see his arse than get an eyeful of his rapidly hardening cock. It didn't seem possible that after this trying night he could even *get* hard, and yet here he was, conscious of her ogling him, and all he wanted was to stride to the bed and press her hands into the mattress whilst he settled between her invitingly open legs.

He already knew what it was like to kiss her, and damn if it wasn't the most passionate kiss he'd ever experienced. Just the remembrance of her tongue lapping at his sent pure heat through him.

Bill had provided him with a man's nightgown—something Duncan was unused to wearing—and thankfully because the innkeeper was taller and stouter than he was, the nightgown hung very loosely. But it didn't fully disguise his erection. He'd no choice but to turn around.

"Please don't say you're sleeping on the floor," she said, her hand over her eyes still providing the fiction that she wasn't watching.

"After the evening we've had, I'm definitely sleeping in the bed." It would be safer, wiser, to make a pallet. But his body yearned for softness, even just to lie beside her, and he was so damned tired of fighting against what he wanted so desperately.

Concentrating on mundane tasks to keep him from lunging for her, he stoked the fire and doused the lamps before sliding into bed beside her. She shifted, the bedclothes making soft noises as they moved against her body. There was a barely audible sound—she wet her lips with her tongue—followed by her long, breathy sigh. One of her toes brushed alongside his.

Today he'd learned that every part of her could be erotic, including her toes.

Only moments ago, his nightgown had been baggy and loose. Now it felt plastered to him, as tight as a sausage casing. He exhaled, as if through his breath he could dissolve into the darkness, leaving behind his overly sensitized body.

The unlit room *was* freeing, in a way. It took away barriers, and words came more easily—including words he'd wanted to say for a long time but been too uncertain to speak aloud.

"I heard something about you," he said in the darkness. "Something that happened in London after you'd come out of mourning. About a wager."

There was a pause, and then she said sardonically, "Ah, yes, when honorable gentlemen make bets on women's bodies, everyone emerges the victor."

"So it's true, then."

"It is. A handful of England's most well-bred lords had a bet to see who would be the first to get me into bed once I'd left mourning behind. The Duke of Lighthorn was gracious enough to come to my aid, protecting me against men who would have tried to seduce me. I emerged with my *honor* intact." Her words were acidic.

Anger on her behalf seethed through him. *Fucking men.* He wished to pummel the teeth right out of their faces, and he vowed that when he returned to London, he would do just that.

Still, his voice was admirably calm when he said, "I see."

"Forgive me," she said tightly, "but what do you see?"

"Something else about why you're going to Nottinghamshire, to that house party." It felt easier to speak into the shadows enveloping the room than talk in bright and unyielding light. "It's *your* choice. *You* decide who to sleep with. When and where. And there's no doubt, no equivocation or wondering at anyone's motivations—it's a sure thing."

Silence reigned for a long while, and then she gave a quiet laugh. "I suppose you're right, Major."

"Duncan," he corrected gently. He reached between

them and found her hand, then wove their fingers together. It was warm and soft but not weak in the slightest.

"I'm sorry about what I said at the ruin, Duncan," she whispered. "It wasn't meant to hurt you."

The memory of Susannah's rejection seeped in, but he fought back against its poison. At this moment, all that existed was now. He could face his old injuries later.

"I know," he said, lowly. There was no anger for Beatrice—she couldn't have known—and he wouldn't give more power to being jilted.

"What—"

Softly, he said, "Let's not discuss it."

She squeezed his hand. "This thing between us, I only wanted something strictly for pleasure. As you said, it would be my choice. Not my obligation, like with Edward, nor a trap to be avoided, like those scoundrels in London. It would have been only you and I, for a short time, and then we could have both moved on, no hurt feelings, no ulterior motives. It would have been only pleasure. As much as we wanted."

Her words shot desire through him, his whole being growing hot with need for her. He loved the sound of her voice in the darkness, husky and rich and seductive.

"*Would have* is finite," he said, feeling his words rasp, "as if the chance has come and gone." He moved onto his side, facing her, and with remains of firelight, he could see the lines of her face, how she had a beautifully bold nose and possessed the most incredible mouth. And, God above, the line of her throat was the embodiment of temptation. "If you don't want me to kiss you, tell me. Because there's nothing I want more than to taste you again. Can I?"

In response, she tugged on his hand, urging him to her.

He savored the clash of their spirits, because she was bold and determined to meet the world without fear. For the time they had together, he would be there beside her, giving her everything.

As for his own heart, he'd keep it safe. This was just two people who wanted each other; it didn't have to be anything more.

He shifted his hold on her so that he pinned her hand to the mattress, just as he'd fantasized about. His other palm found hers, and he slid to grip her wrist, holding it to the bed just beside her head.

Her breath hitched—his dominance aroused her, as it stoked his own need.

"Aye?" he asked in a rumble.

"Yes," she gasped.

He brought his mouth to hers. The kiss was explosive as she arched up into him, their lips and tongues and teeth devouring each other. She was ablaze, and he met her fire with his own. She tasted of tea and warm, musky sweetness. Each stroke and caress of their mouths made him burn, his entire being consumed with wanting her. Their tongues slicked against each other, the strokes going directly to his cock.

He pressed the length of his body into hers. She gave a delighted hiss at the feel of his hot, hard erection against her thigh.

"You like that," he growled. "Like to feel my cock on you."

In response, she moaned.

He hungered to say more, to tell her all the things he'd wanted to do to her, what he wanted her to do to him in raw, explicit detail. And yet he couldn't form the words, a mental muzzle preventing him from freeing himself.

He *could* ask her what she needed, because nothing mattered more than pleasing her.

"I want to touch you," he rasped. "Your pussy. May I?" When she gave another moan in response, he said tightly, "Give me the words, Beatrice. Yes or no."

"Yes," she said huskily. "Touch my quim. Please."

It seemed as though he'd been waiting to hear those words from her for years, not days, because hot desire shot through him to hear her speak them.

He released one of her hands to stroke along her body. Her breast formed a perfect, velvet weight in his hand, and he caressed it. When his fingers brushed over the tight point of her nipple, she gasped and arched upward into his touch. He pinched the tip of her breast, remembering she liked that, and she made a low, pleasured sound.

God, she was so open to sensation, her responsiveness ratcheting his own sensitivity higher so that he couldn't stop himself from rubbing the length of his cock against her. And she pushed herself into him, trying to bring him closer.

He had to slow down or else he'd shoot his seed like an untried lad. Reluctantly, he pulled his hips back from her, and she made a soft whimper of protest.

"I want you . . . want you . . ." she gasped.

"You first," he growled.

Taking his hand from her breast, he trailed it over her soft round belly and then went lower to the coarse silk of her hair. Already, he felt the damp of her excitement. When he stroked her outer lips, she was slick with need, and when he dipped between them to find the delicate folds beneath, her arousal soaked his fingers.

"Christ," he muttered, delighted to his marrow.

She gasped and moaned as he learned her, tracing the lips, finding her entrance and circling it. He slicked his thumb back and forth over her clitoris, and she cried out. Her nails dug into his shoulder, forming tiny points of exquisite sensation as she urged him on.

He sank a finger into her. Heat surrounded him, liquid heat, and the sounds of ecstasy she made inscribed themselves onto him—to his final days, he'd hear and treasure them.

Yet he hungered for more. He added a second finger into her and found the swollen spot within. As his thumb circled her clitoris, he thrust into her. She pushed against him, her movements fast and demanding. Ah, bless, she didn't want gentle—she wanted hard and rough. So he gave it to her, letting the strength of his body serve its true purpose, pumping into her with delicate brutality.

"Yes, God," she cried.

"Like this?" he snarled. "Fucking you with my hand like this? Tell me."

The words had torn from him, and at her long moan of pleasure, he couldn't regret saying them.

"Duncan," she gasped. "Want . . . your cock . . . in my hand . . ."

Never before had he removed a garment as quickly as he did the infernal nightgown. He tore it from his body, and as he tossed it aside, her long, dexterous fingers wrapped around his cock. His eyes rolled back in bliss.

She pumped her hand up and down his shaft, nothing shy or uncertain about her movements. His precome slicked her fingers and palm, and somehow she knew exactly how he needed to be touched, her hold on him perfect in its power.

But he could not forget that this was about her. Her desires. Her needs. Her body. As she fisted him, he continued to thrust his fingers into her passage and stroke her clitoris. He was so close to climax, yet he would not allow himself the release until she'd achieved her own.

Again, words tore from him, and he could no more stop them than he could hold back a hurricane.

"What do you want?" he panted. "You want me to make you come?"

"Yes . . ." Her head thrashed on the pillow.

"Ask for it," he said on a rasp. He heard himself say, "Beg me for it."

"Please, Duncan," she moaned. "Please make me come."

With his hand, he fucked her harder. He took her neck between his teeth and gently bit down, like an animal holding its female for a base, primal mating.

She went taut beneath him as she cried out with her orgasm. He soaked in the feel of her and her sounds, watching her face with each wave.

Then she fell back, spent. "Thank you," she gasped.

It took every ounce of his will to pull from her exquisite grasp, but he did. He slid down her body and knelt between her legs. Gripping her thighs, he widened her legs, his gaze holding hers all the while.

She gasped. "You're . . . ?"

"I am—if you want me to."

"Never had this before," she confessed.

He went still. Her goddamned husband should have been horsewhipped. "I can stop."

Her hand tangled in his hair and pushed his head down. "Don't you dare."

Nothing else existed for him then but his mouth on

her. He glossed his tongue through her folds, lost in her taste and feel. As his fingers caressed and stroked her clitoris, he licked at her opening. She trembled beneath him, but he'd no intention of relenting and wasn't satisfied until she keened another climax.

He wanted more. As he fastened his lips around her bud, he fucked her with his fingers using the same hard force as before.

She came again, the sound washing through him and centering in his cock.

And then she surged up onto her knees. She tugged him so that he knelt as well, and she gripped his head to give him a deep, fiery kiss. His hold around her hips would doubtless leave a bruise, but she fitted her body snugly to his as she arched and rubbed herself along his cock.

"Know what I was thinking about when you found me in the bath?" she breathed into his mouth. "Was fantasizing that you came into the room and put your cock in my mouth and I sucked you."

He made a noise, a kind of bestial noise that he'd never made before. "Then, do it." He thrust against her.

She hummed in agreement before folding herself back to position her mouth close to his straining erection. He grunted when she took hold of him, and he growled when she licked the head. When she sank down, bringing him between her lips and then deeper and deeper until he was almost fully in her mouth, he tipped his head forward and moaned. As she sucked him, she stroked her hand up and down, ensuring that every inch of him was engulfed in sensation.

He couldn't look away. He had to see her sucking him, his shaft disappearing between her lips. And when he saw her free hand slip down to her pussy, he knew he wouldn't last much longer.

Through force of will, he managed to hold his climax back until she cried out around his cock.

"Going to come," he panted.

But she didn't pull back. She sucked even harder, her hand stroking him firmly, unrelenting in her determination—and with a shout, he came. Ecstasy engulfed him as she swallowed his release.

When she'd taken the very last of his seed, he gathered her in his arms and laid them both down. He carefully tucked the blankets around her and smoothed her hair, then glided his fingers over her swollen mouth.

"So fucking lovely," he said, his throat raspy from the force of his shout. "Thank you."

Her breath was warm on his face as she exhaled a soft chuckle. "Think I ought to be the one giving thanks. That was . . . how many orgasms? I lost track."

"Wasn't keeping count." He caressed her cheek as tenderness swept through him. She'd been so open and fully present, lavish with her response, generous in bringing him pleasure. "I can give you more."

"I'd be reduced to ashes." Her lashes lowered and, incredibly, she seemed almost shy. "You liked that."

"How can you doubt it?" A smile touched his lips. He'd never had a stronger—or louder—climax. Nell and Bill likely thought he'd been torn apart, and in a very, very nice way, he had.

She pressed her lips to his, and he rose up to meet her—but she pulled back before he could deepen the kiss. "There's still so much out there I've yet to experience. But now I've enjoyed the sexual attentions of a Scot. Who knows what's next?"

He stifled a jab of disappointment. But he wouldn't let himself fall into the trap of his need for more, so he'd shut craving for emotional closeness into a box.

Unaware of his thoughts, Beatrice continued in a cheerful tone, "The whole evening has been an unfolding surprise—I've had a bounty of firsts. First time someone's hand other than my own made me come. First time I've had a man's mouth on my quim. And my very first fellatio. Really, it's a wonder why we don't celebrate things like this, because I would truly like some cake."

"There must be some in the kitchen." He rolled to sitting. "I'll fetch you some."

"It was merely a jest." She leaned on her elbow, propping her head in her hand. "You made me come like a madwoman. You don't need to bring me cake."

"Don't mind." He stood and walked to where he'd stowed his borrowed clothing.

She sat up. "That would be delightful, but it's not necessary."

He dragged on his trousers, which were quite snug since Mr. Goddard seemed to possess much narrower thighs and calves. "I get hungry after sex, and your talk of cake has made me crave some." Duncan crossed the room and gave her a fierce, quick kiss. "I'll be back in a trice, bearing cake and something to drink. After we have our snack, I'm going to put my mouth back on your pussy and make you come half a dozen times. Maybe more. What say you to that?"

After a moment, she glided her hands up his torso, scratching her nails through the hair on his chest, and making his breath hitch and his heart pound.

"I say . . . forget the cake."

Chapter 11

One should never underestimate the effect hours of cunnilingus could have on one's temperament.

As Beatrice sat in the taproom of the nearby village's inn the next morning, dressed in her own clean and dry clothing, sipping her tea, she couldn't stop herself from smiling. It was as though the world had been bathed in radiant light, rendering everyone and everything exquisitely beautiful. She could barely remember last night's terrible slog through rain and mud—all she could recall was the feel of Duncan's mouth on her quim and the wave after wave of ecstasy he'd given her.

From his kiss, she should have known that he would be talented at sex. And yet she hadn't truly believed it until last night.

He'd also been extraordinarily generous, pleasuring her for half the night before she'd fallen into an exhausted but sated sleep.

This morning, he'd been his usual businesslike self. They'd risen early—she hadn't missed the sly looks

Nell and Bill had given them when they'd taken breakfast in the kitchen—and ridden in Bill's wagon to town. After they had shaken hands with Bill, they secured lodging for Green and Wiggins.

Duncan then went to see about securing spots on the mail coach. Which left her alone in the taproom, enjoying her tea and delighting in a sunny day in the wake of countless orgasms.

She was so pleased, even the nearby arguing between a handful of men over the results of a local cricket match couldn't dislodge her good spirits.

"That's a fine smile, my lady."

She looked up into the angular but friendly face of Duncan's friend, William Rowe.

"It seems our paths are paralleling, Mr. Rowe," she said and waved at the seat across the table. "Please do sit."

He did so, folding his rangy body to fit it into the narrow chair, and then planting his elbows on the table. Despite his cheerful mien, lines of tension bracketed his mouth, as if something troubled him.

"How fortuitous to see you again," she said with a gentle smile.

"We were supposed to be at Sandimas University yesterday but were waylaid by the storm. Should reach there today and give my paper tomorrow, although," he continued, shooting a wary glance toward the bar behind her, "some of my more combative colleagues are here now."

She shifted in her seat to see three men of scholarly appearance gathered at the bar, all of them casting surly and belligerent looks in Mr. Rowe's direction. Turning back to him, she said, "What precisely do they object to?"

"They're displeased with my paper's thesis, which is that England's political history is less sterling than many would like us to believe, and that it's not a linear movement toward progress."

"Though I agree with you, I can see how that hypothesis might ruffle some feathers." Her brow lifted.

He shrugged. "Cannot be helped when one speaks uncomfortable truths." Glancing around the room, he asked, "Has McCameron abandoned you?"

"We've had an accident with my carriage, and so he's looking into securing spots for us on the mail coach. Everyone emerged safely, incidentally. But where's Mr. Curtis?"

Stains of rosy color appeared on Mr. Rowe's cheeks. "Still abed. We had a late night."

His phrasing gave her pause, but she did not know either Mr. Rowe or Mr. Curtis well enough to push for a deeper explanation.

It was difficult to concentrate on what Mr. Rowe had said, though, when the nearby argument about the cricket match became louder, more insistent.

Mr. Rowe said evenly over the growing noise, "Your trip to Nottinghamshire—"

"Rowe," someone called snidely from the bar. "I

said, *Rowe*." One of the scholars detached himself from the group and stalked up to Mr. Rowe. His face was already splotchy with anger, and he puffed out his chest.

"Spare me your boorish, nationalistic platitudes, Gable," Rowe said on a sigh, his posture indolent, perhaps deliberately so.

Yet the man did not back down. He prodded a finger into Rowe's shoulder. "You're truly going to spout your revolutionary, subversive drivel to the esteemed panel? You don't deserve a place amongst the finest minds of England. You ought to be clapped in irons and transported." He jabbed at Rowe again.

Beatrice jumped when Rowe's hand snapped up and grabbed hold of his aggressor's wrist. His tone light, but his gaze intent, Rowe said, "Do that again, Gable, and you'll be wiping your arse with your neckcloth."

The scholar blanched and seemed on the verge of retreating, but he shot a glance toward his companions hovering at the bar. Apparently goaded by having them witness his humiliation, Gable moved to shove his fingers once more into Rowe's shoulder. "You're a traitor to the nation."

With far more speed than Beatrice would have believed possible, Rowe was on his feet. His chair fell backward, hitting the floor. He knocked his knuckles into the other man's chest—more of a shove than a punch. "That's enough."

Gable stumbled and fell right into the group of men

arguing about cricket. As he did so, two quarreling op-
ponents collided, sputtering with outraged indignity.

The room detonated into chaos.

Beatrice did not fully understand how a taproom in
a perfectly respectable inn could turn into a swirling
mass of brawlers, but it did. She crouched low as men
threw punches, tankards, and plates at each other.
Rowe exchanged punches with a man who appeared
to be entirely bald.

The few women in the room scurried out in a panic.
Beatrice tried to do the same, but her path was blocked
by two burly men trading blows. She ducked to one
side as one of the men staggered, on the verge of falling right on top of her.

And then the man was gone, flung aside by Duncan.

He made an impressive sight—his eyes blazing, fists
and body at the ready. He was a weapon. Every other
role he'd played was merely that: a role. First and foremost, he was a soldier.

He stepped to her. "Are you all right?"

"Yes, I—"

There was no time to finish her sentence as a man
in a coarse coat hurled himself at Duncan.

But Duncan gripped his lapels and held him at bay,
dodging punches. Through his teeth, Duncan snarled,
"Be nice."

"To hell with you, Scotsman," Coarse Coat spat. He
tried to kick Duncan in the thigh, but the strike was
dodged.

Duncan's expression was impassive, and then he exploded into motion.

She had never attended a pugilism match, and other than prying apart her scrapping boys when they were young, she had little experience with what fighting looked like, let alone when a man excelled at it. Yet as she watched Duncan turn from passivity to action, she now knew what a born warrior looked like.

He threw a combination of punches and elbows that neatly and quickly incapacitated Coarse Coat. One moment the assailant was on his feet, the next he was sprawled on the floor, blood spattering the front of his shirt. But no sooner had one opponent been felled than another took his place. Duncan appeared calm and focused, his expression both alert and unafraid.

A brute of a man lumbered toward the major, who held him back with a jab to the jaw. Yet Brute flung a massive fist at Duncan's stomach, making him lurch backward to avoid the hit. His evasive maneuver put Duncan right in the path of a thrown plate. It clipped the side of his face, and a red line of blood dripped down his cheek.

Brute took that as an invitation to try again and moved to shoot a punch toward Duncan's face.

Beatrice swung a chair at the brute's back.

Wood splintered, and the chair fell to pieces. She'd never done anything like that in her life, and it was oddly satisfying. But it was less so when there was almost no effect on Brute.

She resisted the impulse to cringe as he turned around, instead holding up her fists in what she hoped was a reasonable facsimile of a fighting pose.

The huge man's belligerent look disappeared when he stared at her. Who- or whatever he had been expecting, it likely wasn't a middle-aged woman in the latest Parisian fashion.

"My lady," Brute said, giving a short bow. "Beg pardon."

She lowered her hands. Perhaps she could try another tactic. "Please don't hurt my friend. In fact," she added, pitching her voice louder and using her most Encouraging Mother tone, "it would be most becoming and gentlemanlike if everyone here *stopped fighting*. Immediately. Or I will be *quite* disappointed."

To her astonishment, the room quieted. Men dropped their fists and looked at each other with the abashed expressions of boys who had been caught being very naughty. They actually helped one another up off the floor and assisted in sweeping away any dust that had collected on their clothing. A few even shook hands.

"My God," Duncan said, coming to stand beside her and looking around in amazement, "they've stopped."

"Of course they did." She sounded far more certain of the outcome than she had been moments earlier. Her limbs felt shaky, but she breathed slowly to calm herself. "No one wants to disappoint me. Oh, your face is bleeding. Come with me, and I'll see to that cut. No arguments," she added when he started to protest.

She sat him down on a bench and bustled over to the bar. "Water, please."

The barkeep rose up from his protective crouch. "Of course, madam."

The room had begun to return to normal as furniture was righted and someone came through with a broom. Rowe sank down onto a nearby chair, looking slightly dazed but largely unharmed, while Curtis strode toward him.

She returned to Duncan who was, surprisingly, still waiting for her. She set a mug of water on a table and fished out a kerchief from her reticule, which she dipped in the water.

"You'll ruin it," he objected as she brought it to his face.

"It's just a square of cambric. Better to ruin it than mar that lovely face of yours." She dabbed it gently against the gouge along his cheek. He did not hiss or complain at her ministrations. "Are you in pain?"

"Pain doesn't hurt."

She rolled her eyes, but to her amazement, he actually smiled at her, a true smile that made her heart race even faster than experiencing a taproom brawl had.

His gaze held hers, his smile fading, and the damaged taproom ebbed away so that she was aware only of him, just as he seemed to forget about everything else but her.

"I like you this way," she said softly. "A little roughened."

"I can be rough," he answered in a low voice.

She shivered. When he'd been in command last night, making her beg for release, she'd never experienced anything like that. As though she'd been the sole focus of his world and nothing mattered to him but her pleasure. She'd had to obey him in his singular pursuit of her gratification.

Edward had been so apathetic about their lovemaking, treating it like a chore that had to be seen to in order to ensure the continuity of the line. She'd always believed that her desire for sex was somehow abhorrent—*he* had certainly made her feel that way— until she began to read the Lady of Dubious Quality's books and she saw that what she wanted, what she felt, was normal and healthy.

And Duncan, bless him, had given her exactly what she'd been yearning for all this time.

She stared at him, this unexpected man with blood on his face, warrior and lover, and affection softened her. As he looked back at her, his gaze turned tender.

Someone coughed and spat out a tooth, breaking the thrall between her and Duncan.

From the corner of her vision, she spotted Curtis seeing to Rowe. The barrister had Rowe's hand cradled in his lap and was carefully wrapping Rowe's abraded knuckles in a strip of clean linen. The tender way Curtis touched Rowe, and the doting expression on Rowe's face as he watched Curtis nurse him, made Beatrice's heart clutch.

She glanced back uncertainly at Duncan. He, too, had seen the almost loving way Curtis attended to Rowe.

Would he be horrified? Would he storm from the room in disgust?

Duncan's expression shifted into something quiet, something bittersweet. "Everyone but me," he murmured.

Seeing his melancholy look, her chest throbbed with sympathy. Mr. Holloway had fallen in love and married, just as the Duke of Rotherby had done. Here now it seemed that there was some romantic affection between Rowe and Curtis, leaving Duncan the only one of his friends to lack a sweetheart. Perhaps he felt left out, or perhaps he wanted someone of his own . . . She didn't know, but there was yearning in his eyes.

Yet what could she say to him? Men could be such prideful creatures, careful and protective of their poor hearts, instructed from birth to shield that muscle. So much so that when they were hurt, they didn't know what to do with themselves and usually lashed out.

She'd seen it many times over her life, with all the men she'd known.

So instead of pressing him, she finished cleaning the scratch on Duncan's face. "What did you learn about the mail coach?"

He snapped out of his reverie. "There's one leaving in an hour that should take us in the right direction. I also spoke with Wiggins and Green, and they've already engaged a few men from this village to retrieve our belongings. They'll rendezvous with us at Lord Gibb's. In the interim, there's a shop here that sells ready-made linen and few other items we'll need for the remainder of the journey north."

"A very thorough accounting, Major." She smiled at his meticulousness.

He straightened, his bearing utterly military. "Ma'am. Just doing my duty."

The urge to kiss him on his uninjured cheek gripped her, but she didn't know how he would feel about public displays of affection. Instead, she smoothed her hand down his lapels and adjusted the folds of his rumpled neckcloth. It felt so perfectly domestic, but rather than being confined and smothered, this was intimate and personal, and a sharp yearning throbbed through her.

The unexpected longing made her blink. She and Edward hadn't ever shared tiny moments of quotidian familiarity, yet she had one now, with Duncan.

He seemed equally caught up in the cocoon enclosing them. His face was tight with wanting, and in that moment, she ached to give him whatever it was he so desperately craved.

"The hero of the taproom," Curtis said, appearing beside them. Rowe stood at his shoulder, and though they did not touch, the feelings between the two men were nearly palpable. The barrister smiled at Beatrice. "I meant you, my lady. You felled an entire room with your tone alone."

She inclined her head. "I'm not angry with every-one, just disappointed."

Rowe snickered, and Curtis smirked.

Duncan got to his feet. "For the first time, Curtis, you missed the fight."

"Between the three of you, everything seems to have been handled, and no one too injured that they couldn't live to fight another day." Curtis's gaze held Rowe's.

A smile touched the other man's lips.

"You'll join us on the mail coach to Nottingham-shire," Duncan said.

"We part company here," Rowe said. "We're headed west."

"That's a pity," Beatrice said sincerely. "I'd hoped we could continue our journeys together."

"We'll encounter each other again, my lady," Rowe answered enigmatically. He bowed over her hand, be-fore glancing at Duncan. "And we're cursed to see this varlet's face wherever we go."

"Get you gone, donkeys," Duncan said affection-ately. He clapped both his friends on their shoulders before the two men ambled from the taproom. Briefly, Mr. Curtis took Mr. Rowe's hand, before letting it go. Then they were gone.

"Are you all right?" she asked Duncan softly. "And don't tell me that pain doesn't hurt."

He inhaled and exhaled slowly as he watched the empty space his friends had occupied. "I'll be fine. Always am."

Chapter 12

Beatrice surprised him continuously.

The mail coach jounced sharply on the muddy road, and the eight people crammed inside it slammed against each other. A baby in a fair-haired woman's arms began to wail. One of the male passengers kept pulling hard-boiled eggs from his pockets, sprinkling them with pepper, and shoving them into his mouth. The smell of sulfur clung to the interior of the vehicle as though it was a portal of Hell.

It was by far one of the least comfortable rides Duncan had experienced as a civilian.

Yet Beatrice engaged every single passenger in conversation, with the exception of the infant. She did, however, ask the baby's mother if she could hold the child, and when given permission to do so, she gently rocked it in her arms. The baby made soft noises as it grabbed for the ribbons on Beatrice's bonnet. All the while, she continued to talk to the others in the mail coach.

"I've never been to Hartlepool," she said to a middle-aged Black couple who said they hailed from that town. They had introduced themselves as John and Lydia Maye. "It must be lovely with the sea just outside your door."

"It is, madam," Mr. Maye answered eagerly. "Why, when we were courting, I took her for walks all about to look at the sea. Do you remember Seaton Snook, my love?" he asked his wife, who blushed.

"Well, I . . . that is . . ." Lydia Maye murmured.

"Clearly, you remember," Beatrice said with a laugh, and the Mayes also chuckled.

So it went for the whole of the day's journey. She engaged the entire party in lively conversation, sometimes singing to the baby, asking questions of each person that showed she was interested in hearing about their lives. Nothing seemed too dull a topic for her, from the best way to bake a honey cake to the proper care of geese to listening, riveted, to an aspiring novelist relate the plot of their work in progress.

It wasn't merely chitchat to fill the time. She truly seemed to care about these people that she would never see again. Things continued in this vein when they paused at a public house for luncheon, losing a few passengers—including the mother and her baby—and gaining new ones, and then on into the evening.

But she didn't chatter. She sensed when the party's energy flagged, and she let the mail coach fall into a peaceful silence. A few passengers nodded off.

Across the interior of the vehicle, his gaze met hers, and heat sizzled along his spine. It was captivating to watch her all day, see how her hands moved through the air as she talked, watch the pink in her cheeks when something somebody said delighted her.

What must it feel like to dive headfirst into every new adventure? To eagerly experience and celebrate what it meant to be alive in this world? Unlike him, she didn't cautiously, carefully assess situations and make meticulous—Rotherby and the others might say *arduous*—decisions.

It was mystifying, and yet . . . her spell wove around him, colorful as a meadow, from which he could not quite free himself. Did he want to?

Fuck if he knew.

The late earl had tried to erase her or bind her to his will—but she hadn't let it destroy her. She rose up in a cascade of fire like a mythic creature.

No, not a mythic creature: a living woman. He could still taste her on his tongue and hungered to know her taste again.

Finally, the mail coach stopped for the night at a small town. As the passengers wearily climbed down from the vehicle, groaning and stretching, he waited for her outside. When she appeared, she took his hand, her fingers tightening around his. They silently approached the inn, a rather ramshackle building that, whilst clean, could stand a few repairs.

Inside, he and Beatrice arranged a room with the innkeeper. It did not escape Duncan's notice that she made no mention of a second room, and like hell would he bring it up. He carried their two small satchels into their chamber, noting how her gaze also lingered on the bed.

Duncan then went downstairs as she bathed. Afterward, she adjourned to a sitting room beside a cheerful fire as he washed off the dust of the day.

With both of them clean and refreshed, they regrouped in the sitting room and walked together to the taproom.

The innkeeper approached them. "Sir, madam. A private room?"

"Yes, please," she answered before Duncan could decline the innkeeper's offer. At Duncan's questioning look, she quietly explained, "It's delightful meeting so many people and learning their stories, but I own that I'm rather tired of cheerful conversation."

"So you'll settle for my dour silence?" he teased.

"Spending time with you is not *settling*," she answered with remarkable vehemence. "And anyone who says otherwise will get a drubbing."

He had no answer to that, so they walked quietly behind the innkeeper as they were shown to a private room toward the back of the building. The room itself had no door, but a heavy curtain hung in the frame, offering the diners inside some seclusion. There was a round table within, surrounded by four chairs, with heavy wooden paneling on the walls, a small, cozy fire, and a vase with purple flowers.

He and Beatrice were soon sharing a decanter of surprisingly decent wine and dining on roast hare with stewed mushrooms and roasted potatoes. A berry flummery had been provided for dessert.

In the glow of candles and firelight, with a fine meal in his belly and a striking woman sitting opposite him, a peculiar sensation crept through Duncan. His limbs felt loose, the muscles of his back and arms slackening, and there was a kind of lightness in his chest that he couldn't quite understand.

"Seem fond of talking to strangers," he noted. "Everyone who rode with you today in the mail coach found a new friend."

"That's it precisely." She tilted her head as she studied the candle's flame. "I was taught that genteel women kept their conversation with unfamiliar people to a minimum—especially if those people weren't highborn. And when we *did* converse, it was to be with disinterested politeness. But that always seemed like rubbish to me."

"How so?"

"It's ridiculous to think that someone's birth has anything to do with whether or not they're a worthwhile person." She made a very unladylike grunt. "I've met countless aristocrats who are absolute ninnies. And besides, their world is identical to mine. What can anyone possibly learn if they talk about the same things with the same people all the bloody time?"

"Thus, chatting up everyone in the mail coach." He

gazed at the remaining wine in his glass. "Officers weren't supposed to encourage fraternization between themselves and their men. Thinking on it now, I probably held similar opinions to yours. Didn't do much lingering in the officers' mess, but I also kept my visits to the men's campfire relatively brief."

"Why's that?" she asked, her gaze full of interest.

"If I was too much their friend, they might question my orders, or think that the chain of command was negotiable—which is a dangerous way to run an army."

"I hadn't considered that," she said thoughtfully.

"Reminds me that I missed the opportunity to tell you how ably you wielded that chair this morning." He leaned back in his seat to watch the way damp tendrils of hair curled around her face.

She gave a quiet snort. "Fine job it did. The blighter barely felt a thing."

"I've a feeling we could have thrown a ship's anchor at him, and his only response would have been to yawn."

"*You* handled yourself well," she said admiringly. "Bloodied noses and put men on the ground."

He shrugged, uninterested in discussing something that didn't warrant praise. "Training, and nothing more."

"Come now," she said, holding up a finger. "I've met my share of officers, and not a one of them knew an iota about fighting."

"It's not a good thing to use one's fists." He couldn't keep the grimness from his voice. "There are better ways of resolving conflict."

"*Be nice*," she said in an imitation of his burr. When she smiled, he found his own lips curving in response. In her own accent, she added, "Until it's time to not be nice."

"Until then," he answered.

She leaned forward, resting her chin on her folded hands. "Can you teach me to throw a punch? I've never learned, and it seems a good skill to possess."

He lifted a brow. "Planning on being in more tap-room brawls?"

"It's not my intention," she replied pertly. "But should another arise, I would like to think I could defend myself. Especially when chairs against the backs of massive brutes are ineffective."

He hesitated. It wasn't precisely proper etiquette to instruct gentlewomen in the art of pugilism, but hell, seeing as how men continued to be oafs without any checks on their boorishness, it made sense that women should have the capability to protect themselves.

"All right," he said, motioning for her to stand.

When she did so, he also rose, and he took one last sip of wine before setting his glass on the table.

"First thing you're going to do is set your feet," he said after they faced each other.

"I want to punch someone, not kick them. I'm very good at kicking," she added with pride. "I had two sisters and three brothers, and the only way to keep anyone from stealing my biscuits at teatime was to let fly with a few kicks."

She demonstrated, lashing out quickly with one of her feet. It was an impressive bit of defensive technique.

"That's good. Kicking is excellent, especially when aiming for significant places on a man." He noted her eyeing his crotch and said on a choked laugh, "Yes, that part. But don't neglect the knees and the inside of the thigh. What I mean about setting your feet to throw a punch is that your power isn't going to come from here"—he tapped her shoulder—"but from down here."

He touched her thigh. Even this light contact with her speared heat through him. He could well picture her leg, having had it wrapped around his head last night.

She sucked in a breath. The languorous postsupper atmosphere quickly disappeared, replaced by a fine and almost exquisite tension.

"Stance is important." His voice went raspy. To demonstrate, he got himself into the proper fighting position.

She attempted to mirror him, but it was not quite right.

"You're going down too low," he said, "and will lose your balance. Here."

He moved behind her, his body close to hers, and he tried to impersonally arrange her limbs—yet when he felt her gorgeously soft, rounded shape, he became rock hard in response. His mind fogged with how it felt to have her come apart against his mouth as he'd held her silken thighs.

Her breath sped at his touch, and her cheeks turned rosy.

Yet he'd agreed to show her how to defend herself, and slavering all over her during his lesson was not fulfilling his end of the bargain. Although, with his cock pressing into the curve of her arse, she surely knew that his mind wasn't fully on fisticuffs.

"The next thing you need is to form a proper fist." He took hold of her hand and curved it into the right configuration. "Never, never tuck your thumb into your hand, or you'll risk breaking it when your fist comes into contact with your opponent."

Unable to stop himself, he stroked his own thumb over the back of her hand, and then around to find the delicate place where her pulse fluttered in her wrist. No mistaking it. She was just as aroused as he was.

"Duncan?" she murmured.

"Aye?" His face was right beside hers, so that if they turned their heads a mere fraction, their lips would touch.

"Last night," she said breathlessly, "you made me beg to come."

"I remember," he said hoarsely. Christ above, his cock was so hard it pained him.

"I liked it." She shifted, turning so that they were chest to chest. He couldn't stop from groaning at the brush of her breasts against him. Her gaze met his, and her words were husky. "I liked how you told me what to do. How you took control."

"Aye," he rumbled. "You want more."

She nodded, her face and chest deeply flushed. "It's as though . . . at that moment . . . I alone was the center of your universe. Nothing and no one else mattered."

The unspoken truth of her words hit him like a punch to his chest. Her bastard husband had never made her feel important, in or out of the bedchamber. That son of a bitch hadn't celebrated his wife.

It would be different with him. He'd give her more pleasure with the brief time they had together than she'd ever experienced in the whole of her life. And if he didn't spill a drop of his own seed he wouldn't care—it was and would be entirely about her.

"Beatrice." He brought his hand up to cup her jaw, angling her head to place her exactly where he wanted her. Brushing his lips over hers, he said, "I'll do what you ask. But you must let me know if there's anything that makes you uncomfortable. Tell me to stop and I'll stop. Aye?"

She swallowed. "Aye," she said, making him smile.

"Now, be a good lass," he said firmly. "Go stand against the wall and lift your skirts."

She sucked in a breath, looking back and forth between him and the nearby wall. For the briefest moment he feared that he'd gone too far—after all, this room had no door, only a curtain, offering minimal privacy.

"And if I'm not a good lass?" she asked impudently.

A reckless joy broke inside of him. He brought his

hand down to the base of her throat, letting her know who was giving the orders. "Then, I'll punish you."

NEVER before had the threat of punishment sent quakes of desire through Beatrice's body. She trusted him enough to know that whatever he planned wouldn't hurt her, not in a way that didn't bring her pleasure.

She wanted to know what this *punishment* might consist of, but she also craved obeying him, ceding her will to him entirely so that she might luxuriate in his attention.

Swallowing thickly, she eased back from his exquisite grip and made her way to the wall.

"Like this?" she breathed.

His stare was dark and potent, and now that she'd seen his warrior's body in action, she knew precisely what he was capable of, and it made her heart pound. He crossed his arms over his chest, and to have all of that virility directed at her and her alone sent her head to spinning, as though she'd imbibed too much wine, yet craved more.

"Lift your skirt," he commanded. "Like I told you."

Hands trembling, she reached for the hem of her dress. She gathered up the fabric, but she had her own power, too, so she raised the material inch by inch, revealing herself in slow degrees. All the while, she kept her gaze on him.

His jaw went tight as she first uncovered her ankles, then revealed her calves, and more. There was no mistaking the thick shape of his cock pressed snug against the front of his breeches.

"Naughty lass," he rumbled. "Taking your time. Tormenting me."

"Is it working?" Excitement made her gasp.

He palmed his erection through his breeches, and the sight of his hand on his own cock sent warmth straight between her legs. "You know it is. Don't think I won't discipline you for being such a tease."

She slowed her pace even more. Even through her stockings, the feel of her dress brushing up her legs made her bite her lip with arousal. How slow could she take it? How far could she push him?

She found out when, with a muttered curse, he stalked to her, crossing the room in two strides.

He planted his hands on the wall just beside her head, bracketing her with his arms. She was overwhelmed but not afraid, and soaked up the feel of him as he enclosed her and shut out the rest of the world.

Leaning close so that their breathing mingled, he growled, "Go faster, lass, or I'll keep you on the edge of coming for hours. And when I do let you come, you'll shatter into millions of pieces."

"That doesn't sound like much of a punishment," she whispered.

"Determined to push me." He bit her neck, and she gasped at the primal act. "Do as I say—or I'll give you my cock."

Oh, but she desperately wanted his cock. She raised

her skirts all the way to her waist, and though she wore drawers, air teased at her aching quim, making her moan.

He moved back slightly so he could see her displaying herself. His blunt fingers stroked against the ribbon at the waist of her drawers. "Take these off."

She cast a look toward the curtain. It wasn't even a door offering complete seclusion, just a drape of heavy fabric that would offer no impediment to someone seeking entrance to the chamber.

"That's right, lass." He leaned closer to whisper into her ear. "Anyone could come right in and see you baring your quim to me. They'd get an eyeful of you showing me your beautiful pussy like a shameless wanton."

A groan tore from her at the mental picture he drew. She did not know why this image aroused her so, but, God, it did. Barely able to control the trembling of her fingers, she fumbled at the ribbon before untying it and shimmying out of her drawers.

Now she was fully exposed to him—to whomever might come into the private room.

"There's a bonnie lass," he said on a rough exhale. He cupped her mons, merely holding her like that with his hot hand, but it was so possessive, so claiming, that she almost climaxed.

His lips grazed along the side of her throat. "I love your neck. Been obsessing how much I want to bite it, to kiss it. Wrap my hand around it and hold you still whilst I pleasured you."

"Duncan . . ." she exhaled shakily.

His fingers dipped between her folds, and he growled when he found her soaking. As he stroked her quim, her legs barely held her. He caressed her bud and circled around her entrance.

"This is what I thought about all day," he said in a rasp. "All through that bloody coach ride. Watching you merrily chat with everybody when I wanted to hike up your skirts and play with your cunt until you screamed."

"Oh, God, yes," she gasped.

"Now I have you all to myself. I've half a mind to fuck you with my hand all night long. Just like *this*." Two of his fingers thrust up into her, and she fought to keep from crying out in case someone was out in the hallway and overheard her sounds of ecstasy. "That's right, lass. Keep quiet. Or else they'll hear you moaning at my touch. Brazen wench."

His touch and words were her undoing. Her orgasm struck with the sudden ferocity of a summer storm. She arched up, the wall unforgiving at her back, his hand still working her quim with unrelenting demand.

"Sir? Madam?" The innkeeper's voice sounded in the corridor. "Is everything all right? I heard—"

"*Go. Away*," Duncan snarled.

"Yes, sir." Footsteps retreated, and Beatrice could only wonder if the innkeeper had looked around the curtain.

She trembled as a smaller climax racked her.

"Liked that, did you?" Duncan said in a low, gravelly voice. When she was silent save for her gasps, he cupped his hand around her throat once more in a wordless demonstration of his power. Knowing how he'd fantasized about doing just this made her shudder with excitement. He bit out, "Answer me."

"Yes," she panted. "Yes, I loved it."

"Of course you did, wicked vixen. And now I'll show you what wicked vixens get."

She looked down to see him tearing at the fastenings of his breeches, and when he pulled out his deliciously thick, hard cock, she wet her lips.

"Want to suck this, don't you?" he growled.

"I do. Please." Pleading with him to take him in her mouth was exquisite.

He shook his head. "Good lasses get to suck my cock. But you're not a good lass. Are you?"

"I'm not," she moaned. "I'm very bad."

"That's right." His voice was so deep she could feel it in her own body. "Have to show you what happens to bad lasses." He released his hold on her throat to grip her thigh in a hold so tight she knew it would leave bruises—and she couldn't wait to see those purple marks on her skin, proof that he'd focused on her so thoroughly and that, for this time, she was all that mattered to him.

He hitched up her leg and hooked it around his waist. When he notched the head of his cock at her opening, they both hissed with anticipation.

"What happens?" she breathed. "What happens to bad lasses?"

"They get my cock in their cunts." He thrust up into her with one stroke.

She was wet enough to take all of him, and she cried out at the magnificent stretching within her.

For a moment, neither moved, both of them panting. She was pinned by him, speared on his cock and reveling in the sensation. His body held her to the wall. She wrapped her arms around his shoulders, holding on to him as though he was her only means of salvation.

Then he moved. Slow, deep glides at first, his pace almost leisurely, as though he could fuck her all night and never tire.

The wonders of a younger man.

"This is what you've been after from the beginning." He grunted with his thrusts. "All this time you've been teasing me, taunting me. You wanted my cock in you."

Had she? Entirely possible.

"Answer me," he growled.

"Yes," she said on a gasp. "I craved this."

"But not so slow and gentle, aye?" He stroked in and out as he spoke. "You want it rough, don't you?"

His words sent heat pouring through her. "Hard as you can. Please."

"Hold tight to me." When she gripped him, he gave another grunt and then—

And then he fucked her. Fiercely.

Her feet lifted from the ground as he drove into her with taut, wonderfully brutal thrusts. She didn't care about the rigid surface of the wall against her back, she didn't care that it would be perfectly obvious to anyone in the corridor what she and Duncan were doing in here. All that mattered was the feel of him within her, and his hot breath against her neck.

She loved the sounds he made—short exhalations of ecstasy that he seemed unable to control. This was what she'd done, made this tightly leashed man give in to the primal need within him.

Her orgasm did just as he'd promised. She shattered into millions of pieces, losing herself in pleasure that had no beginning and no end. She *was* pleasure itself, replete with it, devastated and rebuilt by ecstasy.

His thrusts grew shorter, and then he pulled from her as he groaned his release. She felt his seed on her belly, grateful that he'd had the presence of mind to protect her.

Her eyes grew hot and damp, and she blinked back tears.

Immediately, he released his hold on her leg and gently curved his hands around her face. Worry tightened his features.

"I hurt you," he said, his voice hard with self-recrimination.

"Not hurt," she choked. "It was . . . Thank you . . ." She ducked her head, tucking it against his chest. "That was perfect. Exactly what I wanted."

His thumb brushed away a tear, leaving her cheek damp. Tenderness washed through her. Even at his roughest, she never felt more valuable or cared for.

She stroked her hand across his forehead, grazing strands of hair that clung to his damp skin.

"You're very good at that, you know," she said softly.

His smile was justifiably smug. "I have my uses."

She couldn't prevent herself from asking, "Have you ever done that with anyone before?"

"Since I was sixteen." He added, "Before that, I was quite adept at frigging myself."

"I meant have you ever been . . ." she glanced down at her exposed thigh, which was already beginning to bruise ". . . in command like that?"

To her delight, after everything he'd said and done just moments earlier, he blushed. "Only with you."

More affection swept through her. She had asked him for something, something deeply intimate that required the height of trust, and he'd done it. For her.

She leaned forward and captured his lips with her own, imbuing the kiss with all the sweetness she could wordlessly express. And he returned the kiss gently, warmly.

"We've shocked the inn," she murmured as she pulled back.

"You sound rather proud of it," he said with a smile.

She tipped her chin up. "Perhaps I am."

"Come upstairs with me." His teeth nipped at the place behind her ear. "And I'll give you all the scandal you want."

Chapter 13

Waking with Beatrice in his arms was delightful. Starting the day by fucking her senseless was paradise.

Eventually, they managed to peel themselves off each other to wash and dress before heading for breakfast.

"Breakfast in the private room or the taproom?" he asked her as they descended to the ground floor.

"Taproom. After the thorough swiving you gave me fifteen minutes ago, I find myself quite sated. Temporarily, of course." She shot him a wink over her shoulder.

"Vixen." He'd half a mind—and half a cockstand—to take her against the staircase wall. It didn't make sense. He was a man who could go days, if not weeks, between amorous encounters. He liked sex well enough, and prior lovers had seemed quite satisfied by his performance, yet it was never his consuming purpose.

When it came to her, he just couldn't seem to get

enough. He wanted to be inside her and hungered for her pleasure. Hearing her cry out her release was addicting. It was just like heaven. Despite a whole night of bedsport with her, he needed to take her back upstairs and make her moan.

But he wouldn't be selfish. She needed food after the rigors he'd subjected her to.

The inn seemed remarkably quiet this morning, but he was in too fine a mood to pay the relative peace any mind. He guided her to a table in the almost empty taproom, and when they sat, the innkeeper approached gingerly.

"Good morning, sir, madam," he said with a nervous bow.

"We both require a substantial breakfast, whatever you've available," Duncan said. Recalling what Beatrice had ordered for breakfast in the past, he said, "Tea for my wife. Bring a pot of it so she doesn't run out. Coffee for me."

"Yes, sir." The innkeeper hurried away, and if his demeanor seemed odd, Duncan couldn't find the wherewithal to investigate. Such was the power of energetic, creative sex with a luscious woman.

"My, you're very stern regarding my breakfast," she murmured, and smiled. "I like it."

He shrugged. "Merely making sure you get precisely what you want."

"You've taken care of that quite well, in all regards."

Her smile turned wicked, and she stroked a finger across his wrist.

It was so easy, falling into the desire to give her everything.

A picture flooded his mind of spending countless mornings just like this one. Seeing her sexually satisfied face across from his at the breakfast table after a night of lovemaking. They'd review correspondence and the newspapers and discuss their plans for the day, perhaps making arrangements to meet for luncheon, and he'd spend the intervening hours anticipating seeing her again. He might even bring her a posy purchased from Covent Garden Market.

"It should be a good day for travel," she said, glancing out the window at a sunlit kitchen garden. "At this rate, I'll be exactly on time to arrive at Lord Gibb's."

He clenched his jaw as he fought a crushing wave of disappointment. Of course. She was set on traveling to her orgiastic house party. It meant so much to her, held enormous importance, and he understood that on an intellectual level, but that didn't stop his gut's reaction.

She hadn't said anything about continuing their liaison once this trip had concluded. Foolishly gulling himself into believing their relationship was anything more than temporary led straight to heartbreak. This was just sex.

Other men might have been delighted by such an arrangement. He ought to be, too. And yet . . . because he was fashioned differently from other men, he craved more.

You can't have more, he sternly told himself. *Be grateful for what you've been given.*

The innkeeper appeared, bringing dishes laden with eggs, sausages, and buttered toast. A woman set a pot of coffee and another of tea on the table.

"Is there anything else I can get you and your wife, sir?" the innkeeper asked, hovering.

Duncan's stomach leapt to hear Beatrice called his wife. Yet he replied evenly, "We've everything we need right now."

"Yes, sir." The man and the woman retreated.

Once Duncan and Beatrice were alone again, he apparently needed to prod his wounds and asked in what he hoped was a light tone, "Thought about marrying again?"

When she stared at him as though he'd suggested cannibalism as a viable diet, he continued, "Many women remarry after the death of their husbands, especially if they're young, as you are."

"To begin," Beatrice said, "bless you for calling me young. I'm a mother thrice over. But, to your point, given the choice of taking a seat at a banquet, or resigning myself to a meal of a single dish every day for the rest of my life, I'll take the banquet."

"There's companionship and affection," he felt obliged to point out. "The chance to see a beloved face every day." This was what he'd hoped to gain with his own marriage, and he'd fixated on it in the heart of war's hellishness.

From infancy, he'd been taught the importance of a wedded union. A man might indulge himself for a few years with amours and dalliances, but when it was time to create something lasting, something that would stand through the decades ahead, he found himself a bride. The McCamerons were fervent believers in fidelity—none of his male kin ever kept mistresses. That was the path they all followed, and he had fully anticipated he'd do the same with Susannah.

That future with her had been blown to pieces, and yet he still believed that when you wanted a romantic relationship to last, marriage was the answer.

"I've a few friends who married for love," Beatrice said softly. "They wanted precisely what you described, and, for a time, they got it. But it faded, changed. Even the most doting husband turned distant."

"That doesn't happen with every love match," he countered. His own parents were still affectionate with each other after nearly forty years.

"A distant husband is the best situation many women can hope for." Her gaze was direct as she regarded him across the table. "For me marriage was an extended exercise in losing myself. I cannot, *will not*, endure that again, not when I'm only now beginning to relearn who I am."

He gave a clipped nod, grappling with the fact that

her reasons were sound. Men lost none of their power by marrying, unlike women. Yet . . . marriage was what people did when they cared about each other. There wasn't an alternative.

They finished their meal in silence, and he couldn't help feeling that something slipped from his grasp—despite the tightness of his grip.

When the innkeeper appeared to take away their empty plates, Duncan asked, "What time does the mail coach leave?"

"Sir, it's gone already." The innkeeper twisted his hands together. "An hour ago."

"What?" Beatrice demanded, sitting up straight. "We should have been made aware of its departure."

"I tried, madam. I went to your room to tell you but"—the innkeeper coughed into his fist—"it sounded as though you were both *engaged*, and as sir was most insistent last night on being left alone I, erm . . ."

Duncan cursed under his breath. His hunger for her had wrecked their plans. "There must be another coach later today."

"Day after tomorrow, sir," the innkeeper said contritely. "There's one coming later this afternoon in Wilbrick."

"Surely we can hire someone with a wagon to take us there," Beatrice said.

"There's George Thompson." The innkeeper nodded energetically. "He'll be your man. Uses his dray to make deliveries in town. You'll find him on the main road, in the house in the middle of the street."

Duncan nodded, determined to get things underway. "Thank you for your assistance." He pressed a coin into the innkeeper's hand. To Beatrice, he said, "Remain here, and I'll meet you in the yard. Shouldn't be more than a quarter of an hour."

Smiling, she saluted him, making him realize he'd used his most officerlike tone.

Well—he *had* been an officer for over fifteen years.

Leaning close to her, he whispered in her ear, "Last night, you rather enjoyed me being in command."

"Sir, yes, sir," she murmured.

"God*damn* but that sounds better coming from you instead of my men," he growled.

"Should hope so," she answered pertly. "Perhaps later tonight you can hear it again."

He drew in a breath, trying to calm his body's reaction to her. Right now, he had a duty to carry out.

A quarter of an hour later, he rode toward the inn, sitting beside Thompson on the seat of the lumbering dray. It was an awkward and much-mended vehicle that had seen its prime during the last century, and the horse pulling it was nearly as aged. Yet the wagon had four wheels, and the horse plodded steadily. It would have to. Several large baskets of apples were heaped in the bed.

Duncan cast a glance toward Thompson next to

him. The man had a pair of shaggy white eyebrows with a long beard to match. At the sight of Thompson's whiskers, Duncan ran a hand across his own jaw and realized, belatedly, that he'd forgotten to buy shaving supplies, and his own beard had already begun to come in. He was not enamored of his facial hair, as it grew in quite red, which had earned him a fair share of teasing from his fellow officers. But there was nothing to be done for it. He'd just have to ride through the English countryside looking like one of William Wallace's broadsword-wielding chieftains.

Beatrice stood in the coachyard, their baggage at her feet. She eyed Thompson and his somewhat ungainly wagon but made no word of complaint. Duncan leapt down from the seat and loaded their satchels into the wagon's bed. He handed her up to the driver's seat before jumping into the bed, as there was no room for three people on the bench.

Making a place for himself amidst the apples, he leaned against the back of the driver's seat, his legs stretched in front of him, watching the village buildings thin, until they were finally out in the countryside. Between the rocking of the wagon, the tumultuous morning, and the many hours Duncan had spent last night making love to Beatrice, he found his head lolling forward as he fell into a doze.

He snapped awake as the wagon quaked to a stop. Looking around, he noted that they were in the middle of the countryside, a wood on one side of the road and rolling hills on the other. A lone farmhouse nestled a distance away in a hollow.

"Is this Wilbrick?" Beatrice asked.

"No, ma'am," Thompson replied. "Can't take you as far as Wilbrick on account of me needing to deliver those bushels of apples to Joe Liddle by day's end. But it's an easy journey to get there."

"We agreed you'd take us to Wilbrick." Duncan couldn't keep the irritation from his voice.

But Thompson didn't seem to notice or care that his passengers were irate. He smiled peaceably and said, "Joe Liddle needs his apples."

"Tell us how to get to Wilbrick," Duncan grumbled.

"Well, sir, you just head through that wood." Thompson gestured toward the thickly growing trees. "Go on that way for about a mile and a half, turn at the yew that was split by lightning, and follow the creek until you reach a farm with a blue shed. At the farm you head due east and then you'll join up with the road again. Take that for three miles and at the fork, stay to the right. In no time, you'll be in Wilbrick and can catch the mail coach there."

Duncan tried to commit Thompson's instructions to memory. He'd gotten by with even more uncertain directions and was still alive, so he surely could get himself and Beatrice to their destination.

After grabbing their bags, he climbed down from the wagon's bed. He helped Beatrice descend from the seat. She'd barely risen before Thompson snapped the reins and the wagon rolled into motion. She stumbled, and Duncan held her snugly to keep them both from tumbling into the dust.

Though he cursed Thompson's haste, Duncan didn't mind having his arms around Beatrice.

As she waved goodbye to Thompson, Beatrice asked, "Did you get all of that? Something about an oak tree and a creek and a yellow barn?"

"It was a yew and a blue shed," Duncan answered. "A short detour and then we'll be precisely where we should."

"WE'RE lost, aren't we?" Beatrice asked two hours later.

He turned in a circle as he surveyed a field that was entirely devoid of blue sheds and yews and anything resembling the directions Thompson had given them. "A small misdirection, but we'll get onto the right path in no time."

"I think we're lost." She'd removed her bonnet and fanned herself with it.

"Was a goddamned officer in His Majesty's goddamned Army," he growled. "I don't get lost."

But . . . they were hopelessly lost.

"It's not your fault." She walked to him. Thankfully, she seemed to understand that he was in no mood for gentle touches, so she didn't try to give him a consoling pat on his shoulder. "There wasn't a single yew tree in that whole forest, and the first creek looked more like a stream, so it made sense that we didn't follow it."

He dragged his hands through his hair. "I'm a fucking embarrassment to the 79th." It was intolerable.

"Listen to me." She planted her hands on her hips. "George Thompson gave us rubbish directions. You need to absolve yourself of feeling responsible for where we are now. I don't care if you were an officer. You're human, and humans are not always perfect."

He drew in a ragged breath, and ridiculously, his eyes grew hot. "I take my responsibilities seriously."

"So you do. And we are *both* adults capable of overcoming obstacles." Her expression was kind, far kinder than he believed he deserved. "Right now, Major McCameron, you are going to use all your years of campaigning experience to read the landscape and find us a village where we can get proper directions, perhaps rest a bit. Perhaps a little less rest," she added with a wicked smile that, even in his emotionally fraught state, stirred his desire.

"And then," she went on, "when we know precisely where we are, we'll be able to get ourselves on the right path. We'll be at Lord Gibb's in a few days. Of that I'm certain."

It always kept coming back to that damned house party. As time went on, he couldn't stop wishing she wasn't so fixated on the thing.

The whole purpose of this trip was for her to explore precisely what she desired for herself. And if Lord

Gibb's gathering and the freedom it represented to her was what she wanted, then he'd sure as hell make certain she got it.

He was a soldier and also a son of the Earl of Glenkirk, and he did his duty, no matter the cost.

But . . . "The sun's going to set in a few hours." He knew what had to be done, yet he didn't relish presenting the option to her. "I don't want us wandering around in the dark. The best thing to do is make camp and try again in the morning."

He was reasonably certain that, on his own, he could locate a town or dwelling in the depths of night, but she would not fare as well, and God knew who or what they might encounter. These were lean times, and vagrants and brigands were always a possibility. Making a camp would ensure they had the warmth of a fire and the security of a fixed location.

"Make camp." She looked at him, her face blank. "As in, sleep outside?"

"Aye." He waited for her to try to convince him that they could find a village before nightfall. Surely gently reared ladies did not make a habit of spending the night in the out-of-doors. "Afraid there's no help for it."

"I see." Her gaze swept over the field in which they stood. Try as he might, he could not read her expression. "You have experience with it."

"Considerable experience." He'd usually had a tent, but many times he'd had to sleep outside. And, especially as the war had worn on, he had often assisted his men in preparing the site.

She was quiet briefly. He waited for a long and deserved explanation as to why a countess did not and would not sleep outside.

"I've every faith in your abilities," she finally said. "Where should we make our encampment?"

He only allowed himself a moment's astonishment. But then, it shouldn't be a shock that she readily adapted to adverse circumstances. God knew she'd done it enough on this journey—and in her life.

"Better to get out of the open elements." He squinted toward the horizon, where he espied a stand of trees that they could reach within a quarter of an hour. "We'll head for that copse, and once we're there, I can gather branches to make a rudimentary shelter. I can build us a fire, as well. Won't be able to hunt, but I'm a fair hand at foraging, so our bellies won't be entirely empty tonight. What?" he asked when he saw her smile.

"There's something very alluring about competency," she murmured.

He snorted. "May change your tune when it's two o'clock in the morning, we have no blankets, and you're fantasizing about cottage pie." After another survey of the landscape, he hefted his pack. "Ready to move out?"

"Where you lead, I follow."

———

An hour later, he could reasonably claim that he'd created a decent, safe campsite. He'd been able to locate a small hollow that sheltered them from the wind, and there were enough raw materials from felled branches to construct a lean-to for additional shelter.

Fortunately, late summer meant that they had an abundance of food available for foraging.

"I've done a little foraging," she said, "as a girl, when we'd spend the summer at our estate in Kent. We'd pick elderflowers for cordial, but I could never wait to take the blackberries back home for Cook to make into a fool. I'd pop them into my mouth, and when Cook asked if we'd found any, I'd say no, but my lips and fingers were purple."

"Impatient lass," he said with a chuckle.

She smiled mischievously. "Always greedy for sensation."

He stepped closer to her, and something warm and thrilling swept through him when she immediately closed the distance, wrapping her arms around his neck. As though it was natural and perfectly accepted that they would stand as close together as possible.

"I've the scratches on my back to prove it," he rumbled, enfolding her in his own arms, his hands pressed into the dip just above her arse.

"Poor laddie," she said without any contrition. "We'll forage for evening primrose to put on your injuries, sustained in honorable combat. Although," she added, her eyelids dropping seductively, "I liked that it was quite, quite *dishonorable*."

He groaned when she dragged her teeth across his lower lip. "Lass, I'd like nothing more than to lie you down in the bracken and tup you like a fiend. But the sun's going down, and we haven't much time to find our supper."

She made a noise of protest but released him and took a step back. "I'm not happy about missing out on a fiendish tupping, but my stomach will thank you later."

Their supper had consisted of blackberries, chickweed, mallow, and wild spinach. There was also a creek that supplied cool, fresh water. True, after a long day, he would have preferred roast mutton and potatoes with a tankard of ale, but compared to the conditions he'd faced on the Peninsula, it had been a rare feast.

"I was prepared to be heroically stoic," Beatrice said with self-deprecating humor from her place on a log across the fire. Full night had fallen, so the fire cast her face in golden light. Her shawl was around her shoulders, and she held her hands up to absorb the flames' heat. "But I see now that such performative forbearance was unnecessary. You've made us very comfortable, Major."

Sitting cross-legged on the ground, he only nodded. He enjoyed her praise, but he wouldn't permit himself any smugness. A soldier did his job and didn't expect applause. "This time of year, first light is just after six in the morning, so we can set out early. Should find habitation within an hour or two—and a decent breakfast."

"I've no complaints about the food you provided for us. Though," she added, her eyes sparkling, "I wouldn't spurn a toasted muffin and a bracing cup of tea."

"I'll get them for you," he said at once. Though she'd demonstrated many times that she was capable of taking care of herself, the urge to provide for her drummed through him.

She tilted her head, considering him. Thoughtfully, she said, "You will, won't you? When you say you'll accomplish a task, you do it. No dithering, no prevarication or hesitancy. You make things happen."

"Uncertainty is costly." He hesitated. It was easy to be candid with his friends and reveal things about himself that he couldn't entrust to others. Yet people outside of the Union of the Rakes . . . they were different. Hell, he'd barely given Susannah a glimpse behind the polished soldier. Perhaps that had been a sign that they were not a good match—he hadn't trusted her enough, and maybe that had kept her at a distance.

So, he drew a breath and said, "Early in my military career, I would agonize over decisions, and my men would be restive. I didn't have confidence in myself, so there was no reason for them to feel confident in my leadership. Fortunately, my paths crossed with an officer who bawled at me to wipe my nose"—in truth, Lord Somerby had snarled that Duncan had to wipe his *arse*—"and do my duty by my men."

"And so you did." There was no condemnation in her voice or in her eyes because he was not always the assertive commanding officer. What he saw in her gaze and the gentle set of her mouth was something else: compassion.

His heart expanded and grew, pressing against his chest so that it was a physical ache. She gave him so much, and God, he was grateful for it.

Her regard roamed over him, gentle and probing and intimate. "Tell me something you've done for yourself since returning home."

"Twice weekly I take my clothing to be laundered, and I pay a woman to clean my rooms," he answered. "Oh, and to cook, since I've little ability there. But, other than that, I do everything for myself."

"Meaning, something nice you've done for yourself," she explained, smiling. "Something gratifying, or that you've always wanted to do. Maybe bought a whole cake from Catton's that you shared with no one; it was all for you. Or maybe you went for a midnight gallop beside the Serpentine."

"But . . ." He frowned in puzzlement, trying to make sense of the things she described. "Why would I do those things?"

"Because you *want to*," she said plainly, as though

desiring a thing and then making it happen was as easy as that.

"The law would frown on thundering around the Serpentine in the middle of the night," he pointed out.

"It's fairly harmless," she countered evenly. "Especially in comparison to something like theft or assault."

"Perhaps," he allowed. "But I'd wager there are laws against it."

"Yet there's no law against eating an entire cake by yourself," she said, tipping up her chin.

"Seems like a fairly foolish thing to take to the courts."

She looked at him with exasperation. "You're determined to vex me with your literalness."

Even though it made him a cad, he chuckled. "It's wrong of me to like teasing you, but I do. A bit of trouble for the troublemaker. But to your point, I was told as a lad not to grab all the cakes at teatime, so I'd never devour an entire gâteau on my own."

"And you always do as you're told?" she asked, her question more curious than pointed.

Still, his back stiffened. "If all the people did whatever they wanted, everything would break down, and then no one would get what they wanted because the world would be a smoldering ruin. There'd be no Serpentine to ride beside at midnight, and there'd be no Catton's and no cakes."

His breath came faster merely from the thought of

indulging his every whim regardless of consequence. He'd taken well to the army because of its insistence on discipline, and eventually he'd become a damned good officer with the commendations to show for it.

"A gentle touch of anarchy can be good for anyone," she murmured. "It doesn't have to be all the time, only now and again."

"What if—" He fought to find the right words as he tried to understand himself. "What if I like it too much, and then I'm reckless and careless, and someone gets hurt?"

"I promise," she said with assurance, "you will never carelessly hurt anyone."

He wanted to believe her, so badly. And yet . . . "You can't know that."

"I know *you*, Duncan. You are a warrior and won't hesitate to go into battle, but there's nothing about you that would thoughtlessly wound a soul." Her eyes held the depth of galaxies, fathomless with utter conviction in him, and that meant more to him than any of the ribbons and medals he'd received.

"Your faith in me is humbling—and ennobling." His throat was thick, but he needed to speak. "Might never have a title, but after what you just said, I don't need one."

She had the loveliest smile when she said, "If you won't give yourself something that makes you happy, then I will. Name it."

"I truly don't need anything," he said automatically,

though the fact that she'd even thought about what would bring him happiness sent a current of pleasure along his body, settling between his ribs.

This is just for now, he reminded himself. *Nothing permanent. Nothing lasting.*

"There must be something," she insisted. "You said you've been restless, in search of purpose."

Ah, he *had* said that, damn it. "Taken care of. My position at Carriford, remember?"

"But what if it isn't the answer to your restiveness?"

"It will be," he said firmly. It had to be, because that's what he was supposed to do. Otherwise, he didn't know what else could fill the vastness within him.

She was quiet, contemplative. "The way you spoke about married life . . . Is that something you'd like for yourself?"

"It was," he said flatly.

"Not anymore?" she asked, her voice as soft as eiderdown.

He could evade her question or ignore it. Yet . . . he found himself speaking. "I was engaged to be married. When I'd returned after Bonaparte was sent to Elba, Susannah accepted my suit. Then the Hundred Days happened, and she said she'd gladly wait for me. Only she didn't."

He wanted to halt the flow of words, but now that they poured from him it was like draining a suppurating wound, and he could not stop. "She ended it. Three days before Waterloo, in truth. Not quite how

I wanted to prepare myself for the biggest battle of my life, but her letter came and I read it and"—he shrugged, though the movement felt as though his bones ground together—"she apologized and was terribly, terribly sorry, but she'd found someone else."

"My God." Beatrice pressed her hand against her mouth.

"She'd gone and married one of my fellow officers—another younger son, only Gaines's elder brother died, making Gaines the heir to a viscountcy."

It was odd . . . he'd been certain that telling Beatrice about Susannah would be an agony and mortifying. And in a way, it was. Yet there was something liberating about it, like discarding a part of himself that he no longer needed.

Beatrice straightened, and her face was dark with anger. "She jilted you for her chance to become a viscountess. That horrible—"

"No." He held up his hand, though he appreciated her outrage on his behalf and the gratification in realizing that his own anger and sadness at what happened had been justifiable. "I can't blame her for securing her future, when I had so little to offer."

"But . . ." Beatrice clenched and unclenched her hands. "That she could hurt you like that, when you were off *fighting*, and could have *died* . . . In no way did you merit being deserted for . . . for what? . . . The opportunity to have a country estate? Having someone call her *my lady*? God." Her voice turned hard. "If I ever cross this Susannah's path, I'll slap her face so hard her teeth will fly across the room."

"Thank you for being so vicious on my behalf." He didn't relish seeing her descend into violence, but there was something primally satisfying in her righteous anger.

Horror crossed her face. "Now my comment to you at the ruin and why it seemed to injure you so greatly makes terrible sense. Hell, if there is blame to go around, then I deserve my share for unwittingly salting your wounds. I am so very sorry."

"You needn't apologize for something that wasn't your fault. I am fine now. Truly." There was an ache when he thought of Susannah, and yet, even now, he felt it ebbing away. Perhaps it might not ever fully disappear, but it would hurt less and less. Eventually, what he'd recall was the memory of the pain rather than the pain itself.

She stood and moved around the fire, then sank down to sit beside him and laced her fingers with his. "She did you a great wrong. You deserved better. And I know that you'll find yourself a lovely woman who values you for who you are, not what you can give her."

He looked down at their intertwined hands. Hers were slimmer than his, and smaller, and yet he'd no doubt that between the two of them, hers were equally powerful—or more so.

The ache for more pressed within him. They could

be so much to each other if she wanted it. Yet even now, she said nothing about their brief affair enduring beyond this trip, or becoming something permanent, something official and sanctified.

Take what you can get and be satisfied with that. He could not get greedy and grab everything for himself.

When he spoke, his voice was a rasp. "Recall how you wanted to give me something that made me happy?" At her nod, he gruffly said, "You've just done it."

Chapter 14

It turned out that sleeping in the out-of-doors was extremely pleasant—when one had a solid, warm Scotsman holding you all night.

By silent mutual agreement, she and Duncan had merely slept in each other's arms. With their environment beyond their control, it seemed the safer choice than sex. She had missed the feel of him energetically pleasuring her. Yet having his embrace snug and secure around her, with his lips close to the nape of her neck so she could feel his exhalations against her skin, had been as intimate as sex. More so, because he'd trusted her enough to reveal his heartbreak.

As she sat beside the remains of last night's fire, finishing her portion of the foraged blackberries, she watched him disassembling their camp with his usual brisk efficiency. One could tell, merely by looking at him, that he was a skilled former soldier, except that didn't take into account the fact that he possessed a gentle, caring soul, and that he yearned for a lifelong companion.

Her heart squeezed at the thought. She couldn't be the one to give him that companionship, not in the way he wanted. Having endured the misery of marriage already, she would not again.

"That's the last of it," Duncan said, carefully scraping his boot across the fire's ashes.

She stood and shook out her skirts. "What is our plan?"

"The brook where I retrieved our water should lead us to either a village or a mill, or at the least a croft."

"We can enjoy the scenery along the way. Oh, but wait," she said as he hefted his pack and her valise.

He paused, head tilted slightly in question.

She drew close to him and pressed her fingers against his cheeks. The whiskers there were thicker now, closer to a beard than stubble, and she loved the prickling sensation against her skin.

Softly, as sweetly as she could, she kissed him. She adored how readily he opened to her now, no more tentativeness between them.

She pulled back slightly. "Thank you. For taking such good care of me. And for being vulnerable with me, too. Your trust is something precious, and I will do my utmost to protect it."

He said nothing, but there was gratitude in his

eyes, and his throat worked as though he swallowed emotion.

After one more kiss, she exhaled and put more distance between them. "Shall we keep moving?"

They reached a village shortly, finding the avenues strangely quiet for the morning. The majority of activity seemed concentrated around the church, where people were coming and going at top speed. Many of the women carried armfuls of ribbons and flowers, but the expressions they wore were pinched, as though they were pressed to be in ten places at the same time.

"What on earth can be happening?" Duncan muttered as they stood and observed the frenetic commotion.

"I suspect it's a wedding," she answered flatly. Weddings were part of life, and she'd been to many before, during, and after her own, yet it was difficult to throw herself into a celebratory spirit when she knew how her marriage had turned out. "So long as we can get on the next mail coach, it shouldn't impact us much."

A girl carrying more masses of flowers trotted by, but she stopped at Beatrice's comment. She had a mass of curly black hair and appeared to be about nineteen, though her eyes were weary.

"Won't be catching a mail coach here in Beaumont," the girl said. "They stop in Shermer, the next town over."

Beatrice fought the urge to grind her teeth in frustration. Heavens above, it seemed every obstacle in the known universe kept falling in her path, keeping her from Lord Gibb's.

"We'll hire someone to drive us," Duncan assured her.

"Not today you won't," the girl said tartly.

"Why not?" Beatrice tried to keep the aggravation out of her voice, but judging by the girl's arched eyebrow, she hadn't been entirely successful.

"There's a wedding," the girl replied. "Not just any wedding. An alderman's son is marrying my sister. Got half the town working to make the church look suitably grand, and the rest of Beaumont is getting the grange hall ready for the wedding breakfast." She rolled her eyes.

As tired, grimy, and frustrated as Beatrice was, she couldn't help but notice how there was a little bit of hurt in the girl's eyes when she talked about the town's preparations for the wedding.

"Forgive me, my dear, if I'm overstepping," Beatrice said carefully, "but you seem decidedly unenthusiastic about the prospect of your sister's nuptials."

The girl's expression turned crestfallen. "It's only . . . today's my birthday, and everyone seems to have forgotten."

"Oh, child," Beatrice said earnestly, hurting for the young woman, "I'm so sorry. Speaking from experience, I know that it's terrible to be overlooked. Let me be the first to wish you a very happy birthday."

"Aye," Duncan added. "Happiest of birthdays."

The girl beamed, and Beatrice's heart swelled.

"Is there a special Scottish birthday custom we can do for her?" she murmured in Duncan's ear.

"A smack on the arse for every year," he answered. "But I don't think she'd much appreciate that from us."

"Not without a proper introduction," she whispered, fighting a smile. Turning back to the girl, she said, "I'm Mrs. Frye, and this is Mr. Frye. What's your name?"

Beatrice had no intention of giving the girl's behind any swats, but she also didn't want to be rude and not call her by her name.

"Louisa, but everyone calls me Lou." The girl shot a wry glance over her shoulder toward the church. "Think my family wanted a boy, but they got me instead."

"May I again wish you a very happy birthday, Lou."

The girl blushed and said bashfully, "I'm sorry you'll have to wait until tomorrow to hire a ride to Shermer. In the meantime . . . why not come to the wedding?"

"Us?" The thought of attending a wedding and pretending to be happy, even for strangers, seemed too much. She was too weary to manufacture excitement over another woman's loss of autonomy.

"Thank you, Lou," Duncan said quickly. "Mrs. Frye and I are in need of a little rest and a bath, if you'll just point us to an inn."

"There's the Three Twins on the High Street," Lou answered, pointing. "But after you've rested and bathed, you're welcome to come to the wedding breakfast."

Duncan opened his mouth, presumably to gently refuse, but Beatrice spoke first. "That would be lovely."

The church bell chimed, and Lou grimaced. "I have to go. See you at the breakfast!" With that, she dashed away.

Once they were alone, Beatrice turned to Duncan. "Was I so transparent about not wanting to attend the wedding?"

His gaze was concerned as it roamed over her face. "Given what you'd said about the state of your own marriage and your thoughts about the wedded state in general, it seemed best if we avoided watching Lou's sister walk down the aisle."

Beatrice cupped her hand against his jaw, feeling not just the prickles of his beard but a surge of gratitude. In a short time, he'd come to understand her far more than any man ever had. "You're very kind."

He only shrugged, which endeared him to her more. Then he asked, "Won't attending the wedding breakfast be equally uncomfortable?"

"Given our slender supper and even more trim breakfast, I'll endure the discomfort for roast ham and pudding."

"And cake," he said, eyes twinkling.

She looped her arm through his as they began to walk toward the inn. "And cake."

THE Beaumont grange hall had been festively decorated with bunting and flowers, and tables were set up bearing platters of food, fruit, and even more flowers. Guests milled, chatting and eating, and the bride and groom accepted felicitations from everyone. Even Duncan and Beatrice had congratulated the new Mr. and Mrs. Warnick after Lou's introduction.

He'd tried to ignore the burst of pleasure that had arisen when he and Beatrice had been presented as Mr. and Mrs. Frye. They'd gone by these fictitious names for days, yet something about being represented as a married couple at a wedding gave it more heft, more significance.

But it didn't have significance. It was a convenient disguise for this journey, to be discarded like a domino mask at the end of a masquerade.

Perhaps that was what tinted his mood as he and Beatrice stood in a corner, availing themselves of food from the offered banquet.

"It's a perfectly pleasant wedding breakfast," Duncan murmured to Beatrice as they stood in a corner.

She paused, a seed cake halfway to her mouth, and eyed the celebration. "*Pleasant* isn't an especially effusive word."

"The roasted ham, slices of chicken pie, and tiny fruit tartlets all taste fine," he said quietly, careful that none of the other guests heard him. "The sparse rations last night and this morning whetted my appetite . . ."

"I sense an *and yet* in there," she said, a corner of her mouth tilting up.

"And yet there's a dullness on my palate." He shook his head, baffled by the strange tenor of the room and the people within. "Can't quite understand it. The sparkling wine is fizzing, the conversation seems cheerful enough, but . . ."

"It's like someone let the air out of a balloon."

He smiled at her perceptiveness, and how easily she seemed to understand him. "So it isn't just me."

"Not a bit, Mr. Frye. I should set off some Catherine wheels just to stir up some excitement."

His smile widened. "Here, now. Pyrotechnics are my specialty, and I'd be vexed if you stole my literal thunder."

"Can't have you *vexed*, dearest Mr. Frye." She winked at him, and it was astonishing how such a small movement could be both amusing and arousing at the same time. She must have seen the flare of heat in his gaze, because she murmured, "When we're done honoring the new bride and groom, and when we're finished with our meal, we ought to repair back to the inn and see what happens when I *vex* you some more."

His body came immediately to life as hunger for her knifed through him. Holding her all last night had been delightfully torturous, but now he truly felt the effects of not being inside her for over twenty-four hours.

"Teasing lasses pay for their wickedness," he said in a low, rough voice.

The flush that spread up her neck and into her cheeks made him growl. Breathlessly, she said, "I hope that's a promise."

"I never break promises," he rumbled. "Been planning the next time we're alone, and what I mean to do to you. And I'm a comprehensive planner."

She gazed at him with scorching intent, her lips parted, her chest rising and falling. He was on the verge of taking hold of her wrist and gently but firmly pulling her out of the grange hall, toward their inn, when Lou appeared.

"They'll be cutting pieces of cake soon," the girl said with exasperation, "and then we can finally go home."

Duncan plastered a smile on his face—or an approximation of one, since all he felt at the moment was blazing frustration. Lou looked almost as irritated as he felt, though he doubted she churned with the same thwarted sexual energy as he did.

He needed something to talk about besides the fact that he burned to take Beatrice to bed, which wasn't very polite conversation, especially not at a stranger's wedding breakfast.

"Must be looking forward to tonight, though," he offered.

Lou frowned, puzzled. "What's tonight?"

"The wedding celebration," he answered simply, not comprehending her confusion.

The girl spread her arms open. "This *is* the wedding

celebration. After this, we just go home and that's the end of it."

"But . . . the dancing," he said, his mind churning as he struggled to make sense of the utter nonsense Lou was saying. "There's always dancing at a wedding."

"Forgive me, my dear," Beatrice said gently to him. "That isn't always the case. Not in London."

He stared at both women, appalled. "We're not in London. This is the country, and *every* country wedding must have dancing. That's how we do it where I'm from. A wedding is always followed by a merry feast and much dancing. How can anything be celebrated without it?" It was such a simple, understood truth that to go against it was a horrible rending of custom.

"There's no dancing tonight," Lou whispered, shaking her head, "because dancing isn't legal in Beaumont."

Both Duncan and Beatrice stared at the girl. Finally, Beatrice breathed, "That's ludicrous."

Lou looked around to make certain that they weren't being observed, then said in a tight whisper, "For the past five years, it's been forbidden to dance. Not at weddings or festivals or anything. Ever since our Squire Redmire's son went to an assembly, drank too much, and drowned in the river on his way home. Of course, drinking isn't outlawed, but dancing is." She rolled her eyes.

"My God," Duncan said on a low exhale, attempting to comprehend the fact that one could get arrested for merely *dancing*. "A popular law, is it?"

The girl snorted. "Hardly. We even used to have a harvest dance this time of year, but that's no more since the law was enacted. Nearly everyone hates it—and I hate it the most." Shyly, she said, "I'm . . . I'm a dancer."

Beatrice nodded with approval. "I could tell by the way you moved through the company. Light on your feet and graceful, just like a dancer."

Lou smiled and blushed, her lashes dropping bashfully. "But the only dancing I do now is across roofbeams—my da's a builder and needed help, and since I've no brothers to apprentice, I have to help him."

"And you unable to even dance at a public assembly without fear of being thrown into gaol." Beatrice clicked her tongue in sympathy.

"There *has* to be dancing after a wedding," Duncan insisted. He felt pity for the girl, and the thought of eschewing one of the most important village celebrations made his stomach knot and the muscles of his back tighten. "There *must* be."

Rules had their purpose—yet he saw now that they weren't always there in a person's best interest. They could be outside, and arbitrary, and plain *wrong*. Especially when they were created by someone who had their own frailties and faulty agenda. It made more sense to fight back against a regulation that caused harm rather than adhere to it out of blind obedience.

"What do you suggest, Mr. Frye?" Beatrice asked him, her brows arched. "Organize an illicit assembly just outside of town limits?"

He stared at her for a long moment. And he knew just then what had to happen, what he had to do. What the squire had imposed on the town was *damaging*, in desperate need of fixing.

Beatrice had asked him last night what would make him happy, and he now understood that part of what he needed was repairing harms, shifting the balance from wrong to right, even in some small way.

"That is *exactly* what needs to transpire," he said. "Follow me."

Both Beatrice and Lou trailed after him as he made his way out of the grange hall. Once they were safely away from prying ears and sheltered behind a shop, he said to Lou, "If we arranged for an assembly where people could dance, someplace outside of the village's limits, would you be able to get people from Beaumont to attend?"

"Oh, yes!" The girl's face practically glowed with excitement. "Would you honestly do that?"

Beatrice glanced at Duncan, but she smiled and excitement made her eyes gleam. "Would we, Mr. Frye?"

What he'd wanted from being a soldier was to realign the world, to bring peace to the people for whom he fought. On his best days, that had been true—

though, there had been very bad days when it had felt like the complete opposite.

Here, however, in Beaumont, he could create a measure of harmony, and there would be no bloodshed, no loss. Only happiness.

"If this is something the people want," he said firmly, "then, we're going to give it to them. There's surely a barn or a similar structure just beyond the boundaries of the village. We can find a sympathetic farmer, and if the monetary compensation is adequate, we'll find a venue. But you must get the word out—and find musicians."

"I can do all of that." Lou flung her arms around Duncan, then Beatrice. "Thank you, thank you! This will be an evening no one in Beaumont will ever forget. I'm off to spread the word." She trotted back to the grange hall, giving them a cheerful wave, before ducking inside.

He turned to Beatrice and found her looking at him with admiration. And pleasure.

"Time to make this assembly happen?" she murmured.

"Today is the day," he said, threading his fingers with hers, "and tonight is the night."

Chapter 15

Impatient for the dance to begin, Beatrice eagerly walked the length of the barn, checking on the decorations.

After coming to an agreement to hire out the barn which belonged to a Mrs. Willard, Beatrice and Duncan and Mrs. Willard's children had spent the afternoon making flower garlands and paper lanterns, as well as sweeping out hay and airing out the structure so that it smelled only of sweet grass when the assembly began.

She'd thrown countless balls for London society, but never with this kind of fizzy enthusiasm. This was far more important. While she hoped the villagers had a good time, what truly mattered was *Duncan's* enjoyment.

He'd been the one to spearhead the enterprise, and his determination to make this assembly happen thrilled her to her marrow. It was as though this morning he'd emerged transformed from the wilderness. He was still himself, sardonic and disciplined and purposeful, but there had been an alteration, too, as though he'd found a purpose that had been lacking from his life. He was both freed from his self-imposed yoke and more determined than ever.

She was the lucky woman to see him evolve. And she had no doubt that he would continue to grow, too, long after their time together was over.

The thought that it *would* come to an end made her pause in midstride. She had been so eager to move from one experience to the next, yet she hadn't considered what would happen afterward. What would become of her and Duncan.

The man himself spoke to a trio of musicians, which included a woman with a fiddle, a man with a drum, and another man with a flute. She couldn't hear what Duncan said to them, but his gestures were animated as he likely instructed what he wanted from them that evening.

Thank goodness he still hadn't shaved, because with his beard, he looked very much a rough-and-ready soldier, and she couldn't wait to rub her lips across his whiskers. In motion, he cut a splendid figure. Hell, he was an excellent specimen of masculinity when in repose, too.

"No one is here yet." Lou walked into the barn, wearing a pretty frock and an expression of dismay. "I told *everyone*. Well, most everyone. Not my ma and da, of course, or Squire Redmire, who surely drinks pickle juice."

Beatrice came forward to take the girl's hand. "People will come. Mr. Frye has done everything to make certain that tonight is unforgettable."

The girl started to object, but the sounds of many voices grew closer. As the musicians began to play, groups of people entered the barn. Most of them were dressed in what had to be their finest clothing, and they looked around at the decorations with happy, nervous expressions.

Lou flitted from cluster to cluster, thanking the men and women for coming, agreeing with the assessment that the barn looked lovely. Beatrice was glad to have some part in this evening. She was grateful, too, that she traveled with enough coin to compensate Mrs. Willard for the use of the barn. Kindness was one thing, cash was another.

More and more people gathered in the barn, and jaunty music played, but despite their apparent enthusiasm for the *idea* of a public assembly, no one danced. Everyone clung to the walls, fidgeting and glancing about nervously.

Lou hurried over to Beatrice. "Why aren't they dancing? Was this a mistake?"

"No mistake made," she answered. "Look how they're all tapping their feet in time with the melodies. They want to dance, but no one wants to be the first on the floor."

Surveying the room, Beatrice tried to send the men silent commands to ask women to dance, or if there were some progressive ladies in the company, perhaps they could do the asking. And yet whenever she met someone's gaze, they suddenly became fascinated by the barn's roof or the toes of their shoes.

Beatrice knew what had to happen.

She crossed the room without hesitating, aware of everyone's eyes on her, yet there was only one person whose attention she desired.

Beatrice stopped in front of Duncan, and his intense gaze energized her even more. "Dance with me, Mr. Frye?"

"Defying the custom of having the gentleman request the dance," he murmured with a quietly seductive smile. "I expected no less."

She held out her hand, and his slid into hers. Awareness crackled through her as they walked out onto the floor together. After they bowed and curtsied to each other, he took hold of her other hand, and he began to dance the poussette. It took her less than a moment to follow suit.

Of course he was a marvelous dancer. He was athletic and light on his feet, never faltering in his steps. His gaze held hers, and she felt like the center of his whole world. She hadn't danced in years, not since the earliest days of Edward's fatal illness, and to move like this again—with *Duncan*—filled her with a reckless delight.

"Let us dance!" Lou cried. Moments later, the floor was filled with couples.

Not everyone knew the steps of the poussette, but what anyone lacked in knowledge they made up for in enthusiasm. There was so much unbridled happiness filling the barn as young and old danced for the first time in half a decade.

In the midst of Beatrice's pleasure, a question whispered at the back of her mind. Should she continue on her journey to Lord Gibb's? For so long, attending the house party had been one of her wishes, her hopes. With her goal so close, she didn't want to turn back now.

If she did return, would regret torment her as she sat in her London town house, knowing that she'd had a chance to gain something that she'd dreamed about?

God, she didn't know.

On this journey, she had found happiness with Duncan. Yet for how long could it last, when she could never give him what he truly wanted?

"Here, now," he said lowly, interrupting her thoughts. "That's a melancholy look for such a festive occasion."

Her smile came readily as she gazed at him. "An occasion that you made happen."

"It *needed* to. A country wedding without dancing is like drinking whisky out of a sieve. An incomplete experience."

She stroked a hand over his hair, brushing the coppery strands. "What a scofflaw you've become."

His brows rose. "On the contrary. By helping arrange this assembly, I followed protocol to the letter. We've set things to rights, which is the opposite of violating a law."

"But in Beaumont," she replied, "dancing is against the law. So you've actually *broken the rules*."

He stared at her, though his body continued to move in the steps of the poussette. Finally, he said, "The law is wrong, and this, I hope, helps makes things a little better for the villagers. The people here clearly want to dance, but the squire imposed his will on them and took away something they needed." Quietly, meditatively, he said, "At the beginning of this journey, I'd never have done anything like this."

"Something in you changed," she said softly and watched the play of thoughts and emotions on his face. An edge of worry cut through her. Would he reject this metamorphosis? Or would he embrace it?

"The outside world has its expectations of me," he said thoughtfully, still turning her in the dance. "But these last days, I've pushed against those boundaries. I've discovered something."

"What's that?"

"Not what I expected of myself, but . . ." his brow creased as he seemed to explore his thoughts ". . . what energizes me. This," he said, glancing around at the decorated barn, "was a way to give Lou, and many people in Beaumont, what they wanted."

"And they appreciate it," she said earnestly.

"I'm glad, but this was also for myself, and you, too." His gaze held her as securely as his arms. "I can seize opportunities for happiness, for myself and for others, just as you'd advocated. Like this assembly. The villagers needed to dance, and making certain they could do so brought *me* happiness."

He went on, "Adhering rigidly to regulations is no guarantee . . . of anything. I followed rules, but why? There are *shoulds* and *shouldn'ts*, but I never truly knew who I was in the midst of that. I've tried to obey in the way I thought others wanted me to. But their wants don't matter."

She searched his face, his voice for signs of dismay or uncertainty, but what she found was strength and anticipation.

"*You* gave me the means to question my assumptions," he went on, his eyes bright and brimming. "All of them. And I thank you for that."

"I can't take credit for it," she said, her throat aching with happiness. "It was entirely you."

He gave her a lopsided smile that connected directly to her heart. "We'll share the glory."

THE assembly went on for hours, with the dancing pausing only briefly to allow the musicians a few moments of rest. No one wanted to end the evening. The bride and groom appeared and danced together wearing identical smiles of joy.

Beatrice was torn with the desire to dance until

sunrise and the desperate need to drag Duncan to bed. She wasn't the assembly's hostess—that honor belonged to Lou—but she felt a certain responsibility to stay until the last notes were played.

Still . . . she caught sight of Duncan, paired with Lou on the dance floor. He said something that made Lou laugh. It didn't come as a surprise that the girl had begun to moon over him. Hell, Beatrice mooned over him, and she was a mature woman.

From leading her out of the wilderness to civilization, and the way he'd organized this assembly, he had been remarkable today. He'd been remarkable every day she'd known him, and all the days she hadn't. It stunned her at how mistaken she'd been about him, believing him to be easily defined and utterly without dimension.

They had been together all day, yet that wasn't enough. She needed more of him, to feel his body against and inside hers.

The barn had grown quite heated with so many people within it. After watching the dancing for a minute more, she went outside. She moved across a patch of grass and stared up at the sky. Her mother had been quite fascinated by astronomy and had taught Beatrice how to identify some of the constellations.

There was Cepheus to the north and Boötes to the south, and seeing them again brought a lift of renewed happiness. Though she hadn't been to this part of the country before, the constellations anchored her, making her fully aware of herself.

A smile curved her lips as she looked up to the stars. Mama had instructed her how to find constellations, which was educational, but she hadn't told her everything, such as the fact that women's lives were defined by their relationships to others. Daughter, wife, mother.

But now Beatrice was herself, as free as any woman could be. Even at this midpoint in her existence, there was still more to do, more to feel.

And there was Duncan—unexpected in every way. She'd never known anyone like him, and she never would again. Pain sliced through her at the thought of their eventual parting. Because they *had* to part. He wanted marriage and all the sanctioned trappings, but she would not, could not do that again.

Solid arms encircled her, as an unyielding, warm body fitted close to hers. She arched up to the lips that nuzzled the crown of her head.

"Not concerned about cuddling a stranger?" Duncan asked playfully.

"I know you," she murmured. "In the daylight and the darkness, I know you."

"Keep saying things like that, and I'll be forced to ravish you."

"Then, I won't stop saying them." She turned in his embrace and lifted on her toes to bring her mouth to his. It was heaven to kiss him beneath a starry summer sky, hear his breathing turn ragged, and feel his grip on her tighten as the kiss grew hotter.

"Want you so much," he rumbled. "Been thinking about all the wicked ways I can make love to you. I've got ideas."

Excitement leapt within her. "Our inn awaits."

"Take us there," he answered without hesitation.

The inn was quiet at this hour, and no one was around as they slipped inside. The climb up to the first floor took some time, as Duncan kept stopping to kiss her and scratch his teeth down her neck.

"There's a whole bed just upstairs," Beatrice gasped.

"No one else is around," he said on a rasp. "I can bend you over and fuck you on the staircase."

She inhaled sharply at the image. But the prospect of a mattress sounded exquisite, so she managed to plant her hands on his chest. His heart thundered beneath her palms.

"Bedchamber," she ordered.

One of his eyebrows arched up. "Now you're giving commands? That definitely merits punishment." He reached down to stroke her ankle. "Better run, ma'am, because I aim to chase you."

She needed no further urging and sprinted up the remainder of the stairs. His footfalls were quick behind her as she raced down the hallway. She flung open the door and just caught a glimpse of the handsome, rustic four-poster bed before he was on her.

His hold was secure as she thrashed in his arms. She felt his deep laugh in the soft places within her while he carried her to the bed. "Think to get away from me? Naughty."

The mattress pressed against her back as he lay the length of his body atop hers. His weight on her was delicious, the feel of his hard cock curving into her belly even more so.

He pinned her wrists down, then kissed her, his tongue sweeping into her mouth in a hot, possessive demand. When she rubbed against him, trying to rouse him even more, he grunted.

"You know what happens to teasing vixens," he growled. "They get trapped and tamed."

"Like the sound of that," she said breathlessly.

He glanced at the posts of the bed. "How many pairs of stockings did you purchase?"

The question was unexpected. "Three. Wearing one pair now."

"I'm going to ruin them." He looked between her wrists and the bed's posts.

Her belly leapt as she realized what he meant. "Please. Ruin them."

He made a low sound of approval and need. "Do. Not. Move."

Nimbly, he rolled off her. She raised herself up on her elbows to watch him shut and lock the door, then rifle through her satchel.

"You moved," he said, straightening. Her quim heated when she saw two pairs of her filmy stockings in his large, male hands.

"What if I did?" she challenged, tipping up her chin.

"First punishment, then. Take off your clothes."

God, how she loved the sound of those words in his deep voice. "I can't do that without moving."

He stalked to the bed to wrap his hand around the back of her neck. "The more impertinent you are, the longer you're going to have to wait until I let you come. Now strip. Everything. And be quick about it."

When he released her, she drew in a shuddering breath and slid off the bed. Briefly she debated as to how fast she ought to undress—it might be amusing to keep teasing him—but she wanted to be naked with him more. He watched through slitted eyes as she removed her garments layer by layer. She had the presence of mind to set everything on a nearby chair, and her hands trembled as she disrobed.

Light from the moon gathered brightly in the chamber, and her body was fully exposed to him as she took off her gown, her stays, her shift. He'd seen her nude before, but she felt a quick stab of self-consciousness. She did not have a girl's lithe body. Childbearing and life had shaped her into the woman she was now.

As if aware of her sudden unease, he stalked to her. He didn't pause as his hands clasped her waist and he bent to kiss her ravenously.

"Lie down on the bed," he commanded when they paused to gulp air.

Her legs shook beneath her as she clambered onto the bed and stretched out. He leaned over her to maneuver her limbs, firmly but gently pulling her arms and legs out so she was spread-eagled.

"Don't you want to undress, too?" she gasped.

A grunt was his only reply.

It struck her then, the disparity between them. Her, entirely bare, spread out for him, whilst he was fully clothed. Her on display, him garbed and fortified. The discrepancy made her shiver with arousal.

She shook even more when he used her stockings to secure her wrists and ankles to the bedposts. It was loose enough that she wasn't uncomfortable, yet she was powerfully aware of how she couldn't cover her breasts. Her quim was utterly exposed, and she'd no doubt he could see how wet and full it was. Never before in her life had she been revealed like this. Never had she had anyone look at her the way Duncan did now.

She had no fear of what he'd do to her next, yet the quiet ache in her heart *did* frighten her. Because at that moment, he was all that mattered to her.

Chapter 16

W hat . . ." She licked her lips. "What do you plan on doing to me?"

His face was tight with need, his expression verging on ferocious. "Everything."

She closed her eyes, letting this one word and all its potential soak into her. The bed dipped with his weight, and his mouth found hers. It was a kiss of hunger and desperate need. She could not hold on to him, not with her hands bound, but she arched up to meet his demand with hers.

He stroked his hand down her neck, across her collarbones, and then he cupped her breast. His fingers teased her nipple into a taut point. She gasped as he gave it a gentle pinch, then gasped again when his other hand performed the same service to her other breast.

"A little pain, aye?" he growled into her mouth. "Just enough to make you wet."

She had not thought that a touch of pain could

heighten pleasure. Yet it did. It brought her senses fully alive, sharpening her and making her ache with the need for more. She'd no doubt that if she could touch her quim, she'd find it dripping with arousal.

He played with her like this for long, excruciating, delicious minutes, kissing her and giving her nipples firm squeezes between his fingertips. The throb between her legs grew and grew, her clitoris hot with the need to be touched. But she couldn't rub her legs together to assuage her need.

"Please," she moaned. "Touch me. Duncan. Please."

"Don't know if I should." He dragged his jaw along hers and then went lower, abrading her with his whiskers, and she luxuriated in the sensation. "Ye've been verra bad, Beatrice. Do ye deserve it?"

"Duncan," she wailed. "I'll lose my mind if you don't touch my pussy."

"Canna have that." His accent had deepened as his voice dropped even lower in register. "Poor wee lass and her hungry cunt."

When he stroked his fingers lightly over her outer folds, she hissed. It was like throwing a thimble of water on a fire. She needed more and shifted restlessly in her bindings to bring her into greater contact with his skin.

His fingers slipped down to orbit her clitoris, and she moaned louder.

"Is that enough for ye?" His words vibrated against her as he bit the top of her shoulder.

"More," she managed to gasp.

His thumb stroked her bud, his fingers circling her entrance. "Greedy lass. This is what greedy lasses get."

She cried out when he softly slapped her clitoris. Sensation exploded through her, hot tendrils of pleasure that burst across her body.

"Aye, ye like that," he rumbled. "Can ye take it?"

Sweat bloomed over her skin as she canted her hips up as much as she was able. "I can."

"Good lass." He slapped her clitoris again, this time with more force. Ecstasy careened outward, and she gave another cry, then another as he did it once more.

Release beckoned, and she stretched toward it.

"Not yet," he admonished, and to her dismay, he removed his hand. When she made a noise of protest, he shifted so that he knelt beside her head. His eyes blazed as his chest rose and fell in a hard, rough rhythm. "'Tis my turn."

She couldn't look away as his hands tore at the fastenings of his breeches. He pulled out his erection and gave it a hard, tight stroke.

"Want to see my cock between your lips," he panted.

God, how she loved to hear him use such filthy language, the disciplined officer becoming a man turned crude with lust. She licked her lips. "Give it to me."

"*Fuck.*" With one hand, he cradled her head, lifting it up, and with the other still gripping his cock, he guided it to her.

The crown pressed against her lips, and when her tongue darted out to lick around it, she tasted the slick salt that seeped out. She opened wider for him. He leaned in, sliding his cock deeper into her mouth. The length of his shaft filled her, and she feared, briefly, she couldn't take him completely. But she relaxed into the moment, and he slid all the way in.

He was still fully dressed, save for his bare shaft, and again she reveled in the contrast between them.

She sucked him, savoring his feel and taste, glorying in watching his face contort with pleasure. He panted with each dip of her head, cursing and growling praise as he gave her the gift of his trust. Cupping her tongue around the underside of his cock, she was unrelenting in pleasuring him. It was exquisite to be in service to him, yet she knew that of the two of them, she was the one with the power.

"Good lass," he rumbled. "So good. Will ye take my come?"

In response, she increased her speed and drew on him harder.

He went still and snarled with his release, his seed shooting from him. She closed her eyes, swallowing him, delighting in her strength.

The bed creaked as he moved, and then his head was between her legs. She still stung divinely from his slaps. The stroke of his tongue between her folds soothed—and inflamed. As she twisted and writhed in her bonds, he devoured her. His fingers thrust up into her, finding the pulsing spot deep within her passage, while his lips sucked on her clitoris.

Roused and maddened by need, she fell into sensation, knowing only the feel of his mouth on her. Any last vestiges of control slipped from her grasp, and she did not miss them at all.

She came apart, her cries loud enough to make her throat ache. Yet he gave her no time to bask in the afterglow before bringing her to climax again, even harder than before, and then once more. Golden light dazzled behind her eyelids as she flung herself into the pleasure he gave her.

"Not done with ye," he growled.

She managed to open her eyes to see him fit his cock to her entrance. The touch of flesh to flesh scorched her. His gaze found hers. He paused, and she knew what he asked.

"Yes, fuck me," she whispered. Then louder, "Fuck me, Duncan."

He thrust into her, a hard, forceful plunge that made her bow upward, tugging on her bonds.

She could only lie there and take what he gave her, which was, true to his word, everything. His strokes were fast but deep, and she cried out with each one. His growls and grunts sent her arousal into a frenzy. He brought his fingers back to her clitoris, caressing her as he drove into her.

"Take it," he rasped. "Take my cock."

She came again, so intensely she felt consciousness ebb. Moments later, he pulled from her and shot his release across her stomach.

When awareness returned, she discovered him tenderly wiping her clean with a damp cloth. With the same gentle care, he untied her and rubbed her wrists and ankles to soothe them. He pulled the covers around her. As she settled into the blankets, she heard the sounds of him disrobing. The bed shifted as he climbed into it and curled his naked body around hers. Warmth engulfed her.

"Beautiful woman," he said drowsily, nuzzling her shoulder. "Ye are a wonder."

She could not answer. Spoken words seemed too small to contain what she felt. The whole world was too small to hold the immensity of her feelings, and she feared that they were so gigantic, they would tear her apart.

THE following morning, Beatrice and Duncan went down for breakfast and found Lou sitting in the taproom. The girl looked tired but happy as she cradled a cup of tea.

As they sat down at her table, Lou beamed at them both. "You've added to the lore of Beaumont. What a gift you've given everyone—especially me. It's not possible to thank you enough."

To Beatrice's delight, Duncan blushed. "Had to be

done," he muttered. His voice was gravelly, either because it was still the morning or from embarrassment. "No thanks necessary."

He curled and uncurled his fists in discomfort at the girl's praise, and his modesty touched Beatrice deeply. Such a gentle man hidden within the warrior. She adored them both.

She suddenly realized something—what she felt for Duncan went beyond lust.

Fear clutched at her, edged and cold. It had taken years to emerge from mourning, which had lashed her to Edward even after his death. She relished being her own person, yet the longer she spent with Duncan, the more she questioned her instinctive desires.

Flee? Or ask him for more?

"You want to catch the mail coach, isn't that so?" Lou asked. "I've use of my family's wagon. Afraid I can't take you all the way there, but I can give you both a ride to the river ferry, and that will keep you on the right track."

A server appeared with plates of coddled eggs, toast, and streaky bacon, and poured fresh cups of tea. She must have been at the assembly last night because she winked before moving on to another table of guests.

"That will suit us fine," Duncan said. "Thank you."

Lou reached across the table to lay her hand across his. "Once again, thank *you* for what you've both given Beaumont."

Beatrice smiled into her teacup when Duncan

blushed. For all that he'd been delightfully filthy last night, saying the most delectable things to her, he was still a modest man. The contrasts in him were a perpetual source of delight.

"I wish you could arrange for secret assemblies every week." Lou sighed. "I'd give anything to dance again. Heaven knows I won't have the chance to become a true dancer in this mossy corner of the country."

"You could go to London," Beatrice suggested gently. "Follow your dream and perhaps dance in a proper theater."

The girl's face brightened, but then her expression fell. "Couldn't. I've no blunt, and if I went into service, I'd have no time to dance. And where would I live? I don't know a soul there."

"Miss," Duncan said as the server walked past. "Have you pen and paper?"

"Just a moment." The woman bustled around and finally produced a piece of paper and a writing implement. She set them in front of Duncan, who wrote on them before sliding the sheet across the table to Lou.

"There's a name on there," he said. "A friend of mine in London who hires builders for a construction enterprise. I've written the address of his place of work. Call on him when you get to the city, and give him my name. He'll fix you up with work and a place to stay."

Lou stared at Duncan, her eyes wide. "Truly? You would do such a thing for me?"

His cheeks reddened even more. "You'll have employment and a roof. The dancing part is up to you."

The girl leapt up, darted around the table, and threw her arms around Duncan's shoulders.

"Impossible to thank you enough," she said, her voice thick. Tears streaked down her face. "You've given me a way to seek my dreams."

He grunted, but his jaw was tight, as though he pushed back his own response.

Beatrice touched her fingers to her cheeks and was unsurprised to find them damp. At the same time, she silently cursed him for being so bloody wonderful.

"I'll let you eat your breakfast." Lou let go of Duncan and skipped back to her seat.

As they finished their meal, Lou peppered Beatrice and Duncan with questions about London. Clearly, she was excited to begin her own journey, and Beatrice could only hope that she wasn't disappointed with some of the more difficult realities of what it meant to live in a huge city. She herself had little experience with those realities, but it was impossible to dwell in London without seeing the contrasts of the high and low.

Where there was hardship, there was also beauty and joy.

Finally, after the last bite of toasted bread and sip of tea, it was time to go. Lou went to hitch up the wagon, and then they were off.

There was enough room on the driver's bench to accommodate all three of them, so they spent the ride talking more of London—especially its theaters. Lou was especially fascinated by the idea that the playwright Viscountess Marwood had been a commoner, but she plied Duncan with countless questions about the dancers that took the stage between burletta performances.

Beatrice could not decide whether she was tired of this itinerant existence or if she dreaded being stationary again. It did feel right, though, to travel with Duncan. He seemed made for life on the road, and she could hardly remember what it had been like to encounter him in the Duke of Rotherby's refined study.

Soon, they reached a swiftly moving river. A small ferry moved from one bank to another, anchored by a rope that attached to the boat through iron rings fastened to its side. The ferryman angled the ferry into the current, letting its motion propel the flat-bottomed vessel.

"This is it," Lou announced, nodding toward the water. "Take the road on the other side to the next coaching inn."

More thanks were exchanged before Duncan and Beatrice climbed down from the wagon. They waved goodbye to Lou as the girl turned back toward home.

They approached the ferryman, who had docked on their side of the river. The ferry itself looked a touch precarious, comprised as it was of time-aged wooden planks held together by rusty nails and obstinacy.

"This is safe, aye?" Duncan asked, placing a coin in the ferryman's hand.

"A' course," the man said with an enthusiastic nod. "You and your missus'll be safe as babes in their cradles. Climb aboard."

They were the only passengers, and so once they were on the vessel, the ferryman used a long pole to push off from the shore. The ferry moved in a sideways motion, the current trying to pull it downstream as the rope affixed through the iron rings kept it heading toward the opposite bank.

They had gone a third of the way when Duncan stiffened. "There's a sound."

"What?" the ferryman demanded.

"Something's creaking." Beatrice gulped. "Like . . . strained rope . . ."

A loud snapping noise pierced the quiet.

The rope split in two, and the ferryman lunged for it. He managed to wrap his hand around the line, but it slipped from the rings affixing it to the vessel. Still holding to the rope, the ferryman was dragged off the ferry and into the river.

Duncan dove for the other end of the broken rope, but it slid into the water before he could reach it.

At the least, the ferryman managed to swim to the riverbank. But as for Beatrice and Duncan, they were completely untethered. There was nothing to do but stay on the ferry as the current bore it down the river, taking them farther and farther from where they needed to be.

Chapter 17

❧

This was a fucking disaster. Duncan cursed himself for not having reached the rope in time to keep them from drifting away from the shore.

He eyed the current, but it moved too swiftly for him to ask Beatrice to chance swimming to the bank. He didn't doubt that he could make it, but there was the possibility that she didn't know how to swim, and even if she did, her skirts could easily drag her down.

"What do we do?" she asked, turning to him. She appeared remarkably calm given the circumstances.

"Got to be a rudder." But when he grabbed the tiller, it crumbled in his hand. He swore. This goddamned ferry was a disgrace. "We're stuck on here."

Her face paled, and he gripped her hand.

"It's going to be all right," he said. In situations such as this, belief in one's survival was the most important factor in determining one's success. While he had every belief that the ferry would eventually make its way to the riverbank, there was no telling how long it would take nor where they'd be deposited.

She nodded and fought to smile. "It is."

He gave her a quick kiss for her courage, and then there was nothing to do but wait and hope that they'd hit the shore sooner rather than later.

But the sun crept lower and lower to the horizon. *Hell.* He didn't want to spend the night on this blasted ferry, leaving Beatrice at the mercy of the elements again. Having lost her bonnet in Beaumont, she pulled a shawl from her baggage and draped that over her head to protect her from the wind and sun.

Blessedly, thirty minutes before dark, the vessel ran aground at the edge of a wood. The ferry shuddered as it ground into the muddy bank, and though Duncan had no earthly idea where they were, being off the water was something of a blessing.

He eyed the thick mud of the riverbank, shot through with reeds. The sludge stretched nearly twenty feet before it became solid earth.

"Grab the bags," he instructed her. He stepped off the ferry and immediately sank into the mud. It reached his knees and squished in his boots. "I'll carry you."

"I can walk," she protested.

"You'll wind up with fifteen pounds of mud on your skirts," he pointed out. At her continued objection, he added, "That will slow us down. I can get us both to dry land, and then you'll be able to walk without hefting that weight around."

She looked reluctant but didn't protest any more. Instead, she collected their satchels and then climbed into his waiting arms.

"Afraid that between me and our luggage," she said worriedly, "we're heavy as the world on Atlas's shoulders."

"No trouble at all," he said. Fit as he was, carrying a full-grown woman and two bags through knee-high mud was still a challenge. The mud sucked at him, trying to pull him down like a ravenous creature. By the time they reached the dry earth, sweat coated his back, and he struggled to breathe.

"Rest now," she commanded when he finally was able to set her down.

"Almost dark," he gasped. "Have to keep moving."

"Yes, Major. But I'm taking the luggage."

He would have dissented, but damn if his arms didn't shake and his legs wobble. So, grudgingly, he allowed her to carry the bags—for a while. When he was reasonably certain that he could hold something heavier than a dandelion, he took them back from her.

The woods were thick and full of brambles that tore at their faces and snared their clothing. Uneven ground covered in scrub made the going slow. For all her willingness to take on a challenging situation, Beatrice did not have the same facility with walking through rough terrain as he did. She trudged along slowly. When she stumbled, she cursed under her breath but forged ahead. Their progress was hindered as full night fell. At least a waxing moon hung in the sky to give them some illumination, turning the landscape into shades of indigo and black.

"No signs of human traffic," he said, peering into the dense forest. "Only game trails."

"Well, if we want to spend the night with a deer, we're in luck."

He shot her a glance, and though it was dark, he could hear her laugh.

"No need to disturb the poor, slumbering wildlife," he said as they continued on. "Hopefully, we'll reach a road soon. The prospect of whisky, a bath, and a bed big enough to accommodate us both seems like the closest I can ever come to Heaven."

"If that's what the afterlife consists of," she said, exhaling with each step, "then I hope my sins won't be judged against me so I can join you there. Though I can guarantee that what happens in that bed will not be at all angelic."

"Amen to that," he said fervently, then stilled.

"What is it?" she asked.

"Lights ahead." What he wouldn't give for his spyglass, but that had been lost days ago. Peering at the lights and the dark shape that contained them, he said, "Looks like a large house."

"Thank God," she breathed. "I'm doing my level

best to be a good sport, but maybe we can drink that whisky beside the world's biggest fireplace."

He led the way toward the house, and they broke from the woods to find themselves at the edge of a sloping lawn. The house that sat beside the lawn was indeed a substantial home consisting of two stories and an attic, and it was a measure of the occupants' wealth that most of the windows blazed with candlelight.

Duncan edged around the structure, grateful that he didn't have to tell Beatrice to try to muffle her footsteps. One never could be too cautious when approaching strangers' homes.

They kept to the shadows, but one large window revealed what had to be the dining room. There was a long table covered in fine white cloth, and silver dishes heaped with food and flowers arrayed atop it. Surrounding the table were a number of people in elegant, expensive clothing. Judging by the way everyone placidly ate their soup and the restrained murmurs of their voices, it was precisely the sort of staid and quiet dinner party that Duncan and the other members of the Union tried to avoid.

"Perhaps we ought to call a physician to see if any of those people are actually alive," Beatrice muttered. "Afraid I'm fresh out of black crepe. How about you?"

"Recognize any of them?" he asked lowly, careful to keep from being heard by anyone inside.

She peered into the room. "Not a one."

That was good. He could work with this. "At parties, Rotherby always gets to be the charming rogue, and I've never had the chance. You've been showing me that we all need to try something different now and again to keep from growing moss. So what say you and I liven up that funereal gathering?"

Her smile flashed in the darkness. "Excellent plan, Major."

"We'll charm the master and mistress so much, they'll beg us to stay the night in their most comfortable accommodations." He adored, too, that she was entirely eager to be mischievous at a moment's notice. This would be for her, too. A way to give her more mischief, more joy. "Let's have some fun."

Torches burned beside the main door, but the servants all seemed to be inside. Duncan stepped forward, and after casting a glance at Beatrice to ensure she was beside him, he rapped smartly on the door.

A moment later, it opened, revealing a liveried footman. His eyes widened at their bedraggled appearance, and his mouth hung open.

"Good God, it's as dark as my gangrenous soul out here," Duncan boomed heartily. "My wife and I have been wandering for hours. Take us to your master and mistress."

"Sir?" the footman said bewilderedly.

Duncan smiled widely. "Major Frye, and Mrs. Frye. Of Dundee."

"I'm weary enough to sleep in your privet, and no

one wants me scaring off the grouse with my snores," Beatrice chirped. "Please, do not leave us on your doorstep."

"Yes, my lady." The footman opened the door wider and gestured for them to enter. "If you'll wait in the drawing room . . ."

Duncan dropped their bags on the marble flagstones the moment he and Beatrice crossed the threshold. "Why wait when we can delight the company even sooner with our presence?"

The footman hesitated, but Duncan was already walking with Beatrice down the corridor that seemed to lead toward the dining room.

Behind him, the servant muttered, "Please, follow me," before hurrying ahead of him.

As they trailed after the footman, Beatrice whispered to Duncan, "A cheerful fellow, this Major Frye of Dundee."

"Mrs. Frye can't help but be captivated by her husband," he whispered back, which made her chuckle.

After the slog of this afternoon, hearing her low laugh shot his spirits straight up into the ether.

They approached the dining room, pausing just outside as the footman rushed in and approached the gray-haired gentleman at the head of the table. Conversation continued as the servant spoke lowly into his master's ear. The lord of the manor frowned in confusion.

"Lost travelers?"

The footman nodded.

"Show them in."

The dull drone of voices quieted as Duncan entered the dining room with Beatrice. Everyone stared at the scruffy condition of their persons, but he strutted forward, wearing his cockiest grin. On his arm, Beatrice had never looked more effervescent, smiling and nodding like a celebrated guest, despite the fact that half of her hair hung around her shoulders and she sported a long tear in the fabric of her sleeve. The gentlemen slowly got to their feet.

Duncan gave a raffish bow to the man at thc head of the table. "Sir, what a delight, an absolute *delight* to make your acquaintance. You're as striking and elegant as I expected from the master of this house. Didn't I say so?" he asked Beatrice.

"Oh, you did," she said with a charming smile.

"Major Frye?" the gentleman asked, looking just as puzzled as his servant. "Mrs. Frye?"

"At your service." Duncan bowed again, and Beatrice sank to the floor in an elaborate curtsy. "My wife and I were en route north when our vehicle and servants suffered a series of calamities, dash it. We were forced to continue on foot and wound up at your door, and what a door it is. Like the entrance to a cathedral of taste and sophistication." He kissed his fingertips.

"That is . . . most extraordinary."

"Your home is truly so *impressive*," Beatrice bubbled. She shot a wink at the guests staring at them from around the table. "And these *people*. To a one, the most distinguished and handsome individuals I've ever beheld. Oh, but you're dining, and we have interrupted you."

"Please, join us," the master of the house said. As servants came forward to set two more places at the table, he continued, glancing at the other guests, "I am Mr. Atherton. My wife, Mrs. Atherton. And our friends, who are joining us for the week."

Duncan beamed as Atherton introduced him and Beatrice to half a dozen couples whom Duncan had not heard of—likely they were country gentry who seldom came to London. He gave an approving nod as the servants edged aside the man seated beside the hostess to make room for his chair, just as another footman positioned Beatrice next to Atherton. These were places of honor for the highest-ranking guests.

Once everyone had taken their seats, the meal resumed. The guests kept throwing him and Beatrice curious, abashed glances. But he couldn't let the meal descend into dull silence.

"Confound it, Atherton," he said after taking a bite of roast, "I haven't eaten such delectable food since dining with the tsar in Saint Petersburg." Turning to Beatrice, he said, "Do you remember, my dear?"

"I do, my love!" She pressed her hand to her bosom and heaved an impressive sigh. "That parade of dishes was simply divine, each one more delicious than the last. He has the best cooks in the world, you know," she added for the rapt company's benefit. "And the tsar is inordinately fond of good food. But this is even better—without a doubt."

"Too kind," Atherton blustered as the guests made sounds of appreciation.

"What took you to Saint Petersburg, Major?" one man with ruddy cheeks asked.

"A matter of the greatest importance for international diplomacy," Duncan answered, dropping his voice into a stage whisper. "The tsar and I . . . Well, I cannot say precisely what we discussed. Security purposes, you know, but suffice it to say it involved intense negotiations and more than a few late-night meetings fueled by vodka and a fervent need to serve my country. It was a terrific hardship, but I persevered."

"The major was even forced into fighting a duel," Beatrice threw in, her words hushed but riveting. "Sabers, *on horseback*, in the dead of a Russian winter. I can see it now—the black horses, the white snow, the crimson blood."

Gasps sounded around the table, and Duncan had to bite the inside of his cheek to stop himself from chuckling.

"Did you survive, Major?" a lady in gray asked, eyes wide.

"Clearly, madam, I did," he answered. "Else I wouldn't be here tonight with you gracious, dazzling people."

"But it was a close call," Beatrice added. "Alas that

we are not on more intimate terms, else he might be persuaded to show you his scar. A very dashing scar, at that, in a very dashing place."

"My goodness!" someone exclaimed.

Duncan sipped at his wine to keep his laughter at bay.

When it was time for the ladies to retire from the dining room, Duncan watched Beatrice go, unable to keep his gaze from her.

They'd worked well together, and having her beside him through every step had been perfect.

She winked at him over her shoulder, and pleasure swelled through him.

It wasn't so long ago that he'd remarked on something similar to Rotherby. His friend had watched Jessica McGale leave the dining room as though the sun had set for the very last time. Soon after, Miss McGale became Rotherby's wife.

And now, here Duncan was, staring after Beatrice with likely the same look on his face. But Rotherby had married that woman. There was no possibility of the same for Duncan and Beatrice.

Once the women had retired to the drawing room, Atherton said, "You will stay the night with us, Major, of course."

Mentally, Duncan exhaled. He'd been waiting for this very invitation. "So kind of you, Atherton. The greatest kindness."

Mr. Atherton turned to one of the footmen. "Tell

Mrs. Powell that we'll need the Mahogany Room prepared."

"And baths," Duncan added. He smelled of riverbank and sweat.

"Yes, my lord." The servant bowed and retreated.

"Unfortunately," Mr. Atherton said apologetically, "all of the rooms on the first floor are occupied, and the Mahogany Room is on the second floor. I hope that won't be an inconvenience to you, and that you don't find it uncomfortable."

Spirits at the conclusion of the dinner were welcome, so Duncan accepted a glass of brandy, though he'd wished for that whisky he'd dreamt of hours ago.

"Don't trouble yourself," he replied to his host. "When I visited the palace of the king of Sweden and he made me and Mrs. Frye sleep in a room entirely made out of ice—*that* was uncomfortable. Do you know . . ."

And so it went as he spun yet another outrageous tale. Even without Beatrice in the room, Duncan enjoyed himself, never before indulging in the fine art of braggadocio and bluster.

As the gentlemen conversed, he was grateful that he and Beatrice would retire to a secluded bedchamber. The day had been eventful and tumultuous. He *ought* to be weary beyond imagining. Yet energy pulsed along his limbs in anticipation of sharing solitude with her.

She'd taken hold of his heart—and he didn't want her to let go.

CLAD in only his shirt and breeches after a bath in an adjoining closet, Duncan eased into the bedchamber to find Beatrice curled in a chair by the fire. Her bare toes peeped out from beneath the hem of her borrowed robe, and her freshly washed hair spread across her shoulders, forming waves and curls that he desperately wanted to rub between his fingers.

So he crossed the room and knelt beside her chair and did just as he'd desired, combing his fingers through her tresses. She purred in response, leaning into his touch.

"You smell of honey," he murmured.

She smiled. "McGale & McGale soap, in fact. They purchase it from Birmingham, or so the maid who helped me with my clothing said. I'll have to tell Jess."

He recalled that Beatrice was one of the investors in the duchess's family's business. But the intricacies of the marketplace did not interest him right now. Beatrice did.

"You make for a superb Mrs. Frye, wife of the most significant Major Frye." He nuzzled down her neck, sinking into the warmth of her skin, loving the way her body shook with laughter.

"What appalling tales you told," she said, chuckling.

"What appalling tales *we* told." He nipped at her jaw.

Breathlessly, she said, "I'd no idea you had such a talent for dissembling."

"Blame the Union for first introducing me to a life of nefarious behavior." He dipped his hand under the neckline of her robe and growled when he found her bare flesh. "Yet with you, my taste for mischief has reached its pinnacle."

"I'm not the least bit sorry." She turned her head, and their mouths met.

Whatever lingering traces of weariness he still carried suddenly dissolved at the feel and taste of her. They leaned into each other, opening more and more as the kiss caught fire.

"I ache with wanting," he said hoarsely. "I can't get enough of you."

"Take me to bed, Duncan," she whispered against his mouth. "This is our last night together, and tonight . . . I want gentleness."

"As you wish." He gathered all her softness in his arms and carried her to the bed. Laying her down, he stroked his hands over her hair, down her cheek, along the length of her arm, until he wove their fingers together.

He raised her hand to his lips and kissed it. She gazed back at him, her eyes dark and shining and filled with more than desire—emotion gleamed there, but he did not know *what* emotion.

Time was not his friend. Tomorrow, God willing, they would leave this place and reach Lord Gibb's. Delivering her to the house party's doorstep would mean the end of their idyll together.

He fought against the pain that threatened to slice him apart. She had not asked him to stay with her, and he couldn't press her to do so, not when she'd been so clear that what she required now was freedom.

By the end of the following day, he'd be on his way back to London—without her.

If this *was* to be their final night together, he'd sure as hell make it memorable. Because there would never be another Beatrice, and he hoped that, for her, there would never be another like him in her bed and in her life.

He bent over her and kissed her, long and deep. Desire pounded beneath his skin, and he held the back of her neck to anchor them both to this moment.

"Let me see you," she said breathlessly.

He released her to tug his shirt off and did not miss how she licked her lips when he pulled the fabric to reveal his torso. Her expression became positively avaricious when he removed his breeches.

"I shall miss that beautiful cock," she murmured.

He said nothing, wanting to be more to her than something to fuck. The appendage itself mattered far less than the meaning of her words—this was indeed going to be a goodbye.

This would be what he could give her, how he could imprint himself on her the way she had him, woven into the very fabric of his being.

His hands went to the tie of her robe, tugging on the ribbon until it came loose, and then he peeled back the fine cotton to reveal her nudity.

Her gaze slid away from his—for all that they had

done with and to each other, she still held on to some uncertainty about her body. But it told a tale of the wonders she'd experienced and all that she'd accomplished and survived.

Duncan hated the world just then, how it insisted that women had a very limited window of desirability, supposedly the only part of them that mattered. What a load of bollocks.

Running his finger along her jaw, he gently turned her head so that their gazes held.

"You're so lovely," he rumbled. He cupped her breast. "Here." He then laid his palm atop her heart. "And here."

The look of delighted wonderment on her face would stay with him for all the decades that would follow.

"And . . ." He grinned wickedly as he stroked along her mound. "Here. Definitely here."

She laughed, and he loved to watch how her laughter traveled through her. He bent down to kiss her again. As he did, he lightly, softly stroked her, letting her body tell him when he should slow and when he should go further. His fingers were soon slick with her arousal. She writhed beneath him, filling his mouth with her moans.

After guiding her to sit up, he climbed onto the bed and sat on the edge before tugging her to him. She understood what he wanted, and with a delectable flush across her cheeks and chest, moved to straddle him.

They faced each other, their eyes level as they looked

deeply into each other. She positioned herself so that the head of his cock met her wet, waiting opening. Wrapping her arms around his shoulders, she sank down, filling herself with him. They gasped together, pulling breath from each other, as though they were each necessary for the other's survival.

He went motionless, wanting this moment to last as long as it could.

"I love how you feel inside me," she said huskily.

"I love to be inside you." He took her mouth with his. At the same time, he moved his hips, thrusting.

She gasped, her gaze going hazy. "Oh, yes. Just like that."

He held her hips firmly as he stroked in and out of her. She took up the rhythm, rising and lowering to take him within her.

Pleasure arced up his spine, and he fought the need to fuck her hard and fast. This was to be a slow savoring. Gentle, as she wanted. So he gave her that, his movements unhurried, long, slick thrusts that he hoped touched every part of her.

She'd said she wanted gentleness, but soon she rode him vigorously, and he met her with his own hungry strokes. He knew now the little mewls she made as she approached her climax, so he reached between their bodies to strum her clitoris.

She came with a sound that shot right to his cock. He had enough presence of mind to pull from her, his own release tearing from him.

As she collapsed softly against him, he held her close as their breathing slowed and bodies cooled. He petted her hair, though his hand stilled when she exhaled a laugh.

"Trying to feel if the gray hair is coarser than the brown?" she murmured.

"I like to touch you. And your hair is fucking gorgeous."

She pressed her face close to his neck. "This has never bothered you, the difference in our ages?"

"Don't know why it should."

"Not a common opinion," she said softly.

"The hell with everyone else's opinion." He pulled back enough so he could see her face. "Yours is the one that signifies."

She scratched at his beard, and while the sensation sent pleasure skittering through him, he was more intent on listening to her.

"It's not an easy thing, to be an aging woman. They want me to be invisible. I mattered for a few years, and then I didn't, and I was just supposed to disappear and . . . and I hated that. I hate it still, but I refuse to let it determine who I let myself be."

He moved them so that they lay down, facing each other atop the coverlet.

"Can't blame you for being angry," he said lowly, then added, "and the person you are is a miracle."

One corner of her mouth curved. "*Miracle* implies some sort of divine hand, and I doubt the celestial entity they preach in church would approve of me. I surely hope He doesn't."

Duncan kissed her, tender and fierce at the same time. It conveyed far more of what he felt than his words could ever hope to express. He was going to have to let her go, and he didn't want to. Yet if he was to respect all that she was and all she meant, he would have to walk away.

Duty always had a cost. He'd faced that cost many times, taking each loss to himself as he was supposed to—head down, soldiering on, never truly examining the wounds he amassed. Eventually, those wounds turned to scars, which meant that they stopped bleeding, but he wouldn't be the same person. He was marked forever.

As he drew the blankets around them, and she settled warm and pliant against him with a lovely little sigh, he realized that after he said goodbye to her, the scar tissue around his heart would be thicker.

If someone ever tried to touch his heart again, he would feel nothing.

Chapter 18

A loud noise startled both Beatrice and Duncan awake. He was out of bed immediately.

"What is it?" she asked as he hastily threw on his clothing.

"That was gunfire," he answered, terse and grim, his posture utterly changed. He was alert, ready for battle, turning from her tender lover into a soldier, as sharp and dangerous as any blade. The impenetrability of his expression alarmed her. He checked his timepiece that rested atop the bedside table. "Quarter to six. Atherton said nothing about hunting in the morning. Get dressed."

Heart hammering, she did as he commanded, tossing on her clothing as fast as she was able. She jammed her feet into her shoes as he slipped his knife into his pocket.

He seemed to debate for a moment. "You're safest with me, so stay close, and for God's sake, don't do anything without my express command."

She nodded, fear climbing higher up her throat. "Perhaps we should remove our shoes so that they can't hear us coming."

"Thought of that." He looked down at his boots. "I don't want to be barefoot when confronting an unknown threat. Let's go."

They slipped from the room, and she followed him down the stairs as quietly as possible. She could barely breathe and kept her hand on his shoulder both to let him know that she was close, as well for the reassurance of his solid body.

As they reached the first floor, Duncan froze, holding up his hand in a silent order for her to halt. Following her gaze, she saw a man emerge from a room, but he wasn't one of the men who had been at dinner last night. One of his fists clenched around what appeared to be several pieces of jewelry, as well as small personal items studded with gems. His other hand held a long, terrifying blade. The man seemed preoccupied and didn't see them as he started toward the next room off the corridor.

Duncan motioned for her to stay put. She squeezed his shoulder in agreement.

Feeling shaky with terror, she could only watch as he slipped along the hallway, moving noiselessly closer to the stranger.

Duncan pounced. He wrapped an arm around the man's neck and, with his other hand, gripped the stranger's wrist to prevent him from striking out with the knife. The would-be assailant thrashed, trying to open his mouth to call for help, yet the hold Duncan had on his throat seemed to prevent him from making any sound other than a choking rasp.

Duncan rammed his knee into the stranger's forearm, forcing his hand to spasm open. The knife fell to the carpet, which muffled the sound, then Duncan spun the stranger around before slamming his fist into the man's face.

To Beatrice's relief, the man crumpled to the ground, unconscious. All of the jewels and items he'd taken dropped to the floor, as well. Duncan quickly relieved the man of his weapon.

He stood over the stranger's insensate body, then turned to her, his face completely devoid of expression but his posture loose and capable. He'd transformed into a warrior. The sight would have been fascinating under less terrifying circumstances.

She scurried forward when he motioned for her. As she neared, she whipped cords off from around some curtains. She held them out to him, glancing at the intruder to signify her meaning.

Duncan took the cords from her hands and bent down to efficiently tie the stranger's wrists together, then loop the rope around his ankles so that it would be impossible for him to escape. The whole procedure took less than thirty seconds. How many times had he done this very thing?

Leaning close to her, he said in a voice so low it was

barely audible, "Belowstairs. We'll start with the servants and see if they know what the fuck is going on."

She nodded, and instead of taking the main stairs, he entered the narrow service staircase. With her hand again on his shoulder, she followed him down. The fear that scoured her was unlike anything she'd ever experienced—the fight in the tavern had been mere boisterousness compared to this life-or-death scenario. And yet, if there was any measure of comfort to be found, it came from being with Duncan and the knowledge that he was a superior fighter, trained into ruthless efficiency by years of experience.

She prayed, however, that no one had to die today.

"Doing splendidly," he whispered over her shoulder. "Brave lass."

She exhaled a tremulous laugh. "I'll faint dead away when this is all over."

"I'll catch you."

Of that she was certain.

Once they reached the bottom of the stairs, voices could be heard at the end of the hallway. They sounded frightened, confused.

"What you going to do?" someone wailed.

"Shut up," a man's harsh voice barked. "Or I'll shoot one a' you."

As more terrified sounds rose up, Duncan tensed. "Hostages. Damn." He exhaled, then murmured to her, "Stay very close."

"I will," Beatrice gulped.

There was no one in the world she trusted as much as him, no one she'd rather have with her in a perilous situation.

Together, they slipped down the corridor to the kitchen. They peered around the doorway where another stranger in coarse clothing had the servants collected in a group in the middle of the kitchen. Judging by the footmen wearing partial livery, the staff had been caught unaware by the intruders. Food in various states of preparation was spread throughout the kitchen, indicating that the servants had been in the middle of fixing breakfast for the master and mistress of the house and their guests.

True to his word, the intruder held a mean-looking pistol in his hand. He had it trained on his hostages.

Yet Beatrice and Duncan only had the knife taken from the stranger upstairs. She supposed that the small folding knife Duncan had put in his pocket would do little to help them attack and disarm the invaders.

But what could she and Duncan do? Perhaps creep away to escape from the house and find the local authorities?

Before she could confer with him, a housemaid glanced toward the doorway where Beatrice and Duncan crouched. Her eyes widened in surprise.

"Shit," Duncan growled.

The man with the gun saw her look and spun to investigate. He raised the pistol at Duncan.

Beatrice acted without thought. Moving quickly,

she darted forward to slap at a mound of flour atop a table. The flour flew into the gunman's eyes, and, blinded, he cursed as he stumbled around. The barrel of the pistol veered around the room as he tried to aim and fire.

Duncan flew toward him, knife at the ready.

Beatrice bit back a scream as the assailant moved to pull the trigger. But Duncan slashed the blade across the man's hand, causing him to release his hold on the pistol.

As the weapon fell to the floor, Duncan punched the stranger straight in the face. There was a crunch, and the man fell in a heap onto the flagstones.

Beatrice darted forward to grab the weapon.

"Quiet," Duncan hissed when the servants cheered. Abashed, the staff fell silent. He demanded, "What happened?"

"They came in just before sunrise," a footman said.

"How many?" Duncan clipped.

"Three? Four?" the cook said anxiously. "Couldn't count 'em all. They rounded up mister and missus, and the guests, too. Took 'em into the ballroom and had us down here. Think they mean to rob us all."

That explained all the valuables the knife-wielding man had been taking from one of the bedrooms. But why hadn't she and Duncan been herded with the other guests?

"Someone should go get the authorities," Beatrice said to the staff.

"I'll go," one footman volunteered.

"Be quick," she instructed him, "and be sure you aren't seen." When the servant dashed off, she turned to Duncan. "Now what?"

He took the pistol from her and carefully uncocked the gun before setting the knife down. Grimly, he said, "Now we stop them."

She was both afraid of that, and also she knew that was precisely what a man like Duncan would do.

"The ballroom is on the ground floor?" she asked the cook.

"Yes, madam."

"There's an alternate entrance to the ballroom, correct?" Duncan demanded.

"A corridor the staff uses to ferry to and from the kitchen," a housemaid said. "For serving refreshments and the like during balls."

"Take us there," Beatrice said, then glanced at Duncan. "And before you order me to stay behind, I feel safest with you."

He started to argue but must have seen that she would not be dissuaded, and he nodded.

The housemaid motioned for him and Beatrice to follow. Before they left the kitchen, he turned to the footmen. "Tie up that bastard, and whatever you do, don't let him speak or leave."

"Yes, sir," one of the footmen said. He took a piece of fabric and wadded it up before stuffing it into the unconscious stranger's mouth. A kitchen rag was torn into strips and used to bind his wrists and ankles.

"The ballroom," Duncan said to the housemaid.

"This way, sir." The girl guided them to a passageway that had a series of small windows cut high in the wall. They slipped along the corridor. Thank goodness the stone floor kept their footsteps quiet.

Duncan loosened his shoulders and muttered sardonically, "'Come out to the country, take a lady to a house party, have a few laughs . . .'"

Beatrice pressed her lips together to fight a burst of hysterical laughter. The poor man. Here he'd thought he'd left combat behind, and a simple errand had turned far more dangerous.

A narrow, baize-covered door stood at the end of the passageway. The housemaid signaled to Duncan that he needed to press a latch to open the door.

He nodded, then tilted his head to indicate that she should return to the kitchen. The girl dipped into a quick curtsy before hurrying back the way they'd come.

Duncan drew in a breath before turning to Beatrice. He gripped the back of her neck, kissing her fast and hard, stealing what little breath she had.

"We can do it," he said firmly. "Believe me. We'll survive this threat."

"If you say so." She had less conviction in her voice, but she knew that of anyone she wanted beside her now, it was Duncan.

He rested his forehead against hers. "I do. I'll get us out of this."

"I know you will." And she believed it. He was her island in this tempestuous sea that threatened to drown her.

He kissed her again, then slowly cracked open the door, and they both looked in.

The ballroom was a large, long chamber lined with windows that were, at the moment, covered by heavy velvet curtains, so that the room was streaked with light and shadow. Half-dressed, Mr. and Mrs. Atherton and their guests huddled together in the middle of the parquet floor. A blond man brandished a knife, but Beatrice was more focused on the bearded man with a pistol aimed at his hostages.

"Cooperate," he said tightly, "and no harm will come to you. Any resistance will be met with force."

These men were clearly desperate, and desperate men were capable of anything. Perhaps even shooting another human being.

"See here," Mr. Atherton objected. He yelped when the bearded man trained the pistol at him. Meekly, Mr. Atherton said, "We'll cooperate."

Duncan eased back with a scowl. He growled, "Fucking hate endangering you, but I need your help."

"You have it." She was pleased that at least she'd spoken without hesitation, even though she was bloody terrified. "Tell me what to do."

"Create a distraction."

Frightened as she was, she was eager for the chance to be truly useful. To fight with him, side by side. It was terrifying—and exactly what she wanted. "And then?"

"I'll take out that bastard with the pistol." He gently took hold of her chin, and his gaze held hers. She'd never seen so much gravity in his eyes before. "You'll be all right."

"So optimistic, Major," she said, hoping for levity. "How do you know?"

His expression turned bleak. "Because I can't think about the alternative, or I'll lose my goddamned mind."

This was no time for tears, yet they sprang up anyway, and she rubbed her knuckles across her eyes to banish any possibility of weeping at this moment. She needed to focus for her sake, and for Duncan's.

"Now go," he said, low and taut, gesturing with a tilt of his head that it was time for her to provide some distraction.

She drew in a breath, feeling her own strength, and the strength he gave her, as well. With them working together, they could accomplish anything. Even defeat a gang of vicious robbers.

After one more breath, she opened the door and took some deliberately noisy steps into the room—making certain she didn't surprise the bandits into shooting her.

"I say, are we having parlor games?" she asked brightly.

The men swung to face her, and she fought against a wave of panic when the bearded man pointed his gun at her. But at least he didn't fire it.

"Who the hell are you?" he demanded.

She moved into the room, trying to make her expression bright and vacant. "It's awfully early to do any pantomime, but I suppose if given a cup of tea, I'll join right in. Does look awfully fun."

She looked behind quickly, but there was no sign of Duncan. He'd disappeared.

"Shut up," the stranger snapped.

"Mrs. Frye—" Mr. Atherton croaked.

"There wasn't any Mrs. Frye in the butler's ledger," growled Beard.

A loud bang split the air. The man with the knife sank to the ground, groaning as he clutched his shoulder. Red spilled between his fingers as he lost his grip on his blade.

It was Duncan. Her heart jumped into her throat as he ducked for cover behind a large potted plant. At the same time, the bearded man aimed toward where Duncan hid.

Her body and instincts took over, and she plowed her shoulder into Beard's side just as he fired. The robber's shot went wild, the bullet lodging into the ceiling, with bits of plaster falling like snow.

And then Duncan rushed toward the bearded man. He slammed a punch into the man's ribs—she heard a cracking sound as the intruder doubled over—and then Duncan flipped his pistol around. Using the firearm like a club, he walloped the back of Beard's head. There was a groan, and he sprawled on the floor.

Duncan grabbed the man's spent firearm and tucked it into the waistband of his breeches.

The hostages murmured in relief, and a few even applauded. Duncan barely spared them a glance. He glared at the bearded man, who moaned and cursed as he lay on the parquet.

"Don't understand," the invader muttered. "We snuck into the butler's pantry, got the guest list and all the room assignments. How did we miss you?"

"Last-minute addition." Planting a boot under the brute's chin, Duncan spat, "Robbery? That's what this was all about?"

"I *know* this man," Mr. Atherton said, coming forward. "Rickland? You've plenty of blunt—no need to rob me."

Rickland snarled, "Nothing wrong with wanting more."

"There's plenty wrong," Duncan replied flatly, "when there was every chance you could have killed someone."

"The hell with you," Rickland spat.

Duncan pressed his boot against the man's head. "Shut it." Turning to Mr. Atherton, he clipped, "Servants are all in the kitchen. We already have someone running to fetch the constabulary, but better send your fastest rider, too."

"Yes, Major," Mr. Atherton said, starting for the door. He paused on the threshold. "Never have I been more glad to have a military man beneath my roof."

Then Mr. Atherton disappeared, and his fast footsteps could be heard down the corridor above the wounded man's groans of pain. Duncan grabbed the robber's knife, before glancing back toward Beatrice.

The guests also seemed to be recovering from their shock. Some laughed wildly, while others wept.

Beatrice knew exactly how they felt. She wanted to weep and laugh, too. But she'd wait for a slightly more private time. Instead, she eased close to Duncan, and her hand intuitively sought his. When his fingers wove with hers and gave her a reassuring squeeze, something shifted into its rightful place.

"You did it," Beatrice said in wonderment.

"*We* did it, love," he answered, giving her a tiny smile.

"If you two are going to moon at each other," Rickland gasped from beneath Duncan's foot, "could you at least do me the favor of knocking me out, too?"

"Happy to oblige." Duncan leaned down and, with a neat proficiency, punched the man square in the face so that he blacked out.

Mr. Atherton jogged into the ballroom, though he looked winded by the effort. "Rider's been sent to the village. We should have the law here within the hour."

"Excellent." Duncan faced the guests. "I'll do reconnaissance outside to make certain that there aren't any more of them. Then, we'll drag the villains into a horse stall, secure them, and keep them there until the constabulary arrives."

"How are you so good at this?" Mrs. Atherton asked, her tone both awed and baffled.

"Because he's him," Beatrice said as she smiled at Duncan. It was primal and not very evolved of her, but seeing him in action, ruthlessly dispatching enemies and issuing commands . . . it did something to her. Something that affected her in a very animalistic way.

"Because *we* are *us*," he said, his gaze warm.

She knew she looked at him with girlish adoration but couldn't stop herself. It had nothing to do with his training as a soldier and all to do with who he was, at his very heart. And facing off with him against an enemy had felt so utterly perfect. They'd worked *to-gether*. Never before had she experienced such a fault-less partnership.

She wanted to cling to that, to hold him as tightly as she'd ever held anyone or anything. Yet she'd fought so hard for her freedom, and giving that up went against her every instinct.

Chapter 19

Duncan seethed with emotion and hunger. After a patrol of the house's interior and exterior to make certain he'd taken care of all of the villains, he returned to the second floor room to find Beatrice packing their bags.

The moment the door closed behind him, he stalked to her and wrapped his arms around her. "Need you. Now."

Desire was instant and stark in her face. "Yes."

They sank to the floor together.

It was a fast, fierce coupling, almost a battle as they clawed at each other. She was tight and hot and flawless around him, and though he wanted to last as long as he could, it was impossible. But he made certain that he didn't permit himself release until she came with a sharp cry. Groaning, he only just managed to pull from her as his seed shot from him.

They lay together on the floor, panting.

He dropped his head to the curve between her neck

and her shoulder. A faint trace of honey soap clung to her skin, with the tang of perspiration beneath—no scent had ever been more exquisite, and he drew it into his lungs as deeply as possible as if he could tuck all of her away inside of himself.

Only now did he permit himself a shudder of fear.

The odds had been against them this morning, and there had been every likelihood that she could have been hurt or worse. Of himself, he wasn't much concerned. He'd faced more perilous combat during the war and survived. But she, a civilian with no training and unaccustomed to violence, had walked a risky path. Endangering her had gone against every instinct, but he'd been unable to face the thieves alone—not without something going terribly wrong, imperiling her further.

But she'd been magnificent and was safe now.

Those thieving bastards. He would have gladly beaten all four of them into a mash of blood and bone had it not been for the restraining presence of Atherton and some of the fellow guests. So he'd left them hog-tied in the stables and given his statement to the constabulary and had thought that perhaps he'd gotten control of himself.

Until he was alone with Beatrice.

Now they were tangled together, damp with sweat, and all he could think of was the fact that he had come within a hairbreadth of losing her forever. She'd become everything to him. Her laughter, her light, her wisdom, her passion. Life without Beatrice was unthinkable—he had to do something, anything, to keep her in his life.

"Marry me." Once he said it, his heart surged because it was the answer he'd been looking for.

Her breathing stopped. "What?"

He lifted up on his elbows to look down into her face. The face he'd come to care about so much it physically pained him. "This is good between us, aye? It needn't end. We can be married and have this every day for the rest of our lives. We can have all the things we talked about—a lifelong companion to grow old with."

"I'm already old," she said softly.

"You aren't, and that's not the point." Her words did not elate him—they were far from the joyful acceptance of his suit.

He still lay atop her, his softening cock pressed against her stomach, and their bodies going clammy in the wake of their frantic sex, so he sat up to fasten his breeches and then hunt down a cloth to clean her. He found a kerchief in his bag and handed it to her.

She wiped her stomach clean of his seed, but her gaze was on him. "What *is* the point, Duncan?"

He sank into a crouch beside her. "I want us to be together, for the rest of our days. After what happened here today, I dinna ever want to lose you."

His accent thickened with his urgency, but he didn't care about that. All that mattered was the shuttered look on her face, sending a chill through him.

She tugged her skirts down. Quietly, she said, "And your solution to this is marriage."

This was not going as planned—but that wasn't true. There *was* no plan, and every word from his mouth was forged from feverish desperation.

He took her hand in his. "I'm offering ye me and my heart, forever. As my wife."

"Duncan." She pushed up from the floor so that she stood, and he rose with her. Her voice far too mournful, she said, "You are a *wonderful* man. But to marry again . . . it frightens me. I think of all the things that could go wrong, how it could fall apart, and I . . . I die inside."

"Aye, but it's *me* you'd be marrying." He thumped a hand to his chest. "Not some cold, controlling nobleman who only wants ye as an ornament. I would have ye be all that ye are and never try to crush your spirit."

Her look was melancholy but level. "It doesn't matter *who* I marry. The bonds of matrimony are shackles for women. They take away any scraps of power we might have and give it all to our husbands."

"It wilna be like that with us," he insisted.

"It *might*," she said firmly. "Even if you were good to me, I don't want to *hope* for you or any man to be good to me. I want to be good to *myself*. If I ever thought that you could one day change your mind and become not just my husband but my *master*—I'd live in terror of that day. And what if *I* made *you* unhappy? I couldn't do that to you."

Every word she spoke pierced him like hundreds of bullets, as though he charged the enemy's line. And yet he kept on running forward, into more gunfire.

"That isn't going to happen," he gritted. "I care about you, Beatrice. And I think you care for me."

"I do, Duncan," she said, her voice far too heavy for someone admitting they had feelings for him. "And caring for me means listening to me when I say that marriage is simply not possible."

"We've been Mr. and Mrs. Frye all this time." He knew he sounded desperate but didn't give a ruddy damn. "It could work."

"That wasn't truly being wed to someone," she countered gently.

"But marriage is what people do," he rasped. "When people care for each other, and they want to be together, they marry. It's how things are done. Be my wife, Beatrice."

Her eyes brimmed with a mixture of sadness and resolve. "Not with me, not anymore. If you do care about me, you won't keep asking. It isn't fair to either of us."

He stared at her, churning with desolation and frustration and the terrible, profound knowledge that she held her truth, he held his, and because of this, they had no future.

The knowledge of it nearly made him buckle.

"Then, today will be goodbye," he said heavily.

"It doesn't have to be." She walked to him, color in

her cheeks, her breath coming quickly. "We can be together, Duncan, only not as husband and wife."

He frowned and said vehemently. "I don't want you to be my *mistress*. Mistresses come and go, and their paramours are just as transitory."

"We don't need to use words like *mistress* and *paramour*." Her trembling hands took his, but he couldn't be certain who shook more. "We can be *us*."

His mind and heart struggled to understand what she offered, but he scrabbled against a wall of glass, finding no traction. "No one in my lineage has ever done such a thing. McCamerons marry. It's a maxim that runs deep in my blood."

She looked at him, and in that agonizing moment, he saw in her eyes the truth that he didn't want to acknowledge. His fear became reality when she said sadly, "We're never going to be able to bridge the divide between us. I cannot give you what you want, and you can't live with what I need."

His throat burned as if choked by acrid gunpowder smoke. Impossible not to curse himself, because he'd known the risks of caring for her, but he'd told himself that he would be cautious and protect himself. And now here he was, his heart merely a collection of fragments that he'd never be able to reassemble. Hell, he didn't know if he *wanted* to put his fucking heart back together.

He could be wise, beginning now. The wisest course of action would be to cauterize his wounds and keep moving.

"Fine." The word was as flat as he felt inside. But this was good. He wanted to feel nothing, as he was certain that, should he let a tiny splinter of pain pierce him, he'd simply fall apart.

Duncan had lived through over a decade of warfare and witnessed countless terrible things. He'd buried comrades in arms and had to console his men when their friends had died under his command. And he'd done well to keep it all contained tightly within him. Not even the Union of the Rakes knew the extent of his scars. He survived because that's what he did.

"We should leave soon," he said dully, "if we're to get you to Lord Gibb's today." He threw the words out in a final, futile effort, hoping that she would at the least change her mind about attending the house party, which he hoped meant they still had a chance.

"I see," she said quietly. She straightened her shoulders, like a boxer shaking off a direct hit, and picked up her valise. "I'm certain I can prevail upon Mr. Atherton to lend me a carriage."

He told himself he didn't care that she still intended on going to Lord Gibb's.

Funny how not caring still hurt like a goddamned cannon blast.

He drew himself up to full attention. "I gave my word to Rotherby that I would see you safely to Lord Gibb's. I do not go back on my word, and I don't shirk my duty." *Dignitas, Honestas, Pietas.*

"I'm not your duty," she said, her voice thick.

"You weren't." He closed his baggage with a snap. "But now I find that I must consider you so. I'll wait for you downstairs."

He left the chamber without waiting for her response. Of all the things he'd done today, including hand-to-hand combat and foiling an armed robbery, walking out of the bedroom with his head up and his shoulders back took the greatest toll.

"You've our gratitude, Major," Atherton said as Duncan and Beatrice mounted their horses. "Is there naught more we can do for you?"

"The loan of these mounts is enough," Duncan answered. His voice was flat, hardly friendly, but there wasn't anything to be done about that. He wanted to embrace this nullity of emotion. Better this than the alternative. "I'll have them back to you on the morrow."

Atherton frowned slightly at Duncan's use of *I* rather than *we* but did not remark on it or the frosty silence between a couple who had been so enamored of each other the night before. He did glance at Beatrice sitting stiffly atop a chestnut mare, yet she had her gaze fixed on the path leading from the house and did not notice his scrutiny.

"You're both welcome here again," Atherton said with a forceful attempt at jolliness. "And there should be no burglars or ruffians of any sort. That I promise you."

Duncan bit back a reply that Atherton could offer no such promises, since life was unpredictable, dangerous, and painful as hell. Instead, he nodded. "Again, my thanks." To Beatrice, he said, "Ready?"

She answered tightly, "Let's go."

He touched his heels to his horse, prompting it into motion. She did the same, and they rode down the path, soon reaching the main road.

"You know the way?" she asked as he turned them northward.

No, in fact, he was utterly lost as to what to do with himself or how to feel. But that wasn't what she asked. "Atherton's butler gave me directions that will see us in Nottinghamshire by midday and at Lord Gibb's by afternoon."

Even to his own ears, his words were grim, and he hated that he could still feel enough to hurt. Yet thinking about saying farewell to her made him want to gnaw on flint.

It was, unfortunately, one of those gorgeous English late-summer days filled with sunshine and birdsong. The sky draped overhead in a cloudless span of azure, and beneath it rolled a green quilt of farmland and pasture, dotted with swaying trees and punctuated here and there with gemlike ponds. Shepherds tended flocks of snowy sheep, cows placidly grazed in clover, and everything was so bloody perfect that Duncan wanted to cast up his accounts.

With such fine weather and the roads in relatively good condition and the horses fresh, they progressed quickly on their way. Was time going too fast or too slowly? Each moment in her presence—with the understanding that they had been doomed from the start—felt an agony. He was all too aware of what he'd wanted and what had been lost.

He kept holding himself back from pointing things out to her as they traveled. A doe and two fawns standing at a creek bed, a child and a man flying a red kite atop a hill, a small market in the village square, and a puppet show that had more adults than children watching the characters' antics. All these things he knew would bring her pleasure, and, damn him, he still wanted to give her that pleasure. He'd give anything to watch the play of joy brighten her face and make her eyes shine.

But was it kind to either of them to linger on what couldn't be? Hell and damn, he didn't know what to do, what to say.

At midday, they reached an inn. "We need to stop," he said.

"I've no appetite," she answered.

"It was a difficult morning, and we still have some travel ahead of us. You should try to eat if you can, to preserve your strength."

After they'd handed their horses to a groom, they approached the inn, and a woman of extremely small stature came out. "Take a meal with us, mister and missus?"

He almost bit out that they were not and never would be married, yet that would be the height of truculent foolishness, so he only nodded.

"Lovely table beneath the elm tree," the tiny woman offered. "Perfect for a romantic meal in the fresh air."

"We'll sit inside," Beatrice said and added a moment later, "please. The taproom."

Duncan avoided the innkeeper's curious look. He didn't want to watch her speculate if the mister and missus were having the kind of fractious quarrel that many traveling couples did.

Their luncheon was wordless. She had always showed such a robust appetite and throughout their journey had been fascinated by the food they'd been served, yet now she picked at her meal.

Falling back on his soldiering habits, he ate quickly and without tasting anything. Better to just have done with this agonizing luncheon and get back on the road. And yet that meant their time together was running out. Neither option was a good one.

Soon after, they mounted up and continued on their way.

Before Duncan could fully prepare himself, they rode beneath the large iron gate that marked the entrance to Lord Gibb's property. As they neared the house, he wasn't certain what to expect, given the fact that the next week would see the most unbridled debauchery within its walls. But it was a fine, stately manor house in the style of the last century and seemed as respectable as any large country estate could be.

As they approached the house, Duncan clamped his jaw tightly to keep from asking Beatrice if this was what she truly wanted. She had made her decision plain, and he possessed enough pride that he wouldn't once more beg her to be his wife.

It was amazing what shoddy bulwarks could be formed from tattered pride.

More than preserving his pride, he had to respect her choice. Bullying someone into a marriage was unthinkable, and he was no bully.

Two footmen emerged from the house as he and Beatrice neared and then stopped. The servants held the horses while they dismounted, and no sooner had Duncan's boots touched the gravel than a man with thinning blond hair and a hospitable smile stepped out to meet them.

"Welcome, welcome to my home, Lady Farris." The gentleman who had to be Lord Gibb bowed politely over her hand, which Duncan distantly thought odd, given that likely within a few hours, they'd both be participating in unfettered licentiousness.

"Thank you for your gracious hospitality," she said with a smile that, perhaps to someone who didn't know her very well, might appear warm and happy. But Duncan saw the strain in the corners of her mouth and how her eyes had none of their usual sparkle.

"And you are?" Gibb asked, turning with a curious but friendly look at Duncan.

"Major McCameron," he clipped and shook Gibb's offered hand.

The gentleman chuckled. "That's a formidable handshake, Major. Have you considered crushing coal into diamonds with it? Could yield a fine supplement to one's coffers."

Duncan didn't want to like this man, but he made it difficult to cling to enmity.

"Will you be joining us, Major?" Gibb eyed Duncan like a captain assessing a new player for his football team. "You'll be very popular, I can assure you."

Duncan glanced at Beatrice, but her expression was opaque.

"I'm leaving right now," he answered.

Gibb's eyebrows climbed. "Oh, but I thought that since you arrived together you would . . ."

"He intends to go," Beatrice said simply.

"At the least," Gibb said after a pause, "abide with us for a time whilst your horse rests."

Duncan choked back a growl. It made the most sense to linger for an hour or two as the horses were watered and given some respite after the hours on the road. They were borrowed animals, as well, and it would be poor form to return them to Atherton in shoddy condition.

"If there's a parlor or some corner you can stow me," he finally said, "that should suit me well enough."

Gibb nodded and waved for them to follow him inside. As they walked into the foyer, the gentleman kept up a stream of cheerful chatter.

"Guests began arriving yesterday evening, Lady Farris," he chirped.

"If we were having a competition to see who had the most eventful journey here," she said, "I would win."

"It certainly sounds that way!" Gibb chuckled. "Everyone's currently amusing themselves around the house. Games of billiards and walks in the garden. All of which are available to both of you, of course. Oh, Lady Farris, last night your servants delivered your luggage—somewhat worse for wear, but my maids have seen to your clothing and cleaned and repaired anything that received damage during transit. Your servants told an incredible story of a storm."

"There was a pack," she said. "Belonging to the major."

"Ah, we wondered why one piece of baggage contained a pistol and neckcloths. Mind, we're open-minded here, but it was a bit unusual for our standard bill of fare. Yes, that pack is also in the room we prepared for you, Lady Farris."

"Please have it brought down as soon as possible," she said woodenly, "so the major can leave when he so chooses."

Duncan willed himself to ice over as solidly and thoroughly as a lake in midwinter, but that didn't stop a hairline crack of pain to thread through him.

As Gibb continued to guide them through his home, offering anecdotes about the house and its contents, they passed other guests, and again Duncan was surprised by their very ordinariness. They were of varying ages from late twenties to early seventies, sundry body sizes and shapes, some striking or beautiful and some plain-featured, and all perfectly friendly as though they were greeting people who were there to spend a week merely taking country walks and playing charades, not fucking with abandon.

They passed the billiards room, and Duncan's stomach sank. Inside the room were several men ranging in age from their thirties to their fifties, and they were, to a one, uncommonly handsome and well-proportioned. One looked at Duncan with interest, but the other men straightened when they saw Beatrice. Someone in their ranks would be her next lover.

No scenario could make any part of this situation bearable.

"I'll make introductions later," Gibb nattered on. "It's fortunate you arrived when you did, because our grand gala is only hours away. I like to pride myself as a host and believe that every day under my roof is a delightful one, but you assuredly do not want to miss the first gala. It perfectly sets the tenor of the week. Ah, here we are. The Roman Room."

Gibb opened a door, revealing a parlor adorned with classical-style furnishings and artwork. He gestured for Beatrice and Duncan to go inside, and when they did, Gibb announced from the threshold, "I'll have tea and refreshments brought to you. After the arduous journey you've both had, surely you'll want something to revive you. Major, an honor to meet you."

And then Gibb was gone, shutting the door behind him, leaving Duncan alone with Beatrice.

Chapter 20

All the words that came to mind seemed too small and feeble to bear the weight of Beatrice's unhappiness. She could only dwell in the silence that stretched between her and Duncan.

With ramrod-straight spine and hands clasped behind his back, he stood at a window that looked out on the eastern side of the house. The view was of a hedge-lined path, and a couple strolled down it. They appeared to notice that they were being observed, so they waved at Duncan, who gave a clipped nod in response.

The couple continued on their walk, the woman saying something to the man that made him chuckle. They looked very much like a husband and wife who had spent much of their lives together. And yet they each were broad-minded enough to attend Lord Gibb's house party as a duo.

Beatrice's throat tightened, to think that this man and woman had reached such closeness—they wanted what the other wanted and gave and took with equal measure.

Duncan turned away from the window.

Her heart seized to see how tightly he clenched his jaw and how his eyes flashed with pain. The hell of it was, there could be no way for either of them to emerge from this unscathed. All the choices led to someone being terribly damaged.

"I don't know how to say goodbye to you," she said, her throat raw.

"Was thinking the same thing."

His eyes shimmered, and she realized that he was on the verge of weeping. And while there was nothing wrong with tears, the fact that *this* situation made this impossibly courageous and resilient man cry was torture.

She went to him because she couldn't stand the gulf between them. As she stroked her fingers down his face, his whiskers abraded her fingers, and she leaned into the sensation.

"You are everything good in a person," she whispered. "You are strong and caring and you make me laugh and appreciate me as I am. I will hold you in my heart always."

"And I'll do the same." He captured her hand in his and pressed a kiss into her palm.

Her lips trembled, and a tear tracked down her cheek. She thought she knew all the different varieties of pain a heart could endure, but none of them were like this, threatening to incinerate her and leave her a pile of lifeless ashes. "Duncan."

"Remember that night when we slept outside," he said, his voice gravelly as he continued to hold her hand. "How you asked me what would make me happy?"

"I remember," she whispered. It had been only a few nights ago, when he'd looked at her across the fire with his heart in his eyes, and she'd been its grateful and careful keeper. Closeness had woven between them, potent as any ancient spell, but it seemed so long ago now. Yet the memory of the pleasure caused fresh torment to well within her.

"It won't make me happy, but it's what I need." He released her hand, though his fingers moved stiffly, as if letting her go was an agony.

"Yes?" she answered at once, eager to give him whatever it was he required.

"Open that." Moving as though he was made of heavy iron, he tilted his head toward the parlor door.

Frowning at his odd request, she did as he said.

Once the door was open, he rasped, "Now walk out of this room, and for the love of God, do not come back."

Her legs threatened to give out beneath her, and she held onto the doorframe to support herself. "Oh, Duncan."

"I'd leave on foot if I could, but I have to return Atherton's horses to him. Since I'm stuck here at Gibb's for the next hour, I need you to go." Desperation was in his gaze and a pain so limitless that to see it in him, she couldn't catch her breath. "Beatrice. Please. Be kind and leave me."

Tears streamed unchecked down her face. It was incredible the amount of sadness a person could experience. If there was any fairness in this world, such hurt would simply make you wink out of existence, like a candle in a draft. But the world wasn't fair. It let you keep on going, continue living and suffering, and all you could do was endure it.

Unable to speak, vision swimming, she turned and went quickly down the corridor. If they ever did meet again, they would do so as strangers.

She found a retiring room that was fortunately unoccupied. Wrapping her arms around herself, she sank down onto a low chair and permitted herself the luxury of giving in to her tears. Yet she pressed her knuckles tightly against her mouth to quiet her sobbing. The very last thing she wanted was for some female guest to hear her weeping and come in to ask for an explanation.

She wasn't certain what she'd say to them, anyway. There was no concise way to describe everything she'd experienced this past week, nor the incredible man who'd been with her the whole time. And how could she expect anyone to understand that though they'd come to mean so much to each other, they had to part? There had been no alternative.

Finally, after what felt like decades, her tears slowed and then stopped. Her head was thick and her body sluggish, so she used a provided ewer and basin to splash cool water on her face. She dried her cheeks with a soft cloth before examining her reflection in the tabletop mirror.

Her eyes were still red, as was her nose, and she looked, frankly, puffy. Hardly the sort of siren who'd attract a lover.

She didn't want anyone else. Only him.

Still, she couldn't stay in the retiring room for the rest of the week, so she emerged from the small chamber and absently followed the sounds of laughter emanating from the back of the house. Double doors had been opened to reveal a drawing room. It led to a terrace and a manicured and stylish garden. The drawing room itself contained nearly a dozen people, some of whom she recognized from seeing them earlier in other parts of the house.

Lord Gibb himself was there, talking animatedly with a trio of guests. They all held flutes of sparkling wine, and when Lord Gibb spotted her standing at the entrance of the drawing room, he snapped his fingers at a servant. The footman approached with a tray holding more glasses of wine.

With rote motions, she took a glass and downed it in one gulp before reaching for another.

She drifted through the room, trying to find a place to alight. The guests greeted her with smiles and some looks of interest, yet she could find no group of people that intrigued her enough to stop and talk. Nothing and no one could hold her attention. She didn't want to chat, and she certainly had no sexual appetite.

Lord Gibb approached her. "There's a special evening planned for our first night. It's not to be missed. I've engaged a circus troupe to entertain us before supper, and guests are encouraged to try their hand at tumbling. There's music, as well, with performers coming from as far as Vienna. My French cook and his staff have spent the last three days preparing a lavish meal with food that rivals anything served at Carlton House. Though I was unable to get Mrs. Catton herself to come from London, she's sent two of her best pastry cooks, and they have made an array of cakes and sweets that will make any gastronome's heart overflow."

"How delightful," Beatrice said, attempting to summon enthusiasm. She couldn't have what she wanted—Duncan—so surely, she ought to enjoy all of these things that *were* available to her. Yet hearing this litany of pleasures moved her not at all. Lord Gibb might as well have recited the dates of a recent canal's construction milestones.

"And then," Lord Gibb added, his smile widening, "we fuck." He chuckled.

"Yes, right," she said without enthusiasm.

Lord Gibb rubbed his hands together. "Most guests tend to form specific couples or groups over the course of the week, but for the first foray, there are pillows and couches set up throughout the ballroom. I encourage everyone to experiment and find as many partners as possible over the course of the evening. It's quite a sight, I can tell you. So much freedom in one ballroom. You'll never experience anything like it anywhere else."

"It does sound unique." Her heart continued to beat steadily in her chest—there was no kick of excitement, no tingle of anticipation anywhere in her body. Certainly not in the parts of her that ought to be more interested in the prospect of having her every erotic fantasy fulfilled.

A footman approached Lord Gibb and murmured into his ear. The host nodded before dismissing the servant.

"Is everything all right?" Beatrice asked.

"Indeed. My servant merely wanted to let me know that Major McCameron has departed, taking both horses with him. But you needn't worry—when the week is over, I can easily arrange transport for you back to London."

She barely heard anything Lord Gibb said after the words *Major McCameron has departed*. Nothing else truly mattered.

She and Duncan would see each other no more. Perhaps from time to time, they might cross paths, though she'd never again return to the Duke of Rotherby's estate of Carriford. Securing an invitation wouldn't be a challenge, and the estate itself was delightful, but to go to that place, knowing that Duncan worked and lived there—that would be a torment.

Despite her furious bout of weeping less than an hour ago, fresh tears sprang to her eyes. The cord that tethered her heart to Duncan's pulled tightly, and she braced herself for its inevitable snap, severing that tie.

"Lady Farris?" Lord Gibb's concerned face appeared in her line of vision. "What troubles you?"

"I'm merely fatigued from my journey." Her voice didn't shake *too* much, so that was an achievement. "It was a rather turbulent week."

"So I gathered. I'll have one of my servants show you to your room."

"That would be most appreciated."

He waved over a footman and gave instructions to escort her to her bedchamber. "The gala begins at seven," Lord Gibb added. "If you decide to nap, I can have a maidservant wake you in advance so you've time to bathe and ready yourself for the evening."

"Most gracious of you."

She followed the footman out of the drawing room and through the house. As she trailed after the servant, she tried to distract herself by taking note of the house's interesting details, such as a stained-glass window that would be quite stunning to see when the light shone behind it. But the thought of trying to calculate the proper time to see the window at its best only exhausted her. Besides, she'd seen many stained-glass windows in her life. This one wasn't so special.

The footman climbed a staircase and then walked down a lushly carpeted hallway before stopping in front of a door. He opened it and stepped back to permit her entrance.

It was a pleasant room, decorated in genteel shades of pale blue and gray, with a generously proportioned canopied bed. No doubt all the beds at Lord Gibb's home were of similar size to accommodate the guests' amorous activities. Surely, she and Duncan could use up every inch of that mattress, and he'd be very creative in his use of the bed's posts.

She shook her head. Duncan wasn't here. He would not share her bed ever again.

"The maid's unpacked your belongings, my lady," the footman said, interrupting her thoughts. "Everything's in the press."

She handed the servant a coin. "That will be all."

He bowed and left her alone. Driven more by restlessness than interest, she opened the press and did, indeed, find all of her gowns cleaned and whole. Curious, she looked into one of the press's drawers. Her collection of erotic novels was there, though slightly water damaged from the rain. And her contraceptive devices were there, too. Doubtless the maid was not shocked to find them in Beatrice's bag, but to see them again made her start. When she'd obtained them in London, she'd been filled with anticipation of a week's debauchery, almost naive in believing that seven days of uninhibited sexuality was precisely what she wanted, what she needed.

She knew better now.

Chapter 21

Duncan didn't want to stop. He planned to ride straight on to Atherton's, return the horses, and then find some way to get back to London. If he kept moving, he wouldn't have time to think. To brood. But Atherton's cattle were not sturdy military horses accustomed to long hours on the road. They were delicate creatures, mostly bred to be decorative and admired when ridden to church. So Duncan had no choice but to give the animals a rest.

He found a town with an inn, and its taproom would suit his purposes. Once in the yard, he gave the horses to a boy, with instructions to see to their care.

Inside, the taproom was bustling with the activity of early evening. People looked up at his entrance, but this village seemed large enough that a stranger's presence wasn't entirely unusual.

Much as he wanted to sit with his back to the room, ensuring that no one would disturb him as he drank, old habits and self-protection won out. He took a seat at a table, keeping his back to the wall.

The tapster took his order for ale. "Anything for supper, sir?"

Duncan's response was a grunt. He'd no appetite, and though he knew it was wisest to keep himself fed so that he'd have the necessary energy should anything go awry on his way south, he couldn't bring himself to eat.

"Right, then," the man said before shuffling away.

Duncan observed the merry taproom as though he looked at it through the reverse of his spyglass. It all seemed very far away, and he couldn't feel the warmth of the fire or be cheered by the laughter. He was a visitor from some strange, distant land that knew nothing of conviviality or happiness. His realm was one of endless shadow and harsh, rasping voices that held no emotion.

"Stomachache?" a woman with black hair asked, dropping into the seat opposite him. "Got a hand on your gut, and you made a sound like someone was stabbing you. Since I don't see a knife in your belly, maybe it's a stomachache."

"I'm fine," Duncan muttered.

The woman put a fashion periodical on the table, and it was clear from the publication's worn pages that she'd read it many times.

A moment later, the tapster plunked a tankard down in front of Duncan. "Evening, Nicolette," he said to the woman. "Don't bother the man too long, hear? He ain't looking for company."

"Maybe he is," Nicolette answered pertly. "Looking for company, chap? Would you like to waste some time?" She followed this with a wink.

"The ale's enough company for me," Duncan answered.

She blew out a breath before getting to her feet. "Suit yourself."

Once he was by himself again, Duncan could only shake his head. It would have been a perfectly unemotional fuck with a fine-looking woman, and yet the thought of touching anyone who wasn't Beatrice was exactly like the invisible knife Nicolette had imagined going straight into his gut.

The pain he'd experienced after receiving Susannah's letter had been, in a way, more manageable. Because while he'd been fond of her, fondness had been all he'd felt, and all Susannah had ever shown him. What was between him and Beatrice was explosive, consuming.

Or, it *had been* explosive and consuming. Now it was nothing. No, that wasn't true. Nothing would have meant being numb, and he was one big raw wound.

He respected Beatrice's wish to never marry again. Yet the alternative that she had proposed was utterly alien, existing so far away from the boundaries of the world that he knew and understood. It was one thing to host an unsanctioned assembly in a town that didn't permit dancing, but not marrying the person you cherished above all others, that he could not comprehend.

Duncan threw back his ale, draining the tankard, and signaled for another. He couldn't permit himself to get drunk when he still had a ways to go on the road, but he'd come as close to it as possible and hoped that it could dull the edge of his agony.

Bathed, dressed, ready in every way, Beatrice stood with her hand on the doorknob. It was ten past seven. She ought to go downstairs and join the others. Already, she heard the sounds of revelry—glasses clinking together, laughter, music. She could picture the feast that awaited her with the best food and drink that could be found in Britain. There were many attractive men downstairs, as well. Everything was as it should be. All she needed to do was open her bedroom door, go out into the hallway, and take a few steps before she'd be part of the merriment.

She didn't move.

After a minute, she stepped away from the door. Then took another step backward, one more, and another and another until she sat on the edge of her bed. She willed her legs to make her stand and her feet to carry her back to the door, but her body had other ideas, and she stayed seated on the bed.

She must be tired. Her attempt at a nap earlier had been an exercise in futility. All she had done was try not to think about Duncan and failed miserably. Her efforts at reading one of her rather damaged Lady of Dubious Quality books in an attempt to summon some sensual inspiration had met with similar failure.

It was merely exhaustion.

"Who the hell am I fooling?" she muttered aloud.

Certainly not herself. It was as though he existed inside of her, beside herself, so that when she breathed, she breathed for both of them, and when his heart beat, it beat alongside hers. The fact that he was likely miles away did not alter the bond. It was as strong as it had been when they'd traveled together and when they'd lain with their bodies intertwined in the aftermath of their extraordinary lovemaking.

Because that's what it had been. Not simply sex but a communion between two people. Perhaps at first it had been simple physical attraction, yet that had quickly changed into more than mere bodies finding pleasure and release. He'd been so caring, so attentive to her needs and wants, pushing himself because *she* had asked him to.

She wanted him—wanted all of him. But she could not do something that went against everything she believed in and everything she wanted for herself.

One thing she did not want for herself was to remain at Lord Gibb's. She didn't desire any of the people here, and there was no purpose in staying, not when her heart was heavy with loss.

She moved to the clothes press and began pulling out a few garments. Just the essentials, and she'd ask for the rest to be sent back to her in London.

A tap sounded at the door.

"You may enter," she said over her shoulder as she grabbed a handful of shifts.

"Will you not join everyone downstairs?" Lord Gibb asked, coming into the room. "Supper is about to be served."

"My thanks, but if I might have a tray brought up, I would be most grateful."

"You're staying in your room?" There was genuine puzzlement in Lord Gibb's voice.

She turned to face him. He'd changed into a banyan, likely because it would be easily removed once the actual bacchanal began, and he gazed at her with mystification.

"I am," she said. "Forgive me, Lord Gibb, but I find that I cannot remain at this gathering. What I need is a ride to the nearest coaching inn, and then I can see to my own transport back to London."

"Ah. I see." Lord Gibb blinked in astonishment. "Your letters had indicated considerable enthusiasm for attending my house party, so I find this decision unexpected."

"To me, as well," she said. "Yet it's the right decision."

"My coach and coachman are at your disposal," Lord Gibb replied. "But I ought to tell you that the London-bound mail coach will not arrive at the village until midmorning. If you'll stay one night beneath my roof, I can have my carriage take you first thing in the morning. I promise you'll find the beds here more comfortable than you will at the inn."

"Thank you," she said. "I'll remain tonight."

"Of course."

"I am quite grateful, my lord."

"This will be a first, having someone leave before anything has truly begun. But naturally I will honor your wishes." Lord Gibb took a step toward the door. "Can I not enjoin you to partake in tonight's festivities? It seems a shame for you to go through so much trouble to be here and then not participate. I have heard from a number of other guests that they were looking forward to your presence."

Lord Gibb might as well have asked her if she'd enjoy snuggling a warthog. She'd no interest in embracing anyone or anything that wasn't Duncan.

"That's most gracious of them," she said. "However, I shall remain here in my room until morning."

Lord Gibb inclined his head, then opened the door. More sounds of the guests' merriment drifted into her bedchamber. Later tonight, the laughter would transform into sighs and moans of sexual pleasure, but for now, everyone laughed and chatted. It sounded quite pleasant. There would be new people to meet, delicious food, and exciting festivities—and she'd no desire to be a part of it.

"Good evening, Lady Farris," Lord Gibb said. "I shan't be up to bid you farewell in the morning, but if you ever change your mind and decide you want to return, you are always welcome."

"Thank you again for your generous hospitality." She had no intention of telling him that she wouldn't come back. There was only one man she needed in her bed, yet she could never have him.

Chapter 22

He'd never been more grateful to come upon a sleeping house than he was when he rode up to Atherton's home and found all the windows dark. Even the grooms had gone to bed.

Duncan led the horses into the stable and tended to them, his movements rote and utterly unhelpful in banishing from his mind the thought that at that very moment, Beatrice was likely in someone else's arms, doing . . . he didn't want to think too deeply about what she was probably doing, because if he did, he'd go out of his mind. He could just picture Atherton and the entire household running to the stables, roused from their slumber by his maddened screams.

He pulled a scrap of paper from his pack and scribbled out a note to Atherton, thanking him for the loan of the horses. He stuck the note on the front of one of the animal's stalls before hefting his pack to set off on foot. There was a possibility that he'd meet with unsavory characters at this hour, but maybe a fist to his face could offer some distraction.

There was something both desolate and welcoming about being alone on the road long after the sun had set. The moon was still ripe enough to cast decent light. He debated for a moment whether or not to find a place to bed down for the night. Without Beatrice's comfort and safety to take into consideration, he'd no issue with sleeping beneath the stars, even without the benefit of a blanket.

He *was* exhausted. The day had begun years ago, with the invasion of Atherton's home, and in the intervening hours, he'd experienced devastating heartbreak. And there had been miles on the road.

Yet there would be no rest for him. Any moment's quiet would only give space for memories to come flooding in, and if he *was* able to sleep, he'd doubtless dream of Beatrice and the agony of walking away from her.

Better to keep going. So he did, putting one foot in front of the other, attempting to distract himself by thinking of all the aspects of estate management that would soon engage his attention. That kind of steady employment was exactly what he ought to do with himself. It was reliable and safe and precisely the sort of thing he needed.

When he'd stepped outside the boundaries of sanctioned behavior, he'd made himself too vulnerable.

There was reassuring protection in the rules—or so he told himself.

Hearing the creak of an approaching vehicle, he peered into the darkness. A wagon emerged from the shadows, and two men sat on the bench.

Duncan's hand immediately went to the pistol he'd tucked into his waistband. You could never be too cautious when journeying at this hour, especially if you were a solitary traveler.

Then a voice called out, "Can we offer you a ride somewhere, stranger?"

Duncan frowned at the familiar voice. But that couldn't be possible—he was on the road in the middle of the night, far from London. Impossible that he'd encounter anyone he knew.

The wagon drew closer, and a stunned laugh burst from him. "Rowe? Curtis?"

"Is that . . . McCameron?" Rowe pulled on the reins, and the vehicle came to a stop. "What the deuce are you doing on this stretch of road at one o'clock in the morning?"

"Could ask you both the same question." Even in the darkness, Duncan saw how Rowe's thigh was pressed close to Curtis's. There was plenty of room on the bench. His friends sat close to each other because they wanted to.

"Rowe gave his paper," Curtis said and added with pride, "and fucking obliterated his naysayers."

"Well done." Duncan grinned, though it physically hurt him. "That doesn't explain how you came to be *here*."

"We'd had enough of life on the road," Curtis continued, "and wanted to get back to London and our own bed."

It did not escape Duncan's notice that his friend had used *bed* singular. But, given the pause and meaningful looks from both Curtis and Rowe, that had been intentional.

Rowe had told him that he and Curtis had crossed the boundary between friends to lovers. Now he had his proof that the bond went further than a few nights' pleasure.

The way they both gazed at him now, wariness in both their eyes, they feared what he'd think.

"A sound plan," he said at last.

Curtis exhaled audibly, and tension eased from Rowe's posture.

"You know I only want your happiness," Duncan said. Because it was true. He would give any member of the Union whatever he could to ensure their hearts' desires.

Though he was celebrated as an orator in court, Curtis seemed only capable of nodding.

"As we want yours," Rowe said, his voice thick. "Which brings us to the fact that you're here, in the middle of the night, looking miserable—and the dowager countess is noticeably absent."

Duncan glanced away, down the length of black ribbon that was the road. "We had to walk away from each other."

It was strange how he could condense boundless misery into a single sentence. Stranger still that it could bring back all the pain. His throat worked as he swallowed around the knot that had formed there.

"Damn." Rowe handed the reins to Curtis and climbed down. He laid a hand on Duncan's shoulder. "I'm so sorry. She'd no right to toy with your heart like that."

"She did nothing of the sort," Duncan said firmly. "I could not give her what she wanted, and what I needed was impossible for her."

Curtis growled, "Falling in love is a son of a bitch."

"I don't—" But the rest of Duncan's words died as he realized the truth.

He didn't merely *care for* Beatrice. He *loved* her. Every moment with her was joy, and every moment without her was misery. He became the man he wanted to be when they were together, a man who could live with spontaneity and whimsy and joy. The thought of spending the rest of his life without her in it filled him with pain so acute he could scarcely breathe. But the idea of being with her for the remainder of his days saturated him with the sort of happiness he never believed he could possess.

The knowledge that he loved her was itself an alchemy of elation and dismay.

Because she was worth that, all the pain and uncertainty that came with love. With her indomitable spirit and her warm heart, she was worth it. Yet—

"I don't know if she loves me back," he choked out.

"Did you ask her?" Rowe said pointedly.

Duncan opened and closed his mouth, as he realized he never admitted the depths of his feelings, which meant he never truly gave her a chance to tell him what *she* felt. But what did it matter? "Even so, she won't marry me."

Rowe and Curtis exchanged a look. "There are other ways to be in love that don't include marriage," Rowe said.

"So she suggested," Duncan said grimly. "She wanted us to be together, but not as husband and wife. But that's not how it is in my family. We commit to each other for life."

"Firstly," Curtis said, "marriage doesn't ensure a lifelong commitment. How many people leave their spouses? Men, especially, have a tendency to be the ones who roam or outright desert their wives."

Duncan absorbed this. "Suppose that's true. And secondly?"

"Secondly," Curtis went on, "love stays, no matter what the church or the law insists is required."

"Love stays," Rowe seconded, walking back to Curtis and taking his hand.

Duncan stared at their intertwined fingers. His friends touched each other with absolute certainty, as though they were meant to be exactly where they were—together. In the face of a society that would not condone their union, they held fast to one another, unwavering in their dedication and devotion.

Still . . . "I don't know," he muttered. "Where's the guarantee? Where's the security?"

"It's a leap of faith," Rowe added, gazing at Curtis. "Nothing in this life comes with a promise. You have to trust them on the basis of nothing but how you feel about each other. A rule will never give you that trust because it doesn't come from *within*."

Duncan brooded over what his friends said. "How can it be so simple, and so complex, as trust? How do I walk away from generations of tradition and make my own path? It would be a hard thing to do."

"None of us doubt your courage in combat," Rowe said softly. "There are other kinds of courage."

"I know what I want, and . . ." Frustrated, he struggled to speak, yet if anything, being with Beatrice meant that opening himself up to others led to the greatest rewards.

He went on, his voice a rasp. "I'm afraid. More afraid than I'd ever been on any battlefield, because the risk—my heart—seems even more meaningful than my life."

"Think I can speak for Rowe," Curtis murmured, "but we'd be damned sorry to never see your hideous face again. All the same, it's not an easy thing to gamble your heart."

"There are hazards," Rowe said. "But consider the rewards."

A lifetime with Beatrice—her joy, her strength, her appetite for life. He could watch silver overtake the brown of her hair. He could see her across the table every morning and hold her every night. And he could spend every day bringing her the world.

But he would never be her husband.

"Didn't plan on this," he growled.

"Things don't always go according to plan," Curtis replied with a touch of humor.

There had been many times with Beatrice that they had veered from the known path. It hadn't always resulted in something immediately pleasurable—but he had still learned something about the world and about himself.

Rowe moved back to Duncan and squeezed his shoulder. "I'm learning that the best course is to go along for the adventure." He gazed warmly at Curtis, affection bright in his eyes. "Take chances."

"So easy," Duncan said with a snort.

"Never said it was *easy*," Rowe murmured, "but it's worthwhile. It's not a safe place, this world of ours. We have to do our best to see to ourselves and the people we love. We must be excellent to each other."

Duncan glanced back and forth between his friends. Doubtless their lives together would have struggles, but they would also have joy and pleasure and, most of all, love. That could never be ignored or denied, and to hell with anyone who insisted otherwise.

He'd faced death so many times. It was the work of a moment to end a life, which meant that every second one drew breath was precious and not to be undervalued. It didn't matter if everything followed a careful order. He didn't have to cling to definitions of what should and should not be, when all that mattered was the truth of his heart.

He had also fought many battles—yet never one for himself.

And he needed to show Beatrice that he would fight for her, too. If she wanted, he'd champion her. He would champion *them*.

"How eager are you both to get back to London?" he asked his friends. "Because I've a mind to make some mischief. Perhaps even break a rule or two, and I could use some help."

Rowe grinned. "I am intrigued."

"Been asking McCameron to break the rules for twenty years," Curtis said, and chuckled. "And, damn, I am *ready* for it."

Beatrice had changed into her nightgown and gone to bed, but closing her eyes meant revisiting the horrible moment when Duncan had begged her to leave. The pain in his eyes and words continued to slash through her, and if she did sleep, dreaming would offer no solace. The days and nights with him had been the real dream, yet they were gone now. What she'd produce for herself would be shadowy and ephemeral, tantalizing her with what couldn't be.

After throwing back the bedclothes, she struggled into her clothing, determined to wait out the night. Staying awake wasn't going to make the morning come any sooner, but the alternative was excruciating.

She wanted so badly to just *leave* already so she might put this painful part of her life behind her. Yet it didn't matter where she was—here, or in London, or on the other side of the planet—she'd carry Duncan with her forever and feel the ache of his loss for the rest of her days.

All she had to read were her rain-swollen copies of books by the Lady of Dubious Quality, and for once she'd no taste for reading about someone else's erotic exploits. Especially not when she could hear sounds of many people engaged in all manner of sexual activities, even through her closed bedroom door. On some other night, it might have been arousing to simply listen to sensual abandon.

She pulled the curtains open so she could watch the progress of the night sky, urging the sun to appear.

Where was he now? Hopefully, he'd found a safe and comfortable place to pass the night. An image of him in bed, rumpled and delicious, appeared in her mind. He'd never sprawled on the mattress, clearly too used to constrained sleeping circumstances. As he'd lain beside her, he had been warm and solid, his arm snug around her, holding her through the night and loving her even more thoroughly in the morning.

Groaning, she covered her eyes with her hand.

She would go on living as she had, finding new experiences, but they would be pale echoes without sharing them with him. It had been wonderful to discover the world on her own—and it was so much better having him at her side.

The clock on her mantel chimed four o'clock. Her heart jumped at the sound—dawn was only two hours away. Perhaps she ought to wait downstairs, in case the coachman decided to get an early start. Then again, hearing a long moan of pleasure drift underneath her door, perhaps she should just wait in her room.

She started at the sound of an explosion. The glass in the windows rattled with it.

What could it be?

There—another detonation. Thinking back to Mr. Atherton's home, she prayed it wasn't another group of villains attempting to invade Lord Gibb's house. Looking around her room, she couldn't find much to use as a weapon, though the fire poker might suffice.

Hand shaking, she grabbed the metal rod. God, if only Duncan was here, he'd know what to do. He'd quickly formulate a remarkable plan that would take the invaders out with blinding speed and devastating effectiveness.

But he wasn't here. It was up to her to save herself.

A third explosion echoed, and she realized two things:

The sound was coming from *outside* the house.

The sky was full of light and color.

She ran to the window and let out a shaky laugh when she saw fireworks burst. That's all it was: a pyrotechnic display. A modest one compared to Vauxhall, but here in the country, it was dazzling, a kaleidoscope breaking apart in the dark of night.

This had to be part of Lord Gibb's entertainment for the gala. Yet . . . he'd made no mention of fireworks earlier. And why would he have them go off at this hour, when it was certain that all of the guests were occupied with other matters?

There was one other person she knew who had training in explosives. He'd said so, early on in their journey.

She rushed out of her room and down the stairs. She paid no attention to the guests hastily throwing on robes and loose clothing and exclaiming to each other, but when she found Lord Gibb in his banyan she demanded, "Did you arrange for fireworks?"

Looking sweaty and utterly baffled, he shook his head. "I didn't. I don't know who could—"

"I know who."

She dashed past him, and as the pyrotechnics continued, she hurried through the back drawing room to stand on the wide terrace. Colorful light painted the scene as more guests gathered here, some wearing blankets over their shoulders, and a couple who were completely nude. Everyone had their gazes trained skyward, watching the fireworks overhead.

But she wasn't looking at the sky. She searched the crowd for one man.

"Duncan," she called above the din. "Duncan!"

"Beatrice!" a familiar voice bellowed.

He emerged from the throng, his gaze fixed solely on her. Her heart clenched. Dimly, she took in the travel-worn condition of his garments and the beard that now covered his cheeks and jaw. Hues of red and gold from the fireworks bathed him, turning him into a mythical warrior. Yet all that she truly saw was the look of need in his eyes. Need for her.

They ran toward each other, then collided. His arms wrapped around her, holding her so close she felt his heart thud beneath her cheek.

"You came back," she whispered, clutching him tightly.

Somehow he managed to hear her above the explosions. His gaze was blistering, and his voice was rough. "Of course I did. I love you."

Certainly she would shoot upward into the heavens, like one of his fireworks, and explode with happiness. In the whole of her existence, the only people who had ever uttered those words to her were her children. This was the first time an adult had ever told her that they loved her—and it was all she wanted.

"I love you, Duncan," she said, words ragged. "I've waited my entire life to love you."

He cupped her face, tilting her to fit his mouth to hers. The kiss he gave her was ferocious, deep. Claiming and tender at the same time. She felt his love in every part of her, filling her up so that she knew only what it meant to be with this extraordinary man. And she poured her own feelings into her kiss, telling him with her lips that she would always be his, just as he was hers.

"How'd you manage this?" she gasped when they came up for air. "The fireworks."

"Rowe and Curtis helped me borrow some necessary supplies."

"*Borrow* or *steal*?"

A corner of his mouth tilted upward. "I did leave a promissory note saying I'd pay them back for the saltpeter and other bits."

"Ever the upstanding officer," she murmured, adoring him for being exactly who he was.

"Lady Farris," a male guest said in surprise. "It seems the fireworks have drawn you out of your chamber at last."

"They did." But she didn't look at him, only Duncan.

Duncan gazed back at her, his brows high on his forehead. "You didn't join in."

She shook her head, feeling oddly shy. "The only

one I want is you. But," she went on sadly, "nothing has changed. I can't marry you."

"*Everything* has changed," he said, fierce. "*I've* changed. Kept believing that if I just followed the rules, I'd find my place. If I did as everyone has done before me and kept steady on the known road, I would find happiness. But that's not so—and *you* showed me that. You taught me I don't always need to be the up-standing, dutiful soldier. I only need to be myself, and to hell with the rules."

She stared up at him, discovering new heights of joy.

He went on, "Who gives a damn if you don't call me *husband* and I don't call you *wife*? There's only you and me, shaping the world to what we need. And what I need," he continued, voice aching, "is *you*. Always you."

He crushed her to him again, holding her so firm and so steady, yet she could feel the small tremors that worked his body. She shook, as well, awash in happiness and the sheer joy of being with him.

"Want you in my life," he growled. "However you want. All that matters is that we're together."

"I love you, Duncan," she whispered against his chest, so hot and firm against her cheek. "We're going to have so many adventures together."

"My lass," he said as he brought their mouths together, "depend on it."

Epilogue

Eton College, Eight months later

Miraculous what unlimited money and influence can do for a lad," Duncan said as he surveyed the college library.

The tables normally used for studying had been temporarily moved from the room, and a long dining table covered in fine white damask stood in the middle. A feast prepared by a platoon of chefs and pastry cooks—including Isabel Catton herself—was arranged atop the table, along with fresh flowers in Chinese vases, platters of fruit dusted with edible gold, and a stack of copies of Holloway's latest book, *Courtship Customs of the British Isles*, which no one could eat but warranted celebrating.

"I'd say that it was my irresistibly charming personality that secured us the library," Rotherby said. "Which normally ensures I get whatever I want, whenever I want. However, in *this* instance, it was the heaps of cash I threw at the regents that allowed tonight to happen." He took a sip of the excellent wine he'd provided for the evening.

"But why the library?" Holloway asked. "There are perfectly suitable dining halls that are more properly outfitted for such gatherings. Most cultures keep their books and their food separate for a reason, and I own that combining the two makes me a trifle nervous."

"We're not going to throw pies and sausages at each other." Rotherby opened his arms wide. "I chose this place for our special evening because this is where the Union of the Rakes began. Twenty-one years ago today."

Curtis smirked as he folded his arms across his chest. "An infamous day."

"Rather marvelous day," Rowe said, looking at Curtis warmly. "Bringing me all the people I care about most in the world."

Abashed at this open display of sentiment, Duncan and the others fell silent. Yet Rowe had only spoken the truth of their hearts, because this evening, those Duncan loved more than anything were assembled here.

Feminine laughter drew his attention to the other side of the library, where the Duchess of Rotherby, Lady Grace Holloway, and Beatrice stood. Beatrice said something to the other two women, which set them off in more laughter.

As it always did whenever he looked at her, Duncan's chest tightened as love filled him. The past eight months had seen considerable change in both of their lives. He had moved in to her town house, and though her children and his parents would have preferred that he and Beatrice had married, they had finally accepted that it would not happen. Some in Society were scandalized, yet neither he nor Beatrice much cared. They were blissfully bound to each other for life, and nothing would change that.

And in less than a week, they would be off on a year-long trip around the Continent. They had no specific destination, but he knew without a doubt that wherever she went, there would be a bounty of madcap escapades. He welcomed them.

As if feeling his attention on her, her gaze met his. He did care about the Union of the Rakes, and the people they had brought into their lives, but at that moment, no one existed for him but her.

Clearly, she felt the same way, because she murmured something to the duchess and Lady Grace before moving purposefully toward him. His heart beat fiercely at her approach, and it thundered in his ears when she looped her arm through his and pressed snugly to his side.

"Do you know," she whispered in his ear, "I have all sorts of wicked thoughts in this library. Perhaps later, when everyone's gone, we can play the Naughty Schoolgirl and the Stern Tutor."

He growled in response, adoring her fearlessness in and out of the bedroom.

"If I wasn't so nauseatingly in love," Rotherby said, "I would find the two of you downright obnoxious. But I am absolutely besotted with my duchess, so I give you leave to be as insufferable as you please."

Hearing this, the duchess blew him a kiss. Rotherby gazed at her as though she had literally descended from heaven. Astonishing that a man as urbane and worldly could look as smitten as Rotherby did at that moment, but the world was a rather surprising place. After all, it had brought Beatrice and Duncan together.

"How's your estate manager working out?" he asked Rotherby.

"Carriford is in excellent hands now," his friend replied. "Not that it wouldn't have been, in your oversize paws, but I think I've got a good man in the position."

A thought struck Duncan, and he peered intently at Rotherby. "You knew."

"I know everything," Rotherby answered. "Er, what specifically did I know?"

"That Beatrice and I were meant to be. That's why you asked me to escort her to Nottinghamshire." He stared at his Machiavellian friend as everything clicked into place. "You did that deliberately."

Rotherby stared at him as if he'd just spoken the most obvious truth. "Of course I did, jackanapes. If I hadn't, you would have just brooded and moldered away at Carriford, and I couldn't let that happen."

Before Duncan could reply to that incredible statement, Holloway added, "And he helped Grace and me find each other. Although, technically, she and I already knew one another and had cultivated a friendship for many years prior to his intercession, and—"

"I accept full responsibility for your marital bliss," Rotherby drawled. "Though, I must admit that I wish you hadn't found someone of similarly scholarly disposition, or else I wouldn't be saying goodbye to you tonight."

"We'll be back in a year," Holloway said firmly. The Holloways' expedition that Beatrice, as benefactor, was funding was intended for both anthropological and zoological conservation and preservation, a preventative measure against Britain's thirst for empire. Between Duncan and Beatrice's trip, and Holloway and Lady Grace's expedition, the Union of the Rakes would not be together for a long while.

"I insist that you do return," Rotherby said with his usual ducal high-handedness. He added, after the duchess gave him a pointed look, "Please. In fact," he went on, moving to the middle of the library so he could address everyone gathered within it, "I must extract a promise from all of you, that in a year's time, we will all meet again in this very place and share stories of the past twelve months. What say you?"

"Wouldn't miss it," Rowe said, resting his head on Curtis's wide shoulder. They now resided together in a snug lodging in Bloomsbury and owned a bulldog named Herman.

"I can say with absolute assurance," Holloway said,

"that Grace and I will be present, and we shall provide extensive documentation of everything we learn."

"What about you, McCameron?" Rotherby asked, turning to him. "Will you join us, or will we be forgotten?"

"That won't happen," Duncan said emphatically.

"Don't you forget about me," Rotherby insisted. "Or any of us."

Duncan looked down at Beatrice, who smiled up at him. She'd become everything to him, his light, his laughter, his heart, his passion. They explored every part of England together, always learning, always evolving—from sampling new food to meeting new people to greeting every new experience with curiosity and eagerness.

He'd consigned himself to a strangled existence of precise definitions and narrow beliefs, and then she had burst into his life. She had opened him in every way—his eyes, his mind—and shown him the universe.

He loved her so much it frightened him. But in the face of that fear, he was courageous, too.

And there was still room in his heart for the four men who had, long ago, given him their undying loyalty.

He looked at each of them in turn, recalling the simplest terms and convenient definitions that had been assigned to them: Rotherby—an admired man of influence. Holloway—a shy scholar. Curtis—a defiant miscreant. Rowe—an uncanny eccentric. And him, an athlete who always followed the rules.

They were far more than these superficial descriptors, and he silently thanked whatever cosmic being had brought them together. Because he wouldn't have been able to love Beatrice as he did if he hadn't learned what love was from these four men.

"Forget you and the Union?" Duncan's voice was hoarse, and he blinked back tears. "Never. Don't you know, you damned bastards? We're stuck together. Now and always. To the Union of the Rakes." He lifted his glass.

"To the Union of the Rakes," everyone echoed, also raising their glasses.

"And the people that love them," Beatrice added.

"Hear, hear," the duchess said.

Lady Grace shyly lifted her glass higher. "I like you all much better than lizards. And I like lizards quite a lot."

"To lizards," Holloway proclaimed, looking ardently at his wife.

"To lizards," the group repeated.

They stepped forward so that their glasses chimed together, filling the library with musical sound and laughter.

Duncan had never adored seven people more. Everything was excellent.

Next month, don't miss these exciting new love stories only from Avon Books

Love of a Cowboy by Jennifer Ryan

Skye Kennedy has always loved the close-knit community of Sunrise Fellowship—but when she witnesses the commune's new leader commit a terrible crime, she flees . . . and finds herself in Montana, on the McGrath ranch, and drawn to the stoic yet kind man determined to help her, Declan McGrath.

Dark Melody by Christine Feehan

Lead guitarist of the Dark Troubadours, Dayan was renowned for his mesmerizing performances. His melodies stilled crowds, beckoned, seduced, tempted. And always, he called to *her*. His lover. His lifemate. Fragile, delicate, vulnerable, Corinne Wentworth had an indomitable faith that made her fiery surrender to Dayan all the more powerful.

Scoundrel of My Heart by Lorraine Heath

Lady Kathryn Lambert must marry a titled gentleman to claim her inheritance. Yet she is unable to forget the scandalous Lord Griffith Stanwick, who aided in her achievement—or his betrayal. But when old passions flare and new desires ignite, she must decide if sacrificing her legacy is worth a lifetime shared with the scoundrel of her heart.

REL 0321